reunion
at the shore

LEE TOBIN McCLAIN

HQN®

ISBN-13: 978-1-335-08064-6

Reunion at the Shore

Recycling programs for this product may not exist in your area.

Copyright © 2020 by Lee Tobin McClain

HQN
22 Adelaide St. West, 40th Floor
Toronto, Ontario M5H 4E3, Canada
www.Harlequin.com

Printed in U.S.A.

To Karen Solem

reunion
at the shore

CHAPTER ONE

RIA MARTIN SHOULD have enjoyed the chance to escape the endless bills and even more endless chores that faced her as the owner of a small, struggling motel. She should have relished the soft fall breeze off the bay. But as she hurried toward her teenage daughter's school, her stomach churned.

Can you come pick up Kaitlyn ASAP?

October, and it was the third such urgent text message since Kaitlyn had started eighth grade. Ria's heart ached for her sensitive younger daughter, and she wished she could just hug her and make everything right again. But hugs hadn't helped, and neither had probing conversations nor clear consequences. Kaitlyn's grades were slipping and her reputation as a star student was morphing into that of a star troublemaker. What had happened to Ria's sweet daughter?

The private school's parking lot was small, the two-story brick building surrounded by trees on two sides and backed by the sparkling waters of the Chesapeake. She paused a moment, deliberately making herself look at the natural beauty that usually calmed her. She'd been fortunate to get tuition assistance when they'd moved here last year, part of a displaced homemaker scholarship program. Such a great opportunity for her girls. Or so she'd thought.

Obviously, a highly ranked school wasn't enough to help

Kaitlyn, not now, anyway. She'd always been a daddy's girl, even more so after the divorce.

And he'd gone AWOL as a parent.

She paused at the bench outside the school's front door, sat down and tapped Drew's number on her phone.

This time, it wasn't even him asking callers to leave a message. "The mailbox is full," recited a mechanical voice.

For just a second, worry overrode anger. Had something happened to her ex-husband, the girls' father?

But no. If it had, she'd have heard. Yes, he was two hours away in Baltimore, but his department had her number and would let her know if he'd been in some kind of accident. They'd been divorced only a year and a half, separated six months before that. It wasn't as if she and the girls were off his—or his employers'—radar.

This was just Drew being irresponsible, which was totally out of character, but then, men went nuts when they got divorced. It was the nature of the gender. She thrust the phone toward her purse, missed the pocket and grabbed for it as it fell to the ground.

"Ria! What are you doing?"

Her mother's voice startled her. When she looked up to see Mom's concerned face, her eyes warm and bracketed by fine wrinkles, her tawny hair pulled back into a messy ponytail, she felt like bursting into tears. But she didn't, of course; she was a competent adult. "Being an idiot," she said as she snagged the phone and looked at the face of it. "I think I cracked it. What are you doing here?"

"I got a text about Kaitlyn. When I texted back, the secretary said she skipped out of class again."

Ria stood and frowned. She hadn't called or texted back; she'd just hurried right over here. "Why would they get in touch with both of us?"

Mom shrugged. "Sometimes, when they can't reach you…" She trailed off.

Ria's perpetual mom-guilt ratcheted up a couple of notches. It was true, sometimes she couldn't be reached, caught up in the day-to-day management of the Chesapeake Motor Lodge.

She'd never wanted to be *that* mom, focused on her career instead of her kids. But when she and Drew had split, working only part-time hadn't been an option anymore. Thank heavens they'd moved to Pleasant Shores and were close to Mom, who'd picked up a ton of slack for Ria over the past year and a half. Especially when the disaster had happened, the one Mom didn't even know about, because nobody knew. "I'll take it from here, Mom. You do too much for me already."

"Are you sure? I'm glad to help."

"No, it's fine. You go ahead back to work."

"I'm done for the day. I'll meet you at your place, if you'd like."

Impulsively, she hugged her ever-supportive mom. "That would be great. Thank you."

As Ria watched her mother walk away, she longed to call after her: "Please, stay. I don't know what to do."

All Ria wanted in this world was to help her daughter and thus redeem herself as a mother. But there seemed to be some kind of thin-but-impermeable wall between her and Kaitlyn. She could see her—indeed, the sight of her made Ria weak with mother-love—but she couldn't seem to reach her.

She had to find a way to fix that.

KAITLYN SCRUNCHED DOWN in one of the chairs outside Pleasant Shores Academy's administrative offices and watched her mom talk to the school counselor. Despite the fact that she was sure to get yelled at, seeing Mom—her long red hair in need of a straightener, jeans out of style, black blazer showing she was trying to look professional—was a huge relief.

Both foreheads wrinkled, the two women kept glancing her way. Poor Mom, always so stressed, was just getting more so with this new problem. It was all Kaitlyn's fault. She wanted to throw herself into her mother's arms and cry like a six-year-old, but that wasn't an option. For one thing, her mother drove her crazy these days. For another, she'd be tempted to tell Mom what she'd done.

That could never happen. Thank heavens she hadn't told Mrs. Gray, the counselor, anything substantial. She'd just mumbled something about "friend problems," because counselors always believed that. And it wasn't untrue. Rumors about what she'd done had started to circulate, and the teasing had gotten especially bad today. Her friends from last year seemed to be ignoring her.

That was why she'd skipped out on her classes. She just had to get out of here.

Maybe the woman sensed Kaitlyn's thoughts, because she and Mom both turned and beckoned to her. "There's only one period left, so why don't you go ahead and go home," Mrs. Gray said. "You and your mom have some talking to do."

Kaitlyn stared daggers at the woman.

Mrs. Gray patted her shoulder. "It's not always easy for mothers and daughters," she said, "but communication is so important."

Well, duh. Unfortunately, communication wasn't exactly her family's specialty.

They got halfway across the parking lot before Mom

started in on her. "I know eighth grade isn't easy. But you're old enough to keep control of yourself and stay in class."

Kaitlyn pressed her lips together, because what did Mom know about eighth grade? What did she know about Kaitlyn's life? At a school where everyone had been together since kindergarten, Kaitlyn was still considered a new girl and a summer person after a year and a half of living here full-time. It didn't help that she was the biggest and tallest girl in her class and had gone from an A cup to a D cup practically over the summer.

In the car, she breathed a sigh of relief. Getting away from school felt so, so good. She wished she could get away from Pleasant Shores entirely, just go back to Baltimore for a month like they'd been supposed to do over the summer with Dad.

Not that Pleasant Shores Academy was a horrible place, or at least it hadn't seemed to be when she'd started there last year. It was much smaller than the public school she and her sister had attended before their parents' divorce, and she'd liked that, thinking it would be easier to make friends. It was definitely easier to stand out as a star student.

But when everything went south, a small, gossipy school wasn't what you wanted. She'd learned that the hard way.

"So what exactly happened?" Mom asked as she started the car.

"Don't yell at me!"

Mom opened her mouth, closed it, took a yoga breath. She had no idea how irritating that was, obviously. "I asked a question," she said, speaking slowly and clearly now, as if Kaitlyn were a toddler, "in a normal tone of voice."

The fact that she was right didn't matter. "Just leave me alone," Kaitlyn said, and her voice started to shake.

Just like it had when she'd walked up to Chris Taylor in

the school library and tried to start a conversation, only to realize he was sneering and rolling his eyes toward Shelby Grayson and her clan, who'd looked at Kaitlyn and laughed in a mean way.

"Oh, honey." Mom reached out and rubbed her arm as she had when Kaitlyn was little and scared. "Whatever it is, I'm sorry it hurts."

Tears welled up and Kaitlyn jerked away. "Don't!" If Mom kept on in this sympathetic voice, she would fall apart.

Mom's jaw clamped, and she didn't speak again until they walked in the door of their house. Grandma was there—thankfully—and from the smell of things, she'd cooked a lasagna. Normally, Kaitlyn loved her grandmother's lasagna, and she hadn't eaten anything since the granola bar Mom had forced on her this morning.

But her stomach felt too upset to even think of eating.

She headed up to her room, ignoring Mom's protest, then stopped halfway up the stairs to listen to what Mom would say about the whole scene. She had to wait only a few seconds.

"Is she okay?" Grandma asked.

"I don't think so. I'm going to go up and see if she'll talk to me."

"Give her a little time," Grandma said. "Sometimes Mom is the last person an upset fourteen-year-old wants to talk to."

"But…well." Her mother's voice sounded sad, almost hopeless. "I guess you're right, but it's frustrating not being able to do anything to help."

"Have you talked to her dad? He always connected so well with Kaitlyn."

"No, because I haven't been able to reach him. His mailbox is full and he's not answering his phone."

Her grandmother tsked, and they talked a little bit about whether Kaitlyn's sister, Sophia, could help.

As if. Sophia was too caught up in her own excellent social life to give more than a pitying glance to Kaitlyn.

"You know what?" her mother said to Grandma. "This isn't Sophia's responsibility, and like you said, I'm not connecting real well with Kait these days, no matter how hard I try. I'm going to go find Drew."

"Oh, honey," Grandma said in exactly the same worried, sympathetic way Mom had spoken to Kaitlyn. "Is that a good idea? I'm glad to stay with the girls, of course, but…"

Kaitlyn closed her eyes. *Yes, yes, please yes.* Having her big, strong police-officer dad in the area might get Shelby Grayson and Tyler Pollackson and the rest of the mean older kids off her case.

"It's the only idea I can think of. I know I can get information out of Michael or Barry." Those were the officers Dad was closest to on the force, who'd been coming to their house since Kaitlyn was small.

"But if he doesn't want you to know where he is…" Grandma trailed off.

"At this point," Mom said, "I don't really care what he wants."

"You don't want to catch him in an awkward position."

When she realized what Grandma was saying, Kaitlyn almost gagged. She did *not* want to think of her father in an awkward position with anyone.

"Just because Dad ran around within seconds of leaving you, that doesn't mean Drew is doing the same thing."

"Of course it doesn't, honey, but you still might not want—"

"He hasn't seen the girls for three months. Totally outside our visitation agreement. Just a few texts and some vague excuses. He moved out of his apartment and didn't even give us his new address."

"Are the support checks coming?"

"Yes, he's great about that, but being a father isn't just about money. They need to see him. Kait especially."

They went on talking, but Kaitlyn didn't linger to hear any more. Her mom would go bring her dad home, and Dad would make everything better.

As Ria drove through their old Baltimore neighborhood, memories flooded her. She had walked through these tree-lined streets so many times, holding Sophia's hand and pushing Kaitlyn in a stroller. There was that little corner restaurant where she and Drew had gone on date nights. Their old church, where they'd attended in the early days, before Drew got too busy with extended shifts and Ria got too bitter.

She lowered the window, and the smell of autumn leaves brought back more memories. Her stomach twisted with nostalgia and missed opportunities, but she tried to focus on the city noises: cars and horns and sirens from a busier street nearby. She didn't miss that, she reminded herself. City living could be hectic. She loved the quiet of Pleasant Shores.

There was the park with walking paths, next to the little lake they'd skated on in winter. She and Drew had taught both girls to ride their bikes on those paths.

She drew in a deep breath and let it out, blinking back tears. This was why she avoided coming back to Baltimore. *Thanks a lot, Drew, for making me fall apart again.*

But that was what Drew did. One look at him and she remembered all the good times; spend an hour with him and she got frustrated and remembered exactly why they'd split.

She pulled into the same gas station where they'd always filled their tanks and ran inside to get something to drink.

"Ria! Is that you?"

Ria turned, and there was Sheila Ryan, one of those mom friends with whom she'd been thrown together for years. They didn't really like each other, but they pretended to because that was what you did for your kids.

"Hi, Sheila. How's it going?" Ria prayed that Sheila wouldn't ask her the same question.

Sheila went into a description of her thirteen-year-old daughter's ascent up the cheerleading-squad ladder, her status on the honor roll and the volunteer work she was doing to help shelter animals.

"How are Sophia and Kaitlyn doing?" she asked.

"Oh, just great. We love living at the shore."

"I was sorry to hear about your divorce. That must be a big adjustment, for you and for the girls." Sheila's words were kind, but her eyes were just a little too avid and curious. Whatever Ria said would find its way around the gossip circuit.

She sucked in a deep breath, let it out and forced a smile. "Thanks. It's definitely an adjustment. But I'm running a little motel, and that's fun." *Except that it's always at risk of going under.* "And the girls love their new school." Well, Sophia did, so that was at least half-true.

She made an excuse and escaped, and only when she got to the car did she realize that she hadn't gotten the drink she'd gone in for. She'd never been good at the competitive mom games. They always made her uncomfortable.

As she drove the rest of the way to the police station, she wondered whether it had been like that for the girls, too. Had they felt the competition of their upper-middle-class neighborhood, where she and Drew had stretched so hard to be able to afford their little brownstone?

But none of those status games mattered, she reminded herself. What mattered was helping Kaitlyn.

At the police station, more memories assailed her. She'd come here so often over the years, to pick Drew up, to bring him something he'd forgotten, to just say hello, when the girls had been small and she was a stay-at-home mom.

Now she didn't fit anymore. The new receptionist didn't know her, couldn't tell her anything about Drew, citing confidentiality. Fortunately, she found his friend Michael and begged and pleaded her way into getting Drew's new address.

"He shouldn't have fallen out of touch with you, Ria," Michael said. "But he's had a tough time. If you want, I can try to call him and let him know that you need to see him."

"Thanks, but I've come this far." Then what he'd said registered. "He's not working here anymore?"

"He didn't tell you?"

"Tell me what?"

Michael studied her and slowly shook his head. "He's on a, um, a leave," he said.

"Is he okay?" Her heart pounded wildly.

Michael opened his mouth to say something, then closed it again and nodded. "Pretty sure he is," he said. "Honestly, I haven't spoken to him for a few weeks." He looked like he wanted to say more, but someone called him from the back hallway, and he patted her shoulder and left.

Something was definitely going on. And she was going to find out what it was. It wasn't right that Drew had left her out of his life this far. Not that she had to know everything—they were divorced, after all—but they had kids together, kids who needed him. Her anger mixed with worry, because Drew was usually so responsible. Had he changed that much?

She drove toward the address Michael had given her. The neighborhood wasn't nearly as nice as where they used to live. Unwanted sympathy washed over her. Drew paid regular, generous child support, which allowed her to live in Pleasant Shores with the girls. He'd taken the hit to his own lifestyle, unlike a lot of divorced dads, and she appreciated that.

She turned onto his block and was looking for a parking place when she saw Drew across the street.

With a woman.

A stylish, laughing, tall, thin blonde. She seemed very animated as she talked with Drew, who was looking straight ahead. They were both tall enough that she could see them over the row of parked cars. She pulled crookedly into a parking place, nearly hitting the car parked in front of her, and sat, breathing hard.

He'd replaced her; he really had replaced her.

She had never thought that would happen. Not really, not deep inside. Her chest contracted around a hole that had opened up right where her heart had been.

It was true, then. He didn't love Ria anymore. She'd gotten too stressed, too focused on motherhood instead of marriage, too fat. She had screwed up and made so many mistakes, some of which Drew didn't even know about. Of course a man would leave someone like her.

That tiny flame of hope she'd nursed in her heart of hearts, that they'd get back together, someday, flickered out.

Drew stumbled a little, and the woman leaned closer, seeming to steady him. Drew never stumbled. Had he been drinking? During the day?

What had this woman done to him that he'd be falling-down drunk? Indignation propelled her out of her car. She closed the door quietly and sneaked across the street to watch them from behind. The woman glanced back once, and Ria waited for Drew to do the same, but he didn't. He was focused straight ahead. His walk was a little halting, not his usual confident stride. Now, though, she could see that he didn't have the stumble of someone impaired by alcohol.

Had he been injured?

There was something about the way the woman walked a little bit behind Drew rather than right at his side. Ria edged around parked cars until she was in front of the pair of them, crossing the street so they wouldn't notice her, and her heart nearly stopped when she saw the cane Drew was holding. It was white, with a black handle, a red section near the bottom and a roller tip. He was sweeping it back and forth as he moved down the street, and the truth slammed into her like a gale-force wind.

Drew was blind.

CHAPTER TWO

DREW MARTIN USED his cane to find the curb and cocked his head to the side so he could hear the traffic sounds. *You're going straight ahead, so listen for the cars running parallel.* "Is it…?" he started to ask Meghan, then shook his head. "Wait. I can figure it out."

"Good." She waited with him, and he sucked in a deep breath and started across the busy street.

"Just a little to your left," she said quietly behind him, and he looked down. In his small remaining window of vision, on a bright day like this, he could see that he was veering off the crosswalk. He corrected, then finished his way across and navigated the steep curb easily.

"That was great," Meghan enthused as they continued on down the street, and Drew felt a small rush of pride.

Ridiculous, when all he'd done was cross the street.

"Drew?"

Drew froze. He knew the sound of that voice better than he knew the sound of his own. He had heard it raised in anger, racked with childbirth pain, husky with passion. He had heard it say "I do."

And he didn't want Ria to see him like this. He turned away and started back in the opposite direction.

"Drew! Wait!"

Meghan gripped one of his arms, and Ria—it must be Ria; it smelled like her and it felt like her—gripped the other.

"Hey, you were about to walk out into traffic," Meghan said. "You know better than that."

But he couldn't listen to her when his wife's soft voice drilled into his ears, his mind. "Drew. It's Ria."

"I know," he said. He wished desperately that he could see her face, see how she was reacting to the person he was now. On the other hand, he wasn't sure he wanted to know. "How did you find me?"

"Oh, you know each other!" Meghan sounded happy, and he knew why. She was worried about him, thought he was too isolated. Not that it was any of her business; she was just his orientation and mobility specialist, but she took an interest, as they said.

"This is perfect. Our session was just ending. I'm Meghan," she said, obviously to Ria.

"Ria." His ex-wife sounded a little dazed, and that was understandable. She had just learned that the father of her children was blind. But, warm like always, she reached across him to shake Meghan's hand.

"Do you want help going back to your apartment, Drew?" Meghan asked.

What was he supposed to say? He did need a little help still, but that was humiliating in front of Ria.

"I'll help him," Ria said, and that was worse.

"Great!" Meghan reminded him about their next appointment and left, and he was standing on the street with a rapid heartbeat, his face and neck and ears impossibly hot.

"Do you want to…take my arm, or something? I'm on your right." Ria touched him, lightly. "You're in the brick building, right? Apartment, what is it, 3B?"

"Uh-huh." He put his hand on her elbow reluctantly and breathed in the smell of her, a smell as familiar as life to him. Their hips jostled as they went up the steps to his building, and he was so disconcerted that he stumbled a little going inside. Sweat dripped down his chest.

Between his explanations and her eyes, they got to his door and he pulled out his key. Of course, it took him four tries to unlock his apartment.

Navy gave a bark of greeting and pushed her nose into his hand, and his blood pressure went down a little just from the friendly feel of his former police dog, now pet.

"Navy!" Ria sounded happy—much happier than when she'd seen Drew—and he tipped his head back and could sort of see her kneeling to pet the yellow Lab she'd loved.

"Come on in," he said, hoping his place wasn't too much of a mess. He hadn't exactly focused on housekeeping in the past few weeks. As soon as he'd gotten out of the hospital, he'd gone to a two-month residential rehabilitation program. Since he'd come home from that, his main concern had been to figure out how to navigate the world outside.

Unfortunately, he had no idea how to navigate his ex-wife's paying him a surprise visit.

"Have a seat," he said, gesturing toward his small living room. "Want something to drink?"

"Sure," she said. "Do you have a Coke?"

"Think so." He made his way into the kitchen and leaned into his refrigerator, hoping to cool off. He studied cans, which was mostly what he had in there, as he wasn't much of a cook these days. He found one that he was pretty sure was Coke. Grabbed that and a beer from his beer shelf— he knew exactly where that was and he also knew he really needed one—and carried both to the front room. He felt his way to the couch and sat down, then realized he was way too close to her. He felt her scoot away at the same moment that he did.

"Your friend Michael told me where you were living.

And don't be mad at him—I needed to know. Drew, what happened?" Her voice held curiosity and sympathy, but not pity. It was a fine line, one he'd learned to recognize in the past three months.

"Head injury," he said. At his feet, Navy leaned into him.

"Is the vision loss permanent?"

"They don't know."

They sat in silence for a couple of minutes. He wondered why she'd needed to find him. He kind of hoped it was because she missed him, but he doubted it. Anyway, now he was even less likely to be able to make a success of their marriage.

When they'd gotten married, it had been under duress. All his long hours in rehab had given him time to reflect, and he'd figured out that they'd never really recovered from their rough start.

"Listen, Drew, the girls miss you. They need you."

That was another personal failing: he wasn't living up to what a father should be. "I'll come and see them, make it up to them, after I figure this…" He waved a hand, vaguely. "Figure a few more things out," he finished. "How are they doing?" Truth was, he missed his daughters terribly.

"Sophia is fine, of course." She paused, then added, "She misses you a lot."

His firstborn daughter, beautiful and competent and smart. His throat tightened as he thought about not being able to see his children, not now, maybe not ever. "What about Kaitlyn?"

"She's not doing so well."

An icy hand gripped Drew's heart. He loved both girls equally, of course, but Kaitlyn was his special child. She needed him the most, and when Ria and Sophia had gone off doing girlie things, like shopping, Kaitlyn had usually chosen to stay home with him. When she was small, she'd sat and talked to him for hours while he puttered around the house, and he'd loved it. "What's wrong?" he asked.

"I just can't communicate with her."

"Is that all?" Relief washed over him. Just mother-daughter stuff. "You push it too hard."

Ria sucked in a breath, audibly. "I've had to go in to school three times already this year. She's having some kind of trouble with the other kids."

"Bullying? Fighting?"

"She did get into a shoving match once, but mostly she just skips classes and hides in the bathroom."

That didn't sound like Kaitlyn. "Why would she do that?"

"If I knew that, I'd tell you!" She blew out a breath. "Like I said, I can't communicate with her. She won't talk to me about it."

"Maybe I'll come to Pleasant Shores." The moment he said it, all the problems inherent in such a visit flooded into his mind. He couldn't drive. He would have to learn to navigate a hotel room, new shops, new streets. He was somewhat familiar with the town from their visits to Ria's mother, but knowing a place when you could see it wasn't the same as knowing it blind.

"*Maybe* you'll come? When you feel like it?" Ria let out an exasperated snort. "Nice, Drew. Way to put your kids first."

"We all know *you're* the perfect parent," he spit out as his blood boiled. Could she ever, just once, look at things from his side?

But he knew the answer. They were from different worlds, and they'd never managed to quite cross the gap between them. And she was right—no matter his own issues, kids came first.

"Just don't even bother. I'll manage."

He heard her stand up.

"You always do that!" he said. "Give me a minute to think!"

"Oh, take your time," she said. "It's only your child, after all." He heard her steps click across the floor, heard the door slam shut.

Navy whined a little.

He let his head drop into his hands. Yes, he'd failed on so many levels, and, yes, he blamed himself. But Ria still had the power to totally tick him off.

THE NEXT FRIDAY, Ria walked down to the end suite at the Chesapeake Motor Lodge, wanting to check on the cleaning job done by a new worker. She unlocked the door, walked in…and froze.

What was her ex-husband doing standing in the middle of the suite's small sitting area?

She shoved aside the warm thrum of awareness that swept through her body, but she couldn't ignore the guilt about how she'd talked to him when she'd seen him in Baltimore. She hadn't been wrong, exactly—Drew had definitely neglected his duties as a father—but she hadn't given him any kind of break for the huge fact that he'd lost his vision. That had to be overwhelming, and she'd shown him zero compassion.

The thing was, it was hard for her to think of Drew as anything but strong and competent, even when the evidence of his disability was right in front of her.

"Who's there?" Drew asked. He reached a hand toward Navy, who gave a woof, the whole back half of her body wagging. Drew said something to the dog in a low voice, and she came forward, panting, seeming to smile.

"It's me," Ria said as soon as she could find her voice. She knelt and rubbed on Navy, who tried to lick Ria's face. "Sorry to walk in on you, but…what are you and Navy doing here?"

"I'm here to see Kait, get down to the root of the problem," he said. "Sophia, too, of course. They're both okay?"

Before she could get over her surprise and answer him, there was a sharp knock behind her, and then her mother was calling through the door. "Oh no," she said. "You beat me."

Ria shot a glare back at her mother. "We're both a little surprised," she said.

"I should've called you or something," Drew said. "It was just a lot to pull together, getting the transportation down here, canceling appointments. With this." He waved a hand at his eyes. "And after what you said, Julie, I wanted to bring Navy, too."

"I thought it would be good for Kaitlyn," Mom said to Ria.

"The only ride I could get came earlier than I planned," Drew explained, "and they gave me the key at the desk."

Then there went any option Ria had for being angry at Drew, because how could you be angry at a person working so hard to manage his new challenges? Instead, she focused on her mother, who was obviously in on Drew's coming here. "Can we talk a minute?"

"Sure, honey. Drew, we'll be right back to help you settle in." And her mother led her to the old-fashioned metal chairs outside the door of the suite.

Ria couldn't sit down. Instead, she paced back and forth. "What did you do? How is he here?"

"He needed a place to stay. Just for a week. He needs to be close to his kids, reconnect with them."

"Granted, but he didn't seem at all interested in coming a few days ago. And now he's here, in my motel, without my knowledge?" Her voice rose to a squeak as she glared at her mother.

"He called me."

"He called you and not me?" Heat flashed through her body. "Why?"

"He's worried about Kaitlyn, honey." Mom forked her fingers through her hair, pushing it back. "And I would never have gone over your head like this, but…I'm worried, too."

"So am I!" Her chest tightened, and she glanced toward the house, a white clapboard two-story adjacent to the motel. Sometimes Ria wished she lived on the other side of town so that she could escape the motel and all her responsibilities once in a while. But on days like today, she knew living right beside the place she worked was the best thing for her family.

She could actually see the window of Kaitlyn's bedroom right now. Kaitlyn had pleaded cramps and stayed home from school today, and Ria honestly didn't know whether allowing that had been the right thing to do.

Maybe having Drew here would help—she prayed that it would—but why had he acted so unwilling the other day? Why had he come to her motel without a word of warning? "Did you know he was blind?"

Her mother nodded. "'Visually impaired' is a better term, I think. He told me he still has some sight. But he'll need extra help getting around, and that's the only reason I suggested he stay here at the motel. I'm sorry, honey. I know it was interfering of me, but…" Her lips tightened and she, too, glanced toward Ria's house. "Kaitlyn talked to me about Drew possibly coming, and she brightened up. It's the only smile I've seen out of her in a long time."

Ria had opened her mouth to continue scolding her

mother, but Mom's words snapped it shut. She bit her lip. Mom was awesome at this motherhood thing and had a good sense about what kids needed. Ria, on the other hand, had made so many mistakes, a terrible, secret one in particular. She needed to defer to those who were better at parenting, for Kaitlyn's sake.

"I'll help Drew as much as possible," Mom said. "I was planning to come in and do a quick clean of the place, because that new cleaning guy didn't get to it yet. He seems a little...eccentric." She gestured down the row of rooms to where a frizzy-haired man in a tie-dyed shirt was rocking out to music on his earbuds, twirling a towel in rhythm.

Ria puffed out a breath. One more thing to worry about, but it paled in comparison to worry about her daughter.

Her mother put an arm around her shoulders and squeezed, gently. "I know it's got to be hard for you. I'll just run in and make up the bed, help him get oriented, and then I have to scoot. Mary has an emergency and needs me to come in and cover for her at the bookstore."

"Go on. I'll help him settle in." Ria wasn't going to let Mom do *all* the heavy lifting. She already did so much for everyone, Ria and her kids most of all.

But as she hugged Mom, dread knotted her stomach.

Being around Drew while he visited Kaitlyn was going to be tough. Of course she was glad he was here for Kaitlyn's sake. In fact, she wondered if a weeklong visit would be enough to make a difference. For herself, though, she could only hope the week would go fast.

Because no matter what little remnants of attachment remained in her heart, Drew wasn't what she wanted. She wanted someone who could love and accept her as she was.

"Listen," Drew said as soon as she greeted him, "you

don't have to clean. I can do that. I could just use a tour of the place so I can get my bearings."

Ria looked around. The place wasn't dirty, but—she checked the bedroom and bath—they needed to put out clean linens. "Why don't you unpack, and I'll put sheets on the bed and towels out for you, at least." Then she hesitated. "That's if... *Can* you unpack for yourself?"

"I can unpack." The words were said through gritted teeth.

"Sorry! I just don't... You let me know if you need help, okay? Otherwise I'll assume you don't. During your whole visit." She headed into the bedroom as she spoke and pulled linens out of the closet.

He came into the bedroom, and she watched him move around touching the furniture. Strange to see this big, proud man who'd always stridden rather than walked now moving tentatively. "I've been doing orientation and mobility training pretty heavily," he said when he got to the side of the bed where she was. "And I have some limited vision. I do okay."

"What's going to happen with Navy?" She dreaded the answer, knowing how much Drew loved his dog.

"They're letting me keep her. Some grant that helps the department buy a new K-9, so disabled officers can keep their dogs." He winced and started taking clothes out of a duffel and putting them in drawers, all by touch. "'Disabled officers.' Hate that term."

She finished making the bed, watching him furtively. He was still so handsome. And her body remembered how wonderful those powerful arms had felt around her, how strong his chest was when she'd rested her cheek against it, how warm his lips...

She puffed out a breath and looked away. Lack of attraction had never been the problem between them, although she'd lost her confidence about actual intimacy. Even their last fight had been fiery, and when he'd grabbed her shoulders in frustration, she'd wanted him and she'd seen in his eyes that he wanted her, too.

But the physical side of things wasn't enough. They'd never communicated all that well in actual words, and as the hurt had built up on both sides, their ability to understand each other had declined even further. He'd wanted another child, and she hadn't been sure, and they hadn't been able to talk about it without getting defensive. Add to that his long hours of work, the tensions of raising teenagers, and her insecurities about her body, and she'd started to lose hope. When she'd brought up the idea of a separation, really just to see whether he was thinking along those lines, he'd gone cold and silent on her. Their marriage had collapsed under the added-up burden.

When people—even good friends—asked what had happened to their marriage, she'd never been able to say, exactly. It wasn't cheating or drinking or abuse. But it had been conclusive, just the same.

"Tell me about Kait," he said as he moved to the doorway. "What's been going on the past few days?"

"Your guess is as good as mine. She won't talk to me." She paused, then admitted, "It's good you came, Drew. Maybe you can break through to her, get her to communicate."

"When can I see her?"

"Anytime. She's home from school today, in fact."

"You let her stay home?" Drew moved around the room, restlessly exploring. "Why?"

Her chest tightened. "She said she has cramps."

"That's not an acceptable excuse. She can take medicine for that, right?"

"Right, but—"

"You argue with her and then give in to her. It's not a good strategy."

"I've been doing the best I can, alone!" She forked her fingers through her hair. "Believe me, I question myself every day, but I just have to make a decision and go on. She looked so miserable this morning that I let her stay home."

"She's not going to solve a problem by running away from it."

"Neither are you," she snapped. "Look, I get that you've had a major challenge with this...this blindness thing—"

He made some sort of noise in his throat.

Insensitive, her conscience warned, but she ignored it. "That doesn't absolve you from responsibility, nor give you the right to question my decisions. She's more than I can handle alone, Drew, so I hope you can do some good, at least, with this visit."

She spun to leave, then froze. There in the doorway was Kaitlyn, looking from her to Drew, her face stricken.

CHAPTER THREE

LATER THAT AFTERNOON, Drew climbed out of his ex-mother-in-law's car and snapped his folding cane out to full length. The smell of brackish water and the faraway shouts of the watermen filled his senses.

He remembered liking this part of town when they'd visited Ria's mother with the girls. Beach Street ran for half a mile along the shoreline, and next to the bay was a wide bike path dotted with inviting green benches facing the water. During the season, it could get crowded with bicyclists and joggers and people headed for the beach, but now, in early October, it was quiet.

Across the street from the bay, he remembered, were small shops and a couple of cafés and restaurants, but apparently most were closed for the season. The lunch-and-ice-cream shop they were headed for, Goody's, stayed open year-round and was a favorite of the locals.

He listened but didn't hear the rear passenger door opening. "You coming, Kait?"

She didn't answer, although she did open the car door and climb out. She'd been silent ever since she'd discovered him and Ria fighting back at the motel this morning. She'd taken off, and Ria had run after her, but from what Ria had reported back, Kaitlyn hadn't wanted to discuss what she'd overheard.

His visit wasn't off to a good start.

"Thanks, Julie," he said. She'd come home from her job

at the bookstore in time to drive them here. He was trying to learn to accept help, but it wasn't easy. The lack of independence rankled.

"No problem. I'll be back in an hour to pick you up. Kaitlyn, help your father."

"How?" she asked.

Drew opened his mouth to answer, but Julie jumped in. "Just let him hold on to your arm and warn him about curbs and other obstacles."

Kaitlyn slammed the car door and then was beside him. "I'm here." She nudged her elbow into the side of his arm.

As he gripped it, he smelled fruity perfume, the type that Sophia favored but Kait had always scoffed at. Love and sorrow washed over him. What had he missed while he'd been selfishly ignoring his daughters to deal with his own problems?

He needed to find out what was wrong so he could fix it. Needed to *see* her, but he couldn't.

They made their way inside and ordered ice cream at the counter. As he fumbled with his money to pay—there was a system to the way he folded his bills, but he wasn't quick and automatic with it yet—he heard Kaitlyn sigh.

"This way, Dad," she said when he'd finally figured it out and picked up his dish of ice cream. She led him to a small table and then sat down across from him.

"Thanks for helping me," he said, feeling awkward but needing to get it out. "I know it can't be easy seeing your dad like this."

She didn't answer, but he heard her spoon clink against the sundae bowl.

"So how much did you hear this morning?"

"Oh, nothing," she said.

"Mom said you might have heard us talking about you. We're worried and we want to help."

"Right." More clinking.

He took a couple of bites of his own ice cream, and even through his concern he was blown away by the rich chocolate laced with chunks of brownie. "Wow. I'd forgotten how good the ice cream is here."

"I know, right?" Kaitlyn's voice took on the only animation he'd heard in it so far. "Everything here is good."

They enjoyed their food in silence for a few minutes. Then Drew tried again. "So how are you doing?"

"Fine."

He wished he could see her face. "Mom says you got in trouble," he said.

"Why didn't you tell me you were blind?" The words seemed to burst out of her.

"Fair question." He put down his spoon. "I wanted to get better than this before I saw you. I didn't want to be a burden or ask you and your sister for help." He paused, waiting for a response that didn't come. "I was hoping my vision would come back, and it still might. Some of it, at least. But I was wrong to leave you and Sophia and Mom out of the loop."

"I wanted to come to Baltimore this summer and stay with you for a month. I thought we were supposed to, and then you blew us off."

Guilt poked into him, a million little pins. He'd texted and called, making weak excuses and even weaker apologies. She was right to be mad, but at least she was talking to him. "I'm sorry about that. I got hurt, and I guess…all I could think about was myself."

She sighed heavily. "It's okay."

But it wasn't. He could hear that in her voice. He longed

for the days when she and her sister were little, when he and Ria had been solid, or at least somewhat so. "Are you having problems with your schoolwork?" He didn't expect that to be the issue. She was more book smart than he ever was. Took after her mother in that regard.

"No, it's fine."

"Other kids, then?"

She didn't answer. He heard her push her dish away. Around them, the little dining room was getting louder. Kids' voices rang out, talking and laughing. Someone jostled his chair and muttered "Sorry."

"Are your classmates being mean? Teasing you about something?"

"Don't worry about it."

It wasn't an answer, but he suspected he was getting closer to the truth. "You just have to act like it doesn't bother you. Give it right back to them."

"Dad, you have ice cream on your shirt."

Heat rose in his neck. "Where?"

She reached across the table and touched a spot on the middle of his chest. "Right there. Hey, let's go."

"Don't be in such a hurry." He scrubbed at the area of his shirt that she'd indicated, turtling back his head to try to get the spot into his limited window of blurry vision. No luck, though, and he was probably smearing the ice cream more than removing it. Just one more thing to hate about not being able to see.

But that problem paled in comparison to his real concern: figuring out what was wrong with his precious, complicated younger daughter.

"Let's go. Now." Her voice was low and then she was standing beside him, taking his arm, urging him to his feet.

He started to stand, and his cane clattered to the ground.

He cursed internally as he knelt and felt for it, found it, straightened. Surprising how dependent he'd become on something he basically hated.

Kait tugged at his arm. Around them, more kids' voices rang out. He pushed the button on his talking watch. "The time is three seventeen p.m.," it said. School must be over for the day.

"Dad! Stop it!" Kaitlyn's voice was low, intense.

"Stop what?" he asked, confused.

"Your watch! It's embarrassing!"

Suddenly, Kaitlyn lurched into him. There was a muttered comment in an adolescent male voice. "Shut up," Kait hissed.

At the same time, a girl's voice rang out. "Hey, Martin!" Kaitlyn's head jerked.

"Why weren't you in school? Something bothering you?"

"Let's go, Dad!" Kaitlyn's voice quavered, and she tugged at his arm.

Drew's fists clenched. Did they think he was deaf, too? He opened his mouth to interrogate these kids Kait seemed so bent on escaping, get to the root of the problem.

"This way. Door's over here." She was hurrying him along, her voice breathless, the same way it used to be when she was small and on the verge of a meltdown.

"Did you really need that ice cream?" someone else said.

"Nice *shirt*, Kaitlyn." There were a couple of laughs at that one.

Kait flinched but didn't stop walking. They were at the door now.

Drew wished he hadn't insisted on coming here, and he hated not being able to help his daughter. "Do you want me to talk to them?" he asked. If he could see, he'd have given them one good glare and they'd have shut up, all right. And if they were hurting his baby girl, he wouldn't stop at a glare.

She didn't answer. She just pulled him out onto the street and led him away from the restaurant.

Once they'd gotten across the street and onto the bike path, Drew tugged her to a stop. "Wait a minute. What just happened back there? Are those the kids who are bothering you at school?"

"Grandma, could you come get us now?" he heard Kaitlyn say and realized she was talking on her phone. "At the benches, not at the shop."

She took his arm and steered him to the right. As they walked, he could smell the water beside them. "What are the benches?" he asked.

"That little park where they sometimes have live music. Here it is." She led him to a bench, sat down beside him and refused to speak, despite his efforts.

The whole thing left Drew feeling more confused, more concerned and more inadequate than ever about his beloved daughter.

KAITLYN FINALLY, finally got rid of her father, escaped her mother and made her way down to the shore.

Not the beach part where Sophia and her friends, and all the popular kids, liked to hang out. That way spelled disaster, just as Goody's had been a disaster.

No, Kaitlyn liked to go to the harbor side, where long, narrow wooden docks poked out into the bay, most of them fronted by small, tumbledown sheds. The old-timers were mostly ashore at this time of day, but they didn't go directly home; instead, they stayed near the water awhile, talking to friends, describing the day's catch, sorting the different types and sizes of crabs or doing something with oysters—she wasn't sure what. Fall was transition time, from a summer of crabbing to a winter of oystering; she did know that much.

It was a different world. The weight of her problems got lighter as the salty, fishy fragrance tickled her nose and the bay breeze lifted her hair off her neck. None of her enemies would come here. No one she knew, not her mom, her sister, her father.

Her father. Blind. Done being a cop.

No matter how bad things had gotten at school, she'd always had a solution in the back of her mind: Dad. Dad's size and strength, plus the fact that he was a cop, would stop Tyler and Kyle and Shelby cold. They'd realize they couldn't mess with her.

But it turned out that Dad couldn't even walk across a room by himself. No one was afraid of him now.

And she was a jerk for thinking about how his blindness affected her, not about how it was affecting him.

"Hey, city girl." That was what the watermen called her, but it was kindly meant.

She didn't mind. She *was* a city girl, more than most of the kids here in Pleasant Shores. "Hey, Captain Eli," she said to the man who'd greeted her. He wore a ball cap, and his barrel chest and large stomach protruded out from between his suspenders. "Do any good today?" It was a pathetic attempt to talk the waterman's lingo, but aside from a chuckle now and then, they didn't make fun. She got the feeling they liked having someone outside of their usual community taking an interest.

"Arright," he said and chomped down on the fat cigar he always held in his mouth. He didn't light it, ever—something about a family member who'd died of COPD after a lifetime of smoking.

"Where's Bisky?" Her favorite of the waterman families had the dock next to the captain's, but it was deserted today.

"Took sick," he said.

"Bisky did?" Bisky was the strongest woman Kaitlyn had ever known. Six feet tall, with shoulders broad as a man's, she hauled and carried great buckets of crabs and oysters and gear as if they weighed nothing, and still had the strength to laugh at the men's jokes or give a shove to one of the teenage boys who wasn't doing his share.

"Just the flu. There's Sunny now." He waved down the road that ran along the shoreline, and sure enough, Bisky's daughter, Sunny, walked along, wearing the same overalls and braids she'd worn to school today. She was carrying an empty crab trap, which she set down beside the dock.

"Hey," Sunny said to Captain Eli, giving Kaitlyn a nod before pulling a wad of cash from her overalls pocket and thrusting it toward the old man. "Here's what I got from Richardson. Mom said to give you two-thirds, since we used your boat and your traps."

"How'd you work if you were at school today?" Kaitlyn really wanted to know.

"I get out early. Work release." Sunny didn't offer any other explanation. She was the kind of girl who went her own way and didn't feel the need to explain everything.

"Sounds good to me."

"Does it?" Sunny raised an eyebrow. "Sounds good to me, sitting around in school all day."

"Kaitlyn!" Sophia's impatient voice rang out over the docks, causing several of the watermen to look, then look again. Sophia had that effect on men. And boys, and pretty much everyone. Now, though, she wasn't smiling; she was mad. "I've looked all over for you!" Suddenly, Kaitlyn's phone, which she'd had in her back pocket, was in Sophia's hand. She checked it, then glared at Kaitlyn. "You turned it off!"

"I hate when you do that!" Kaitlyn said. Sophia was a skilled pickpocket where Kaitlyn's phone was concerned. Kaitlyn grabbed her phone back, looked at it and realized she had, in fact, set it to Do Not Disturb. For good reason.

"You have to come home now." Sophia hadn't greeted Captain Eli or Sunny.

Bad manners were unusual for her sister. "Why?" Kaitlyn asked. "I just got here."

"You just have to."

"Is something wrong?"

"Tell you on the way." She tugged at Kaitlyn's arm, then gave Captain Eli a wry little tilt of the head.

And just like that, the old man was on her side, smiling. "Go on home with your poor sister," he said.

Sunny, still ignored by Sophia, shrugged and walked down toward the bay to the spot she often sat at to read.

Kaitlyn envied her but gave in to her sister's greater powers of persuasion and followed her, waving to Captain Eli and Sunny, even though Sunny's back was turned.

"So what's the big emergency?" Kaitlyn asked once they were out of earshot of the others.

Sophia shrugged. "I don't know. Mom and Dad want us to come home and have dinner with them, is all."

"You dragged me away for *that*?"

"I'm in a hurry. I want to get this family dinner over so I can go see…" She paused, then turned to Kaitlyn with a brilliant smile. "Guess who?"

"Don't try to change the subject." They walked rapidly along the road toward Pleasant Shores' downtown. A few blocks after that, they'd reach the motel and their house. "You were rude."

"Rude to who?" Sophia sounded distracted.

"To Captain Eli and Sunny."

"You shouldn't be hanging out there. With *her*," Sophia added, gesturing back in Sunny's direction. "It's just going to make things worse for you at school." She tossed off the advice as if Kaitlyn had asked for it. "Anyway," she said, "Tyler Pollackson asked me to come over tonight. He's so cute! And he's, like, the most popular guy at school."

"I heard he's kind of rapey," Kaitlyn said.

"I'll be careful. I'm not having sex with him, no way. I just want to date him to, you know, boost me up."

Kaitlyn lifted her eyebrows. Sophia's strategies for popularity always took her by surprise; they were things she'd never think of herself, not in a million years.

But for Sophia, at least, they worked. "Why do Mom and Dad want us to have a family dinner? Are they getting back together?"

"Who knows?" Sophia lifted a shoulder. She was walking so fast that Kaitlyn had to half jog to keep up with her.

But she *did* jog, because she wanted to know what Sophia was thinking. "Do you want them to?" she asked.

Sophia didn't answer.

"Do you?"

"Do I *what*?" Sophia asked.

"Do you want Mom and Dad to get back together?"

"I don't know." Sophia's tone was impatient. "I have other things to think about. And so do you," she added. "You need to get some friends, or you'll never make it through middle school."

"How do *you* know I don't have friends?" If bad gossip had passed from eighth grade to eleventh, things were worse than she thought.

On the other hand, maybe Sophia could help her.

"I see you walking around alone, eating alone."

That was because the few friends she'd made last year had dumped her when the gossip started. "That's why I want to get to know Sunny. She's cool."

"She's *not* cool. She's a dock kid," Sophia said ruthlessly. "She'll just make your reputation worse."

Was that possible? But Kaitlyn glanced back toward the shore, a new uneasiness filling her. If she couldn't make friends at the docks, and everyone at school hated her, then what options did she have?

Her family. Everyone always said family came first.

As they reached the house, the windows to the dining room were illuminated, like in a movie. Mom stood on one side of the table, Dad on the other. Mom was glaring at Dad, whose face was turned away. They weren't speaking.

This did *not* look fun, Kaitlyn thought, her mood sinking even further. Mom and Dad had issues of their own. They didn't have time or energy to help her deal with hers.

"Did you hear that Dad's blind?" she asked her sister.

Sophia shrugged and waved a hand. "Yeah, I know, but he said it might go away soon."

Kaitlyn stared at her sister. "Don't you care?"

Sophia's phone buzzed, so of course she ignored Kaitlyn's question. After all, *she* didn't need help from Dad. She was going to be the girlfriend of Tyler Pollackson, no doubt, because Sophia always got everything she wanted.

All of it left Kaitlyn where she'd been before, if not worse off: completely alone.

CHAPTER FOUR

SO FAR, it seemed to Ria that things were getting worse, not better, now that Drew was here.

The family dinners they'd tried to have, Friday night and then Sunday after church, had been a disaster. Completely awkward, with both she and Drew trying to make conversation with the girls while studiously avoiding asking each other anything of significance. Sophia had been stealing glances at her phone and left as soon as possible, claiming study sessions with friends.

Kaitlyn, on the other hand, had sat quietly, not talking, but not seeming to want to leave the table, either. She seemed gloomy, depressed.

Thank heavens for Mom, who'd joined them for the Sunday dinner. She'd kept at least some conversation going and had cooked a truly spectacular dinner of beef Burgundy, followed by coconut cream pie.

Monday morning, Ria was talking with one of the cleaning staff when she saw Drew emerge from his suite, white cane in hand. He made his way down the sidewalk and went into the office. A moment later, the desk clerk came out. "He wants to talk to you," she called, beckoning to Ria.

Couldn't he have called her? Her heart sped up as she hurried into the office. "Hey, what's up?" She touched his arm to indicate to him where she was.

"Wanted to let you know that I'm going over to the

school," he said. "I have an appointment with Kaitlyn's guidance counselor in half an hour."

She frowned. "Are you sure that's wise? Kait will hate that."

He lifted a hand, palm up. "We've got to try everything. Kids are everything."

Her heart warmed toward him. His simple appreciation of family, of kids, was one of the things she'd always loved about him.

On the other hand… She reflexively touched her lower abdomen. Drew would have given anything for another child. Maybe it would've even kept them together.

If only she hadn't made the mistakes she'd made.

"Kait won't talk to me," he went on, oblivious to her inner turmoil, "so I'm going to see if I can get anything from the counselor. I didn't like what I heard Friday afternoon at the ice-cream shop."

It figured that Drew, coming newly into town, would get more information than Ria had. He'd always been the better parent. He was a natural. Ria had to work at it.

She shook off her self-centered worries. "How are you getting there? Do you want me to drive you?"

"I'm walking," he said.

She studied him skeptically. Could he really make it the four blocks to the school, considering the rutted road and that he was unfamiliar with the route?

"I'd like to go with you," she said, surprising herself. But as soon as the words popped out of her mouth, she knew it was the right thing to do. Drew could use a walking companion, at least this first time. And she should swallow her pride and see if there was new information to be gleaned from the counselor. All Ria's conversations with Mrs. Gray had been conducted in haste, with Kaitlyn waiting in a nearby office. She'd gotten a sense that Kait was having trouble with her peers, but nothing specific.

"Are you just afraid I'll fall on my face?" he asked bluntly.

She wasn't good at lying, especially not to Drew. "That's part of it," she admitted. "But I think it would be good if we could present a united front to the counselor. We might both get more ideas of how to help Kait."

"All right." He held his watch to his ear, and apparently it talked to him. "We'd better get started," he said.

"Let me grab my purse and comb my hair."

Minutes later, as they walked down the motel's sidewalk and started to cross the road, a silver Tesla pulled in front of them and stopped.

"Wait—there's a car," she said to Drew. "Electric, no engine sounds."

"Thanks." He stood still, head tilted like he was trying to listen for traffic.

The driver parked and emerged, and Ria did a double take. "Ted Taylor? What are you doing here?"

Her head spun. She'd lived here in Pleasant Shores for a year and had never encountered Ted; she hadn't even known he still lived in town, or was back in town. Now, when Drew was here for a visit...

"I was coming to talk to you," he said. "You look good!" He glanced over at Drew, opened his mouth, then closed it again.

Beside her, she felt Drew stiffen. Understandably so.

Manners were what you fell back on when you didn't know what else to do. "Ted, do you remember Drew Martin? He's in town for a few days."

"How could I forget?" His question was just a little snide, but he reached out to shake Drew's hand, touching it first—he'd obviously seen the white cane and surmised the visual impairment.

The handshake went on a little long. No doubt in a contest of strength, because that was what men did. Especially men like Drew.

"I thought you two were..." Ted trailed off.

"Married?" Drew said, his voice ever so slightly hostile. "We were. And we're still parenting together."

"Of course, of course." Ted looked at Ria, gave her a once-over, actually, and smiled as if he liked what he saw.

Ria didn't believe it, but it still felt a little good. Almost like flirting, and it had been a while since anyone had flirted with her.

"Can we set up a meeting?" Ted asked her. "I'm in real-estate development now, and I'd like to talk to you about your motel."

"You *would*?" Ria's voice squeaked. "That's a little hard to believe. Nobody wants to talk about the motel, unless they're trying to collect on a bill."

"Don't underestimate your business or your property," he said. "Can I give you a call?"

"Sure." She punched her number into his phone. She didn't exactly have faith in anything he said making a difference, but the motel was struggling. She needed all the help she could get.

After Ted's car glided off, they crossed the road and headed down Sunset Lane together. It was a collection of smallish clapboard houses that adjoined the school, and many of the town's older residents lived here.

Drew walked at a good clip with his cane, but when the sidewalk disintegrated into rubble, she offered him her arm. "Street's a mess," she explained. "Watch your step."

He held her arm, and the heat of his large hand there felt familiar and right.

She looked up at the clouds, trying for serenity. She guessed it wasn't that unusual that you'd have a lot of emotions around an ex. They'd been together fifteen years.

Gulls flew overhead, cawing out their warnings and greetings. A breeze from the bay cooled Ria's warm face.

"Ted Taylor doesn't want a meeting with you," Drew burst out, finally breaking the silence between them. "At least not a business one."

He was still thinking about Ted? "What do you mean?" she asked him.

"He's hitting on you. It's obvious."

"I don't think so," she said. "And if he has a way to help, some kind of refinancing or something, I'd be crazy not to listen."

"You shouldn't listen to him." Drew's stubborn tone was as familiar as his hand on her arm.

"I'm always on the edge," she said. "You don't know what it's like, trying to keep an old motel going, trying to update, competing with all the newer, trendier places. It's been…" To her surprise and horror, her throat tightened up. She cleared it harshly. "It's been hard."

And that, too, was a function of having been married a long time. She'd missed having someone to confide in. Oh, there was Mom, and she'd been a rock, but it wasn't the same as a life partner. Ria didn't like to worry her mother.

"Aw, Ree." It was his old, affectionate name for her, and he squeezed her arm. "I'm sure it *is* hard. But a guy like Taylor isn't going to help matters."

She blew out a breath. "I'll handle it." He was acting possessive, as if he was jealous, and it probably had to do with their history and the fact that she'd been with Ted right before Drew. Drew had never liked blond, wealthy Ted. Moreover, Drew was the macho type; he wanted his woman to be his woman.

The only problem was, she *wasn't* his woman. She didn't fit with him. He was gorgeous, one of the handsomest, coolest men she'd ever met, and she, by contrast, was overweight and easily flustered.

That was why he'd been able to sweep her off her feet that long-ago summer. He'd swept her right away from Ted, with whom she'd had a spat, and she'd gone out on the beach with him because, well, he was *beautiful*.

And warm, and kind, and she'd gone along with his seduction, which had been both skillful and sincere. But she hadn't known, at that time, how incredibly fertile they were together. One moonlit night, and bam. She was pregnant.

Drew, being honorable, had married her, but she knew why; it was his sense of obligation. Not love. He'd never told her he loved her, unless in the heat of passion, which had been increasingly rare in the last years of their marriage. Not that that was his fault; it was hers.

"Why, Ria Martin, is that you?" A door slammed, and then Primrose Miller, church organist and gossip extraordinaire, came wheeling down the ramp in front of her house.

Ria was pretty sure she kept her groan internal. "Hi, Miss Primrose," she said, the *Miss* in deference to the woman's advanced age. "Have you ever met my...met Drew Martin?" she finished on a fumble. It just felt awkward to introduce him as her ex.

"I haven't had the pleasure," Primrose said. "I'm guessing this handsome man is the father of your two beautiful girls?"

"Yes," Drew said, not going into any explanations. "It's a pleasure to meet you." He held out a hand.

Primrose clasped it in both of hers, briefly, then looked at Ria. "I hear you have a little half sister," she said.

"Really? Ashley had her baby?" She hadn't known that her father's new wife had delivered, and even though she wasn't keen on the woman or the marriage, a little excitement surged. She'd always wanted a sister. Not that she was likely to be involved with the baby. She and her father weren't exactly estranged, but they weren't close.

"You lost me," Drew said. "How do you have a half sister?"

"Her father, dear," Primrose explained, clearly delighted to have such news to share. "He remarried and has a new child. His wife is a tiny little thing, half his age."

Of course Ashley was a tiny little thing, Ria thought glumly. That was her dad. He was incredibly appearance conscious, was always telling Ria she needed to work out. She was pretty sure issues about body image were part of the problem that had led to the demise of her parents' marriage. Her mom was, as they said, curvy. She always worried about her weight.

Like mother, like daughter.

But why was she focusing on her parents, on Primrose, on Drew even? The important thing was Kait. "We need to go," she told Primrose. "A meeting at the school."

"About your Kaitlyn? I hear she isn't doing well."

Ria's heart rate accelerated. "Wait a minute. You heard that? How?"

"You're right—we should go," Drew said, giving her arm a little tug. "It was nice to meet you, ma'am."

Ria frowned, shrugged, then waved to Primrose and followed Drew along.

Once they got out of earshot, he spoke. "Why are you listening to that woman's gossip?"

"Oh, I don't know. Watch—there's some weeds." She slowed while he used his cane to navigate around the autumn-brown clumps of grass.

"Primrose is hard to escape. And you hate to be mean to a woman in a wheelchair."

Drew made a disgusted sound. "Just like you hate to be mean to a blind man?"

It took Ria a minute to get the connection. He was identifying with Primrose's disability. "Do you *want* people being mean to you?"

"That's not what I meant. Just... I want to be treated like a person, just like she probably does, too. How does she know about Kait's problems, though?"

"I was trying to ask her, but you made me leave." They were bickering like they always had, mixing it up with real conversation, and Ria almost enjoyed the sparring.

They approached the school and got buzzed in. Locker doors banged amid loud teen voices. "It must be the class change," Ria said. "Let's just wait here until it settles down."

"Why do schools always smell the same?"

"Disinfectant and sweat," she agreed. And then she looked down the hall and there was Kaitlyn, walking alone, head down.

Ria knew better than to greet her—no fourteen-year-old wanted that kind of attention called to her—and she hoped they wouldn't be seen.

"Hey, Martin! Your mom's here with some blind dude!"

Drew stiffened beside her.

Kaitlyn looked up and saw them. She lifted her hands and eyebrows in the universal teen "Why?" Then she spun and walked a different way down the hall.

"Aren't we going to talk to her?" Drew asked.

"She doesn't want the attention. She took off."

"It's like you're walking on eggshells around her," Drew said. "Get her over here. Sophia would've come."

"Sophia's Sophia. No way am I chasing Kait down. Let's go on in." She led the way, thinking that Kait wasn't the only person she was walking on eggshells around. She seemed to be living on a carpet of them these days.

EARLY WEDNESDAY AFTERNOON, two days after the unproductive meeting with the guidance counselor, Drew heard his parents' ancient Chevy from the bench where he sat in front of the motel. He stood and tilted his head back, wanting to see them in the worst way.

Was his tiny window of vision a little bit bigger now, a little less blurry? Or was that just wishful thinking?

"Oh, my baby boy," his mother said, and he was enveloped in her arms, smelling her familiar perfume. Feeling the tears on her face. "I can't believe this happened to you."

He had avoided seeing his parents since the accident, knowing it would cause them pain. But the opportunity to have them visit the girls had made him overcome his own feelings of discomfort. He supposed he was glad he had.

"Son." His father's deep voice came from beside his mother, and he loosened himself from her grip and held out a hand for his father's handshake, vigorous as always.

The sound of Dad's voice and the feel of his calloused hand took Drew back, back to his younger years of trying to impress his strong, cool cop father.

For that matter, he *still* wanted to impress Dad.

Behind him, he heard the door of the motel office open. The hairs on the back of his neck prickled and he half turned.

"Hi," Ria said to his folks. "It's been a long time." He could tell that she was hugging both of them from his mother's teary "Oh, sweetie" and his father's uncomfortable-sounding "Okay, okay."

He was pretty sure that his father stood stiff as a board. Things had been awkward with his dad and Ria ever since the divorce.

Not so much his mother. "We're going to lunch, dear," she said. "Can you come?"

"That's such a lovely offer," Ria said, "but I'm stuck here today. Lots of work, keeping a motel running."

Could his parents hear the discomfort in Ria's voice the way that he could?

"Any suggestions about the best place we should go?" he asked Ria. She knew his parents' tastes at least as well as he did.

"On the Waterfront," she said promptly. "You and Papa can get a beer there, and the view will be pretty. Plus, it's one of the only places open during the off-season." She hesitated, then added, "Do you want me to let Navy out, walk her?"

"I already took care of it." He felt his jaw clench. If she didn't think he was able to meet the needs of a dog, how would she trust him to help his daughter?

Twenty minutes later, he and his parents were seated by a window at On the Waterfront, looking out at the bay. After they'd ordered, his mother rhapsodized on how beautiful it was.

"Lot of good that does you," Dad said to Drew, his voice gruff. "There's nothing for you here. You need to get back to the city. See some specialists, get your eye troubles taken care of."

"This is just a short visit to see my girls." Drew wasn't going to go into Kaitlyn's problems. That would just worry his parents.

"Well, right now you can't see them," his father said.

Drew frowned. "What?"

"Your girls. You can't *see* them."

There was a slapping sound, his mother smacking his father's arm, no doubt. "Tony! What a thing to say! You'll hurt his feelings."

Drew smiled, though it felt forced. "That's all right. It's a figure of speech. I use it all the time, still."

"You should have told us what happened to you. You could have come home." His mother gripped his hand. "I would have taken care of you."

"Thanks, Mom—"

"He didn't want to come home. He's a man," his father interrupted. "He wants to get back on the beat ASAP."

"Pretty sure I can't do that." Drew consciously relaxed his shoulders. He'd known he'd have to explain the extent of his disability to his father, but he hadn't anticipated how hard it would be. He'd spent a lifetime trying to make the man proud, and now he was going to disappoint him bigtime. "There are vision tests for cops, and there's no way I can pass."

"This is temporary," his father said. "It has to be."

"It may be," Drew said, momentarily buoyed by the confidence in his father's voice. But almost instantly, realism, in the form of his doctors' words, rushed back in. "More likely, I'll improve some, but I won't get all my vision back." He hadn't ever said that out loud before, but he must have been thinking it on some level for a while now.

Dad let out a curse, then another.

Drew heard the condemnation and pity in his father's voice and understood it. He, his father and his father's father had all been cops, prided themselves on it. They'd also prided themselves on not getting hurt, staying on the job all the way through to retirement.

It looked like that wasn't going to happen for Drew. His stomach clenched.

"You know, honey," his mother said hesitantly, "you could still come back home for a while. I could take care of you, help you get back on your feet."

Dad pounded a fist on the table, rattling the glassware. "No son of mine is going to crawl back home so his mother can take care of him!"

"I wasn't planning—"

"Of course, dear." His mother's conciliatory voice interrupted Drew's effort at self-defense. Though he couldn't see it, he knew Mom was patting Dad's arm. "You know best." She hesitated, then said, "You know, I was wondering..." She trailed off.

"What?" Drew tried to keep the impatience out of his voice. Mom always tried to change the subject in order to keep Dad calm.

"Is there a chance you and Ria might get back together?"

The question hung in the air, making it clear that Dad wanted to know the answer, too.

Drew wanted to know the answer himself. "Very doubtful," he said. "Nothing's changed between us, except that now..." He trailed off.

Neither of his parents finished the thought for him, but he figured they knew what he'd started to say.

Now he was blind. Now he couldn't drive a car or be a cop. He had less than ever to offer Ria and the girls.

Their meals came, lots of fried seafood, and picking at it gave them all something to do. Both he and his father downed beers. Mom talked about Drew's brothers—Mike, who had a promising new job and a pretty new girlfriend, and Stevie, who was enjoying his work in nursing so much that he was thinking of taking his education further, into a PA or nurse practitioner program.

Mom kept reaching out to squeeze Drew's arm, though, and Dad barely said a word.

This was why he hadn't wanted to see his parents, why he'd avoided telling them about his disability as long as possible. He had known the reactions. Pity from his mother and disappointment from his father. He had needed some time to get his own emotions under control before dealing with theirs.

Back in the city, living alone except for his dog and doing his O&M training, he'd started to get himself together. Found some kind of equilibrium. Yeah, he'd been depressed, but he'd felt stable.

Coming here to Pleasant Shores, being around the girls, Ria, and now his parents, was shaking him up big-time.

"It was good to see Ria," his mother said in a hesitant tone. "She's such a kind person. Couldn't you at least try to, you know, work things out?"

Drew lifted his hands, palms up. He didn't want to disappoint his mother. Didn't want to disappoint himself, for that matter. But the odds of him working things out with Ria were minuscule.

"How do you let your marriage fall apart, anyway?" Dad added, his tongue obviously loosened with the alcohol.

There was no good answer to that question. "It just happened," he said, mildly. In his mind he was thinking how Ria had never really wanted to marry him, even back when he was whole. It had just been the pregnancy that had pushed her into it.

Fast-forward to their actual separation, and all he knew was it hadn't been his idea; in fact, he'd been shocked when she had brought it up. Shocked into a cold silence that had seemed, somehow, to seal the deal, even though he hadn't really wanted the marriage to end.

"It only happens if you let it," his father said. "The one time Mama wanted to leave, I wouldn't let her."

"I remember," his mother said with a little laugh.

"Wait—what? You wanted to leave Dad?"

"I thought I did, but he wouldn't allow it."

"Dad," he protested, "you can't force people to stay who want to go." Especially now. What did he have to offer Ria now?

"Maybe not," his father said gruffly. "But you can't give up at the first sign of trouble, either." He paused, then added, "Ria is a good woman. Pretty, too. She won't stay single long."

Unbidden, the image of Ted Taylor came into his mind. Rich, blond, smooth. Wanting to have a so-called business meeting with Ria.

With Drew's wife.

Except she *wasn't* his wife. Shoving away the image of Ria and Ted together, he texted his daughters and told them to come by the restaurant when school let out. That led to a conversation about his phone's VoiceOver feature, which he'd gotten pretty adept at using after the tech training they'd offered in his rehab program.

His daughters finally arrived and there were hugs all around, and it was really the first time Drew was glad his parents had come. Kait and Sophia hadn't seen much of their grandparents since the divorce. Hearing his parents exclaim over how pretty they were, ask them about school, share news about their trips and the repairs they'd done to their house, he vowed to do better with helping the girls keep up that relationship.

He was shocked that Kait sat down with them and kept up a conversation, more of a conversation than she had had yet with Drew. Maybe she was turning the corner, getting things together.

A short while later, his parents stood. "We have to go," Dad said. "Want to beat the traffic. Can you girls help your father get home?"

"Of course," Sophia said.

Drew wished he didn't have to be led around, but he knew his limits. He wasn't familiar enough with the town to make it home on his own, not yet.

And he probably wouldn't stay long enough to *get* familiar. It was Wednesday, and he had been here six days already. The initial plan had been to stay for a week. He'd worried that it wasn't enough.

But Kait was being great. Maybe it had helped her in ways he hadn't expected.

As his mother and his daughters hugged and chatted, his father pulled him aside. "You need to figure out what you're going to do with your life," his father said. "You can't just live off the government. Or get back together with Ria so she can support you."

"I wasn't planning to do that!" Realizing he had spoken louder than he'd intended, Drew lowered his voice. "I'll work it out, Dad. Don't worry," he said. The last thing he needed was to get into a shouting match with his father.

But as his parents said their goodbyes, as his daughters helped him sign the check and guided him down the stairs to the street level, Drew felt sadly dependent and way less of a man than he used to be.

CHAPTER FIVE

"SO, YOU'RE STILL set on leaving tomorrow?" Ria asked Drew.

It was Friday night, and she had invited him to go along while she did a couple of errands and picked up something for the girls for dinner. They needed to talk, and she hadn't wanted to sit and face her gorgeous ex and think about all she'd lost. All he'd lost. All they'd lost together. So they parked and then walked along Beach Street, where the drugstore and the dry cleaner and a couple of restaurants were open late. It had been a balmy day, and a soft breeze blew in from the bay, just across from the shops.

When Ria's heart was so filled with turmoil about both Kait and Drew, how could the sky be so gorgeous? Deep purple clouds moved lazily against a lavender-and-pink background, with a hint of gold where the sun had disappeared an hour ago. The colors were reflected on the bay, flat as a mirror. A pair of waterbirds made a *kuk-kuk-kuk* sound as they swooped overhead, en route to the bay.

"I think Kait's doing better." Drew walked along beside her, and she noticed he was even more adept with his white cane. They were keeping up a pretty good pace.

"She does seem like she's doing better, yes." Ria bit her lip.

"But…" Drew prompted.

"I don't know." She glanced over at him to see if he was impatient with her slower way of thinking through emo-

tional things, like he'd been before. But there was more curiosity than annoyance on his face. "Maybe I'm just being
a worrier," she said, "but I can't believe everything got resolved so fast, and we still don't even know what caused
her problems at school."

"She did say she's fine, and that she wouldn't skip class
again."

"I know." But there was something in her daughter's
eyes...

"Sophia told me she thinks she's fine, too."

"Sophia was just mad that we made her stay home with
Kait tonight. She wants her babysitting duty to stop. But I'm
just not comfortable leaving Kait alone." When he didn't
answer, she sent him a sidelong glare. "You think I'm being
a worrywart, don't you?"

"I don't know." His mouth twisted a little. "The truth is,
I haven't been around the girls very much lately. And now
I can't see them. I used to be able to read Kait's face, but I
can't do that anymore."

There was pain in his words and it tugged at Ria's heart.
She couldn't imagine not being able to see her children.

"Look, I hate to go, but I have some meetings set up
next week with vocational and rehabilitation services and
a technology education program. And with my orientation
and mobility specialist. I need to get moving and figure
out what I'm going to do. Otherwise, it's going to be hard
for me to keep sending the same amount of child support,
and the last thing I want to do is let you and the girls down
that way."

"Thank you." She knew he was an honorable man. She'd
always admired that about him.

If she wasn't careful, her emotions would get involved

again, which she couldn't allow to happen. It was better that he left, and soon.

Because Drew didn't love her. He hadn't loved her before, and he would love her even less if he knew about the miscarriage.

She couldn't erase it from her conscience, but she could do everything in her power to help Kaitlyn and thus redeem herself as a mother. That was what mattered, not some shadowy attraction she still felt for her ex.

They ordered a pizza from the girls' favorite spot, but it was backed up and they had an hour to wait for it. "Let's go over to Goody's, get a cup of coffee and figure out how we're going to do visitation," she said. "I think it's really important for the girls that you continue seeing them more often. They've loved having you here."

As they passed the Lighthouse Lit bookstore, Mary came out to flip the sign from Open to Closed. She was one of the town's mysterious figures, a benefactor to the Healing Heroes cottage for wounded police officers and their canines. No one really knew much about her background, including Ria, even though Mom had been working at the shop for more than a year. Mary was lovely, her shoulder-length silver hair always impeccably curled, her skin and makeup beautiful, her figure slim. Word had it that she was pushing seventy, but you couldn't necessarily guess her age. She had true timeless beauty.

They stopped, and Ria introduced Drew.

"Oh, I know all about you." Mary smiled and shook Drew's hand with both of hers.

He smiled, obviously sensing Mary's charisma. "I'm flattered, but I can't believe you've heard of me. My life isn't interesting enough for people to talk about."

"Your mother-in-law—well, former mother-in-law—works here." The implication being that Mom talked about Drew.

Oh well, Ria couldn't blame her. News was sparse in Pleasant Shores.

"I can stay open another fifteen or twenty minutes if you want to browse," Mary said. "Almost anything we have in the shop is available on audiobook, as well, if that's easier."

"Thanks for that," Drew said. "I may come in another time, but right now, we're headed for Goody's and some chocolate ice cream."

"Black coffee for me," Ria said regretfully. She loved Goody's ice cream, but she *had* to lose a few pounds before the holiday season.

"Would you stop with the calorie counting," Drew said. "You look great the way you are."

How would you know, Ria thought but didn't say. It was actually a little refreshing that Drew couldn't see her. She didn't worry as much about wearing clothes that hid her hips and thighs.

"He's right, you know," Mary said. "You're gorgeous just as you are, and life is too short to drink black coffee when there's chocolate ice cream available."

"You have a point. Great to see you." She gave Mary a side-arm hug. And as they headed down the street toward Goody's, Ria thought about what Drew had said.

She had grown up so weight conscious because of her father's frequent comments and her mother's endless diets. She'd started restricting food when she was a teenager, and since then, there probably hadn't been a six-month period in which she didn't do some kind of dieting.

After she'd had the girls, things just got worse. Drew had always said he liked the way she looked, but she'd felt that he was just talking. She was far bigger than women on TV, in magazines and on social media. For that matter, she was far bigger than a woman like Mary.

In the last few years of their marriage, she'd become so self-conscious that she didn't like to get undressed in front of Drew. She'd found excuses to avoid going to bed at the same time as he did.

Not that she hadn't been attracted—she had been and still was, if she was being truthful with herself. But she'd felt too self-conscious to relax and enjoy, and so their intimate times had gotten fewer and farther between.

Drew had never been much of a communicator, and he'd gotten more tight-lipped the more she rejected his advances. And she guessed she hadn't been much of a communicator, either. She hadn't told him why she was hesitant to get undressed in front of him. She had just found ways to avoid it.

When she saw couples who were mismatched weight-wise, she sometimes wondered how they managed, and whether she and Drew could have worked through their issues, too.

Inside Goody's, Drew approached the counter as if he was familiar with the place. "Large bowl of chocolate and a medium butter pecan, both with hot caramel," he said.

"Drew!" She couldn't deny that sounded delicious, but really...

"Come on. You're in a tense situation, talking about visitation with your ex. You deserve a treat." He leaned closer. "And you're beautiful the way you are. Really."

The little growl in his words sent a charge through all the pleasure points of her body. Not just that he'd said she was beautiful, but the way he encouraged her to treat herself and indulge. He'd always been that kind of man. Confident enough in his masculinity to let him understand a woman's state of mind.

At least, he was that way when he wasn't angry or defensive. So it was good he was feeling more comfortable here, and with her, right?

She studied his face, the strong line of his jaw, the dark stubble he always got by evening. It would be *so* easy to fall under his spell again, but being under his spell didn't mean a successful relationship. That took openness and communication and trust.

And now, given that she was keeping the miscarriage a secret, she *really* didn't want to fall under his spell. No way, no how. That would only lead to pain.

They carried their dishes to a table in the corner, a little away from the busy crowd that was gathering.

She got out her phone. "So should we set some dates?" she asked, going for a businesslike tone.

"Ree. Let's just enjoy our ice cream. It's not like we're in a big hurry."

She relented, took a bite of butter pecan with caramel sauce and let out a groan. "Oh, Drew, this is fabulous."

"Enjoy," he said, his voice a little choked.

She wasn't sure why he sounded that way, and she decided not to worry about it. If she was going to have high-calorie ice cream, she was going to relish every bite. She'd worry about the consequences later.

"Did you know you're on some guy's Frock account?" It was Friday night, and Sophia had come into Kaitlyn's room and plopped down on her bed, uninvited.

"I don't pay attention to Frock, so no." Frock was the network of fake accounts kids at school used to hide their questionable social media activity from their parents. Kaitlyn had looked at Frock, of course, but she'd found it full of dumb things: people posting pictures of the insides of their nostrils, or the alcohol they'd supposedly stolen from their parents, or their latest lacy underwear.

"Maybe you should." Sophia was studying her phone.

Kaitlyn barely glanced up from the book she was reading, a superwoman fantasy that was the best escape ever. She'd discovered that it made her much happier than scrolling through Frock.

"It's bad."

Kaitlyn rolled her eyes. She knew Sophia's definition of *bad*. "What did I do, wear the wrong socks?"

"Look." Sophia held out her phone.

There was a photo of Kaitlyn, and thank goodness, she didn't look awful. She was wearing a green sweater that brought out the color of her eyes, and her hair was good that day.

And then she remembered the last time she'd worn that sweater. A cold hand of fear gripped her chest. "Whose account is that?"

Sophia lifted a shoulder. "TomDickandHarry. Do you know him? Or them?"

"No." Relief that it wasn't Chris washed over her, but it was short-lived. He could go by TomDickandHarry, for all she knew.

"Hit Play," Sophia said.

The cold grip tightened. "It's a video?"

"Just look at it." Sophia hit the play button herself.

And there was Chris Taylor, smiling at her in that charming way of his, moving close to her in the secluded area behind the stage at school, saying something that couldn't be discerned.

Kaitlyn knew what he'd said, though: "Take off your shirt." And "You're so pretty." And "No one will ever know."

And "I just want to see for a minute." And "I really want to go out with you, but I just want to see you first."

She'd held out for a little while, but in the end, the idea of a boy being attracted to her and wanting to date her, the chance to be popular and cool for once, had been too persuasive to withstand.

She watched, horrified but unable to look away, as she slowly stripped off her shirt for him.

What he said next was audible: "Bra, too?"

The Kaitlyn on the screen—who already seemed so much younger than Kaitlyn felt in real life—shook her head, cheeks pink, hair going over her face.

He reached out and gently brushed back a strand of her hair, tucking it behind her ear. "Please?" he said.

And she started to do it, reaching behind herself to unhook her bra, which caused her breasts to point out like she was some kind of porn star, right out there on social media for everyone in the world to see. Their embarrassing size was obvious, and so was the fact that she needed to lose a few. Her side flab hung over the edge of her jeans, now unprotected by a shirt.

"At least you had on a pretty bra," Sophia said now.

"Shut *up*."

He reached out, and she jerked away. That had made her come to her senses, and she stopped before unhooking the last hook, grabbed for her sweater and covered herself.

He'd pouted and begged, but she hurried away, sweater covering her front, her back fat visible for anyone to see.

"He was *filming* it?" was all she could say through a throat thick with horror.

"It wasn't him filming. It had to be one of his friends. Didn't you know to look around? Boys *always* film that stuff. I could have told you…" Sophia trailed off. "Man, if kids made fun of you before, this makes it twenty times worse."

Kaitlyn was hearing her sister's words, but it was through what felt like thick cotton. She couldn't believe it.

But as she started thinking about what had transpired after she'd stupidly taken off her shirt, it was suddenly more believable; in fact, everything clicked into place.

Her hope that Chris would actually become her boyfriend had faded quickly; he'd avoided her, and when she'd finally worked up the courage to talk to him last week, he acted like he barely knew who she was.

Right after that, Chris's older friends, especially popular Tyler, had started teasing her, so she'd figured out that Chris had told other people that she'd taken off her shirt for him after school. That had been awful enough, but she'd denied everything. After all, guys lied all the time.

And then Shelby Grayson, one of the almost-popular girls in tenth grade, had started making remarks about the size of Kaitlyn's chest.

Now, though…

Now there was proof. Now there was this image—she wrapped her arms around her stomach and bent forward, feeling sick—this image of her body, out there for anyone to see.

For all the school to see.

Had Chris known they were filming that awful encounter? And was the person who'd filmed it one of the mean boys who'd been teasing her, or someone else entirely?

The ramifications rained down on her. "Don't tell Mom and Dad." She gripped her sister's hand, hard. "Promise me you won't show them." If either of them saw what she'd done, they'd never forgive her. Mom, always trying to teach them to be proud of themselves, respectful, feminist. Dad was just…Dad. She was his little girl. If he learned about this, not only would he hunt down all the boys and strangle them, but he'd be so terribly disappointed in her. "Promise!" She squeezed Sophia's hands tight.

"Ow! Fine. I promise."

"Delete it from your phone. Unfollow him, so you can't show it to them no matter what."

"Fine. I will."

Kaitlyn glared at her until she actually did unfollow TomDickandHarry.

"What are you gonna do?" Sophia asked.

Kaitlyn crossed her arms over her sick-feeling stomach again and looked up at the ceiling. Tears pooled in her eyes. She shook her head. "I don't know," she whispered. "What *can* I do?"

"I mean, we can't change schools, not really. We could get bused to Jefferson Public, but with as small as the shore is…"

"The kids there would find out."

"Yeah." Sophia's phone was dinging, and she picked it up and looked at it. She glanced over at Kaitlyn and then turned off her notifications.

"What?"

Sophia shook her head. "Just dumb stuff."

"It's not about me, is it?"

Sophia glanced down at her phone again, shook her head, then nodded. "Just a few people asking me what's going on." Sophia patted Kaitlyn's shoulder, which she wouldn't normally have done.

It just showed how bad things were, that Sophia would comfort her and be affectionate.

"At least you're *built*," Sophia said. "You're not gonna have any problem getting a date now."

"I don't want to date anyone who likes looking at something like that!" She didn't want to date anyone, ever. Didn't even want to face anyone.

Going to school on Monday was going to be horrible. Maybe Mom would let her stay home. She'd already used up the cramps excuse, but if she gargled hot water, maybe she could convince Mom she had a fever. She *felt* like she had a fever.

But staying home and wondering what people were saying wasn't exactly going to be fun. Even now she had a sick desire to listen in on people, to grab Sophia's phone and see what the general attitude toward the video was.

"Maybe I can get homeschooled," she mused out loud.

"And hide in the house until you're eighteen and can leave?" Sophia shook her head impatiently. "Besides, Mom and Dad won't let you do that. They think socialization is too important."

"Then what do I do?" The last word came out on a quaver.

"You should have thought of that before you took off your shirt!"

"Well, I didn't!"

Sophia picked up her phone and studied it, and then her cheeks got pink. "Now people are texting me to see if I'll take off *my* shirt or send a nude." She blew out a breath. "I'm gonna get that thing taken down."

"Can you?"

"I can try."

"Don't rat him out," Kaitlyn begged. Chris had shown he was willing to do something awful, letting someone film that encounter. Whoever TomDickandHarry might be, they were undoubtedly popular and influential, and she didn't dare get them in trouble.

"I won't—I'm not stupid." Sophia stood and stalked out, slamming the door behind her. A minute later, Sophia's bedroom door slammed.

Kait looked around her room, her heart beating faster and faster, a loud drumming in her ears. She couldn't go anywhere tonight, no way. Tomorrow, she and Dad were supposed to do something together before he left Pleasant Shores, but that couldn't happen; someone might say something that would spill the beans. Church on Sunday was out, because by then the video might have made its way to the religious crowd.

Couldn't go to school Monday. Couldn't not go to school Monday.

She thought about the video again, how she'd looked in it, what a fool she'd been. Then she stood and, as if sleepwalking, went to her desk drawer.

She pulled out the little bottle shoved way to the back.

She'd been sneaking Mom's sleeping pills for a couple of months now, one here, a couple there. When she couldn't sleep, she'd take half a pill, sometimes a whole one.

She had six in the jar now.

She shut her eyes. If she took two right now, she'd go to sleep for sure. Normal dosage was just one, according to Mom's pill bottle. Quickly, she opened the bottle, shook out two pills and swallowed them.

The image of herself, her chest sticking out without a shirt, pushed back into her mind. She wasn't the kind of girl who liked showing off. She mostly wore loose T-shirts and hoodies.

Now everyone would know what was underneath. What if boys did ask her out, but only to make fun of her and see what they could get?

She was still holding the pill bottle in her hand.

What if she took them all?

It might make her sick, really sick. Might even…

But wouldn't the family be better off without her? Sophia wouldn't be embarrassed. Mom and Dad could work out their problems and get back together.

The guys at school, including that horrible TomDickand-Harry, whoever he was, would get in trouble. They'd feel terriblc, sorry. All the other kids would hate them.

The girls who'd been mean to her, the kids who'd shoved her in Goody's…all of them would be falling over themselves to say how great she was, how ashamed they were. Their parents would condemn them.

Before she could think more about it, she poured the rest of the pills into her hand, grabbed a half-empty can of soda and swallowed them down.

CHAPTER SIX

"So it was touch and go for a few days," Drew said. They'd ended up staying at Goody's talking for longer than Drew had expected. Ria was drawing him out about what had gone down when he'd had his accident. "Apparently, they didn't know if I'd make it or not. They actually induced a coma for a little bit."

"Why didn't someone call me?" Ria sounded distressed. "Drew, you could've died!"

"I put down Mike as my contact person," he said. "That's who they called, and the guys in the department rallied around."

"It's not the same as family."

"We're divorced, Ria." It was sweet of her to act concerned, but the reality was that she had no obligation to him, not anymore. "I had no right to burden you, and Mom and Dad have their own struggles. I managed. The social workers at the hospital set me up with all kinds of services."

"It must have been terrifying. To wake up and realize you couldn't see."

"It was." Drew remembered digging at his face and eyes, trying to rip the bandages off them, before he'd figured out that there weren't any bandages, that he was in the hospital and that he had lost his vision. He shook his head rapidly, like Navy after a bath. "I don't even like to think about that time."

She put a hand over his. "I'm so sorry, Drew. If there's anything—"

His phone buzzed, but he ignored it. "Like I said, you have no obligation. I should have let you know what was going on, and I should've figured out a way to keep on visiting the girls even despite my issues. I…I wasn't thinking I was that important to them." Which sounded pitiful, but it was true. Ria always seemed to have everything under control, and he'd felt like more of an extra than a main actor in the show of their lives.

Plus, he hadn't wanted any of them to see him this way, to pity him.

"You're *really* important to them."

He was starting to believe it. "I apologize. Really. I should have been there for the girls." He almost wanted to say "for you," but that wasn't his right. As he'd emphasized to her, they were divorced.

"Water under the bridge," Ria said, but she sounded worried. "I know Sophia will be fine. And Kait will, too. It's just…it's been such a tough phase for her. Much tougher than anything Sophia ever went through."

Her phone buzzed, and he heard her grab her purse and fumble through it. He had to grin. Ria always had a giant, overstuffed purse, and she could never find anything in it.

"Where is that thing…? Okay, here." She was silent a few seconds. "It's Sophia. Hi, honey." Another couple of seconds of silence. "What? No! Call 911!"

Drew stood and he could hear Ria standing, too. She thrust her phone into his right hand and grabbed his left one, tugging him toward the door. "Talk to Sophia. Kait told her she took a bunch of sleeping pills and now she's passed out. Sophia already called 911, so…"

A sudden coldness hit him at the core. He pressed the

phone to his ear as he followed Ria out, banging into tables and chairs in his haste. "Sophia, it's Dad. How is she?"

"She's breathing and everything but I can't wake her up." Sophia's voice was panicky.

"Try," he urged. "They're sending an ambulance, right?"

"Yeah." She paused. "Kait! Kait, wake up!"

"Do you see the bottle?" His heart was pounding out of his chest. As they practically ran through the parking lot, he could hear Ria's gasping sobs.

"I hear the sirens and… I think they're here. Let me look." There was a pause, and then Sophia spoke again. "It's the ambulance."

"Stay on the phone," he ordered. Calm in the face of terror, a skill any cop had to learn, was all that was keeping him together. Ria didn't have that. She flung open the passenger door and half shoved him toward it, then ran around the front of the car. A moment later, as he climbed in, she started the engine.

"Wait." He put a hand on Ria's arm. "Take a breath."

"I have to get to her!" She was breathing fast, panicky.

"You can't drive like this. And we don't know where to go yet." He reached in her direction and found her hand. Shaking. He squeezed it. "Sophia, what are they doing?" he asked into the phone.

"They're checking her vital signs and…" She spoke to someone and then came back on the line. "After that, they're taking her to the hospital." He heard more voices, then Sophia's again. "They say I can ride along. Should I do that?"

"Yes. Ride with her and we'll meet you at the hospital. How is she?" He fumbled with the phone but couldn't figure out how to get it on speaker without risking losing the connection.

"I don't know. They're hooking her up to oxygen." Sophia's voice caught. "They want to ask me questions. I have to go."

"Tell her to get my sleeping pills out of my medicine cabinet," Ria said in a choked voice. "Maybe we can tell how many are gone."

"Good idea." He relayed the message to Sophia and she agreed.

Then he turned back to Ria. "Are you okay to drive?"

"Yeah." She blew her nose. "I can do it." In her voice he heard the resolute bucking up that she'd always been able to muster when her daughters needed her.

They drove in silence for several minutes. He could tell Ria was pushing the speed limit, but she wasn't squealing around corners or braking hard. He listened to the phone, but Sophia had ended the call and he didn't want to call her back, didn't want to interrupt whatever was going on.

His heart was racing, his adrenaline spiking, but he drew in deep breaths. He couldn't freak out now.

Images of his younger daughter played like a movie through his mind. The day she was born, wrinkled and tiny and beautiful. Her first steps, which they'd watched on video many times. Birthday parties and first days of school and gymnastics competitions. "I wish she didn't have to quit gymnastics," he said.

"What?" Ria accelerated and then reached a steady, faster pace. They were on the highway now.

"Gymnastics. That was so good for her. I'm sorry she had to stop." Inane to talk about something like that now, but Ria usually preferred conversation to silence. It might help her to stay calm.

"No gymnastics on this part of the peninsula. She said she was ready to quit." Ria's voice sounded defensive.

"Look, I'm not blaming you," he said. "I'm just thinking about what would cause her to do such a thing, to try to…" He broke off. "Are we almost there?"

"Five minutes. And you *should* be blaming me. I'm blaming myself. Why in the name of heaven didn't I lock up those pills?"

He'd thought the same thing but dismissed it. The horse was out of the barn now, and who'd have pegged Kaitlyn for stealing pills out of her mother's medicine cabinet?

"Will they pump her stomach? She'd…" Her voice caught. "She'd hate that so much."

"Doubtful," he said and reached over to squeeze her arm, just a quick, light touch meant to comfort. It comforted him, too. "Depends how much she took and when, but they don't do that as often anymore. They may just monitor her, or they could give her something to absorb the drug. Activated charcoal, probably, or maybe there's a counter-medication."

The car slowed, came to a stop, then turned, and a moment later Ria was parking it. "I'll come around for you," she said, and Drew felt a flash of humiliation. How many times had he said that to her, wanting her to let him be a gentleman and take care of her, something she wasn't quite comfortable with? He should be opening her door for her, not the reverse, but there wasn't time for him to make his way over to her door by touch. He got out of the car and she offered him her arm. They hurried into the emergency room.

Drew's heart was pounding harder than ever, almost out of his chest. Was his little girl okay?

RIA RUSHED TO the ER check-in desk, Drew holding her elbow, her heart nearly exploding out of her chest. "We need to see Kaitlyn Martin. Right away."

"You can't—" the tight-lipped receptionist began.

"We're her parents," Drew broke in.

"Oh! Hang on." She looked at Drew, then looked again with open admiration and ran a finger down a list. "Yes, she's here. We'll need to get insurance information ASAP."

"Sure thing," he said. "We're pretty eager to see her now."

Thank heavens for Drew's calm demeanor, his easy way with people. He was good in a crisis. His amazing good looks didn't hurt in terms of getting the cooperation of females from eight to eighty. *Let us in, let us in*, she telegraphed mentally to the receptionist.

"Well, I'm technically supposed to get all your information first, but…" She waved a hand to the right. "I'll buzz you in at the double doors."

Two minutes later they were walking down the hall. When Ria saw Sophia looking out from one of the curtained cubicles, she broke into a run, and Drew jogged alongside her.

Ria gave Sophia a quick hug, then passed her toward Drew and rushed to the hospital bed.

Kaitlyn lay there, face pale, eyes closed, hair damp with sweat. An IV was hooked up beside the bed. She looked sick and vulnerable. But the absence of medical professionals suggested that she wasn't in immediate danger, praise God.

"Honey, it's Mom," she said, gently rubbing her arm, her heart settling a little. Kait was alive, breathing, in a place and with people who could help. Her shoulders sagged with the relief of it.

Kait tossed her head a little. Her eyes flickered open, then closed again, and her hand tightened on Ria's.

So she was responsive. More weight shifted from Ria's shoulders. Something dripped onto Kait's arm, and she realized it was her own tears.

Sophia had guided Drew to the opposite side of the bed and he sat down on it, his hand on Kait's other arm. "Hey, baby girl," he said. "How are you feeling?"

The deep rumble of his voice was reassuring to Ria, and Kait must have felt the same way; a faint smile lifted the corners of her mouth for the briefest second. But although they both asked her questions, she didn't answer, seeming to drift off again.

"How's our patient?" The big, hearty doctor's voice sounded familiar, and Ria realized he was the father of one of Kaitlyn's classmates. "Dr. Smith. Ria, right? And I've already met Sophia."

She nodded and introduced Drew, told him about the doctor's connection to Kaitlyn's schoolmate. The two men shook hands.

Five minutes later, the doctor had explained the activated charcoal that should safely help remove the remaining medicine from Kait's system, and said it seemed likely there would be no lingering damage. He told them he'd tried to speak with Kait, to ask her about what had happened, without success.

"She needs a little recovery time," he said now. "We'll see where a room is available, preferably in the pediatric unit, but if not there, up on eight, in the psychiatric unit."

"Why that unit?" Drew asked quickly.

The doctor leaned his hip against the sink. "When someone takes an overdose of a prescription medication," he said, "we treat it as a suicide attempt."

The words, spoken aloud, pushed Ria back into her chair. She'd thought it herself, but for a professional to confirm it shot horror through her.

Oh, Kait. She leaned over her daughter and wrapped her arms around her, gently so as not to dislodge her IV.

"You said you treat it as one," Drew interjected. "So you're not sure?"

"When she first told me what she did, back at the house, she said it was an accident," Sophia said quickly.

But how could you accidentally take an overdose of someone else's pills?

"She only took five or six, from what we can estimate," the doctor said.

"Still, five or six isn't an accident." Drew said the words flatly. He was stroking Kait's arm, lightly. "Listen, Doc, we have a lot of concerns, but one of them is confidentiality. This is a small town, and your children attend Kait's school—"

"My lips are sealed," the man said quickly. "They would be anyway, just as an ethical thing, but the HIPAA regulations bind me, and everyone else who works with Kaitlyn, to keep her records and medical information private."

"Thank you," Ria said. Drew echoed the words and the doctor left, promising that they'd hear soon about a room for overnight.

Ria just wanted to hold and comfort her daughter. But Drew had other ideas. "Tell us what happened, from the top," he said to Sophia. "Did something upset Kait?"

Sophia hesitated, then spoke. "I don't know of anything specific."

"But you know something." Drew must have heard it in Sophia's voice.

"Tell us," Ria said. "Please. It's important. It's *really* important."

"It's just…some kids have been teasing her."

"I thought so." Drew slammed his fist into his open hand. "It happened at the ice-cream store, the first day I came."

"What happened?" Ria glared at him, even though he couldn't see her. "Why didn't you tell me?"

"I should have. We all have to keep the lines of communication open."

Yeah, yeah, Ria wanted to say. Drew was upset and angry, and like a lot of men, when he felt like that, he started giving orders. But orders weren't going to help anything, not now.

"What are they teasing her about, honey?" she asked Sophia.

Sophia lifted a shoulder. "Oh, you know. Her…" She glanced at Drew. "Her chest, and stuff."

"Her *chest*?" Drew exploded. "She's fourteen!"

Ria looked at Sophia and raised an eyebrow. Sophia rolled her eyes.

Drew didn't know much about how advanced kids were these days. Either that, or he thought his own daughters to be exempt from the way society had been moving.

And although he'd hugged Kaitlyn, he must not have considered the impact her 34D chest would have on teenage boys.

"I'll talk to her about it," Ria said, almost relieved to know that was the issue. It was one she was familiar with herself. Genes didn't lie; Ria had been in the same situation, an early developer.

"But is that enough for her to want to take an overdose?" Drew asked, shaking his head.

"I wouldn't have thought so," Ria said. "But Kait's… sensitive."

"She is." Sophia sounded relieved, and Ria frowned. There was something a little off in the way Sophia was acting, but you could hardly blame her; she'd discovered her sister in danger, ridden to the hospital in an ambulance and spoken with the medical professionals enough to get them started treating Kaitlyn.

Love for her older daughter welled up, and Ria crossed the cubicle to kneel beside Sophia. "Poor kiddo," she said. "You've had quite a night. You did a really good job."

"It was awful, Mom." And then Sophia teared up, and Ria put her arms around her and held her and stroked her hair.

She looked over Sophia's shoulder, and Drew was patting Kait's arm, leaning forward, talking to her quietly. Even though Kait wasn't awake, it was probably the right thing to do.

Why had they let their family fall apart? This was where they needed to be, together.

She should have worked harder to resolve her issues with Drew. If she'd done that, maybe they would still be an intact family, all together. Maybe Kait wouldn't have been driven to this desperate act.

Maybe Ria wouldn't have miscarried their baby, and they'd be a family of five. The thought of that was a knife twisting in her gut.

She looked at Drew, so handsome and so concerned, trying so hard to be the father his daughters needed, and her heart warmed even as her stomach churned.

She wanted to lean on him, but she shouldn't. Couldn't. The issues that had caused their marriage to disintegrate hadn't gone away, and her miscarriage stood as a secret and a barrier between them.

She had to back away, but how could she when their daughters needed both of them? When, truth to tell, her own heart was melting toward him?

Sophia pulled away and grabbed for a tissue, then another. "I'm sorry, Mom. I'm just losing it."

"Of course you are. You were incredibly strong and you

did what you needed to do to help your sister. We're proud of you."

Sophia looked away and got very busy wiping her eyes and checking for smeared makeup via the camera on her cell phone.

"You know," Ria said, "if there's anything you need to tell me, tell us, we won't judge. We just want to know how to help Kait."

Sophia shook her head rapidly. "No, there's nothing."

"Are you sure, Soph?" Drew said from Kait's bedside.

"Yes, I'm sure!" She scooted her chair back against the wall and studied her phone. "I have, like, twenty million texts and Snaps. Can I just answer them?"

Ria glanced at Drew. "Sure. Your father and I need to figure out what to do next, once Kaitlyn's assigned to a room."

"If there's a pop machine, maybe we could go get some sodas while we figure it out," Drew suggested. "Want something, Soph?"

"Anything with caffeine," she said without looking up.

"Will do. We'll be back in five." Drew stood and made his way carefully around the bed.

Though Ria was reluctant to leave her daughters even for a minute, she knew it was the case that she and Drew needed to talk. "Text me if she wakes up or if they come in with news about the room," she said, squeezing Sophia's shoulder.

"I will." Again, Sophia didn't look up. Obviously, she needed a break from the intensity of the past few hours.

As they walked out of the ER and headed toward the vending machines, Drew wrapped an arm around her and hugged her against his side. He kept an arm loosely around her shoulders as they made their way down the hospital's long hall.

She was grateful. She needed to feel his strength.

Turmoil churned inside her. Every minute she was near Drew, she wanted to confess the mistakes that had deprived him of another child. But she also wanted to throw herself in his arms. It was important for the girls that he was here, but his presence was a disaster for Ria's peace of mind. "It's good you were here when this happened," she said finally.

"I think so, too," he said. "Kaitlyn needs both of us. In fact…" He hesitated.

They'd reached the vending machines, and Ria dug for bills and change in her purse. "In fact what?"

"I think…" he said slowly. "I think I should stay in Pleasant Shores."

Ria's hand went nerveless, the coins she'd been holding showering to the floor. Of course, he was right. The girls, Kaitlyn especially, needed him, and that was paramount.

The fact that his presence rubbed salt in Ria's wounded heart…well, that was insignificant next to their children's needs.

CHAPTER SEVEN

SUNDAY AFTERNOON, Drew walked into the motel lobby, Navy at his side, feeling wary.

He'd planned to talk to Ria once she got home from church, figure out what to do about living here and about Kaitlyn's upcoming release from the hospital. But before he could have that conversation, while he'd been walking Navy, Ria had called out from the motel lobby, asking him to come to some sort of a meeting. He didn't know who would be there nor what the meeting was about, except that it related to Kaitlyn.

More than anything else in the world, he wanted to help his daughter. He'd committed to stay in town for the next few months at least. But the truth was, he was a disabled stranger in a strange town, with no job. Right at this moment, going into a situation where he didn't know what to expect… Yeah. He was definitely on edge.

"There's a couch two feet to your right." Ria was suddenly standing next to him, and he felt a sharp tingle of awareness. Her slightly husky voice, the flowery perfume she wore—it had always had its effect on him. Plus there was the fact that she was beautiful and didn't even know it.

Thinking of her beauty stabbed him, because he couldn't see it. Couldn't read the expression on her face, couldn't watch her tilt back her head when she laughed, couldn't look into her eyes.

The loss pressed down on him, making it hard to breathe.

He sucked in air, pushed the negative thoughts away and sat down, and Ria sat next to him. After a short, quiet bark, Navy settled at his feet. He heard a few voices around him, including that of Ria's mother, Julie. "Who all is here?" he asked, but Ria was talking to someone else.

There were multiple reasons he didn't want to stay on at the motel, but Ria was one of them. He'd had to face the fact that he was still attracted to her, but she didn't want him and didn't love him. He hadn't been enough for her when they'd married and he definitely wasn't enough for her now.

"Okay, everyone," Julie said, clapping her hands to make the chatter stop. "Thank you for being willing to meet up. We're all concerned about Kaitlyn and want to make sure she's fully supported when she comes back home."

Drew stiffened. Way to leave him out of it. He loved Julie, and she was a wonderful grandmother to the girls, but she could definitely be too take-charge.

She must have read his body language. "Drew, I'm sorry I didn't discuss this with you first. Ria and I ran into these folks at church and it just came into my mind that we should all meet."

"Who's we all? And what about my daughter's privacy?" He emphasized the *my* just a little.

Ria squeezed his arm very briefly. "Besides Mom and Mary, who you met before, there's Trey and Erica here. You've probably heard us talk about them. Trey was at the Healing Heroes cottage for a while—he's a part-time cop in town now but formerly was on the force in Philly. And Erica's a teacher in the behavior support program at Sophia and Kait's school." She paused, then added, "Everyone will respect Kait's privacy, right, guys?"

There was a chorus of assent.

"Hi, Drew," came a cultured voice. "It's Mary. We met in front of my bookstore a few days ago. I'm here because I know everyone in town and am generally considered a good resource." A soft, thin hand clasped his, briefly, and then there was a snuffling against his leg, the feeling of small paws clawing at his calf, as if a small creature was standing on back legs, propping itself against Drew's leg. He reached down and encountered fur and a sloppy lick.

"And that's Baby, my dog. You'll have to forgive her manners. In dog years, she's even older than I am."

He reached a hand down to Navy, making sure the small interloper wasn't disturbing her or vice versa, but Navy was panting and relaxed. So he rubbed a hand over each dog's fur and some of his tension eased.

"Here's the situation," Ria said to the group. "Kaitlyn told the doctors that she took six sleeping pills because she wanted to get some rest, not because she wanted to end her own life. They believe her, and so she's coming home tomorrow. But Drew and I aren't convinced she was telling the truth, nor that she's going to be able to just reintegrate into her life at home and school so easily."

"You must be so worried," said a gentle female voice. That had to be Erica, the teacher. "Anything Trey and I can do to help, we're happy to."

"I think the problem has to do with other kids at her school," Drew said. "Is there another option? Can she switch schools, get a fresh start?"

"There's nothing that wouldn't involve a long drive each day," Ria said. "Which I'm totally willing to do if that's what we decide, but I'm not sure whether that would be the best."

"Something could be set up with car pools," the other man in the room, Trey the cop, said. "But has anyone considered having her enroll in the behavior support program right here in town, at the Academy?"

There was a silence.

"What *is* the behavior support program?" Drew asked.

"It's the part of the school where Erica teaches," Ria said. "For at-risk kids. And I'm not sure Kaitlyn… Well, I'm not sure she qualifies, and I'm not sure whether she'd like it."

"It's an interesting idea," Erica said. "We have students of middle school and high school age. Most of them have some sort of behavioral or social issue—that's why they're assigned to our school."

"But they're really just kids," Trey said. "I don't see why Kaitlyn shouldn't join in."

"Because she knows the stigma," Mary said. "The behavior support kids do mingle with the rest of the students, but there's also a bit of a dividing line, isn't there, dear?"

"There is," Erica said. "And some teasing. But if she's getting teased already…"

"That's just it," Ria said. "The behavior support program is a part of the same school where she's faced all of these problems. I'm not sure having her there would spare her the teasing."

"She'd be out of the classroom with the kids who've teased her," Julie said. "That would help."

"Would she get the education she needs?" Drew asked Erica. "I don't mean any offense by that, but she's very bright and needs to be challenged. If it's a mixed-grade classroom, with some tough kids, is that possible?"

"I'd do my best," Erica said slowly, "and I do have one other highly gifted student who'd be a good learning partner for her, but my co-teacher and I couldn't teach her alone. We'd need to find her some extra enrichment, extra projects."

"There are plenty of things that need done around this town," Mary said. "Drew, Erica's class already does a lot of service projects. I could imagine Kaitlyn getting involved in those and more."

"How would doing extra service projects challenge her?" he asked.

There was a short silence, and Drew wondered if he'd offended Erica. But someone had to ask questions. His daughter's education, as well as her happiness, deserved attention.

"It's all in how it's presented," Erica said. "There's background research that goes into each service learning project, and follow-up reports. I already have Rory, that's my other gifted student, doing some of the work, but he has issues with social skills. Kaitlyn could be a big help, and in the process, she'd be researching, writing, calculating, meeting with people—"

"That would be perfect for Kait," Julie interrupted, sounding excited. "She's very practical and she hates busywork. If she saw that the research she was doing had a real-world function, I bet she'd love it."

"It's worth running by her, to see what she thinks," Ria said doubtfully.

"No." Drew waved a hand. "Let's don't run it by her. If that's what we decide is best, we need to just tell her, not ask her. And she needs to start right away. Sitting around at home, making too many decisions for herself…it can't be good for her."

"I have to agree," Mary said. "She's young to make her own decisions. And she'd benefit from the protection of being in a familiar environment right now."

"You and Ria need to talk about it and decide," Julie said, "but I think it's a terrific idea. Between that and Drew staying on in town for a while, maybe she can get back on track."

As everyone talked on, weight lifted from Drew's shoulders. Helping his daughter wasn't going to fall solely on him and Ria. This was a good community and people were willing to help.

In fact, listening to them brainstorm made him wonder if maybe they'd help him, too.

He wasn't good at asking for help, or at least, he hadn't been in the past. But as his O&M instructor had constantly reminded him, nobody could handle a visual impairment entirely alone. He cleared his throat, and when there was a break in the conversation, he jumped in. "I'm staying in town for a while, like Julie mentioned," he said, "but I need to find another place to rent. Do any of you know of an apartment that's available?"

"You can stay here at the motel," Ria said. There was some kind of tension in her voice. Of course there was. Having him stay here couldn't be easy.

He wouldn't inflict that on her. "You need to have full-paying occupancy. And I need a place where I can be independent. Ideally, I need to find work here in town, as well."

"Hey," Julie said.

"You know…" Mary said at the same moment.

Then there was a silence. "What?" Drew asked.

"Healing Heroes," Trey said. "It's standing empty." His voice shifted, and Drew could tell Trey was leaning toward him, facing him. "It's a cottage for disabled cops and their K-9 partners, funded by an anonymous donor. You get a few months to rehabilitate and get your life together, rent free. In exchange, you do some significant volunteer work in the community."

That sounded an awful lot like charity, and Drew opened

his mouth to refuse, but Trey went on talking. "I did it. That's how I ended up here in Pleasant Shores. I was re-habbing my back after an injury."

"Tell him about your volunteer work," Julie urged.

"I worked at the school, in the behavior support pro-gram." Trey's voice softened. "Had a pretty tough cooper-ating teacher, but in the end it worked out."

There was low laughter all around. "His cooperating teacher was Erica, and he married her," Julie explained. "Is there a need for another volunteer in the Academy?"

"I couldn't do that," Drew broke in. "Nope. Not if Kait's going to go there. Last thing she needs is her father look-ing over her shoulder."

Mary cleared her throat, and just like that, everyone quieted. It was obvious that the older woman commanded respect among the others. "Another possibility is the oral history project," she said. "The historical society has a grant for it, but the intern who was going to do the work just backed out on us."

"Drew majored in history," Ria said. "And he's good with people."

Her words warmed Drew, but he didn't want to get into something over his head. Maybe he'd been good with peo-ple once, but when he couldn't see them, connecting was harder. "What kind of people?"

"Mostly the local watermen," Mary said. "We're gather-ing data for a small museum here in town. Trying to capture the lifestyle here before everything goes modern. Sharing information about the bay, the issues it faces—overfishing, pollution, climate change."

Drew had always loved fishing and the outdoors, and he liked talking to people, got along well with older folks. He sat up straighter, catching the excitement. The possibility that he could work, support himself, felt like a precious gift. And doing something that actually appealed to him was even better.

"I'd be interested to hear more about the job." He already knew there were services he could get to help him with any employment opportunities he could find. "Meanwhile, is the cottage nearby?"

"It's my old house, so you've been there before," Julie said. "Remember the beach cottage? I didn't want to live there anymore after Melvin left, and someone came forward wanting to buy it for the purpose of helping K-9 officers. The condition was that I'd manage it."

Now Drew remembered hearing something about the whole situation, from the girls. And the idea of living in the little beach cottage, of having that independence… Yeah. It was pretty much perfect, and he said so.

"Call me later this afternoon," Trey said. "Hand me your phone and I'll punch in my number. I can show you around the Healing Heroes cottage. Nice place."

Soon Drew could hear that people were getting up, gathering their things. He felt someone stop in front of him. "It's Trey. Great to meet you, man. We'll talk later."

"And I'm Erica. Just let me know if you have any questions about the school. I'd love to have Kaitlyn in class, and if you and Ria want that to happen, best to get the paperwork started right away."

Mary and Julie both greeted him on the way out, too, and then it was just him and Ria.

"Do you want to talk about Kait's schooling now?" he asked Ria.

"You could've stayed here, you know," she said instead of answering his question.

"It wouldn't be good."

There was a pause. "Sure, I guess."

He heard the hurt in her voice. Maybe it was the emotions of the day, but he reached out and pulled her closer, into a hug, patting her back and, he had to admit to himself, enjoying the way she felt there.

Which was the problem. "It's too hard to be this close together," he growled into that familiar neck, and he felt her body respond in the way it always did, moving marginally closer and settling perfectly against him.

He'd ached to hold her, and now that he was doing it, the memories flooded him—from the first time he'd kissed her, young and full of bravado, pretending arrogance but secretly afraid, to the last time, when he'd put everything he had into it, hoping to save their marriage.

They stayed that way for a moment, and then she tugged loose. "Maybe it's better if you *do* go," she said.

"Yeah. Listen, let's both think about this a little and then I'll give you a call." He was trying to keep his tone cool, but it wasn't working.

And, yeah, it would be best to get a little distance on Ria, but that sure wasn't what he felt like doing.

"I'M NOT GOING to the behavior support class!" Kaitlyn stopped, still, on the front porch of her house, looking from her mother to her father in disbelief. Everything in her rebelled against their ridiculous suggestion. "No way. Forget about it."

"Come on. Let's walk and talk." Her mother started down the steps and then paused. "It's five steps down," she said to Dad.

Kaitlyn's fists clenched. "He *knows* that." Why did Mom have to treat Dad like a baby?

Neither of her parents answered; they just waited for her at the bottom of the steps.

She'd gotten home from the hospital earlier today, and already they were on her. She just wanted to take a nap, but they'd insisted she come out and walk and talk with them about something important: apparently, their wacky idea that she should enroll in her own school's behavior support program.

She walked down the stairs and followed, kicking at stones, as they led the way past the motel and toward the downtown of Pleasant Shores. The sun was trying to shine through a low layer of clouds, which was part of the point: until her newly prescribed meds kicked in, she was to try natural means of improving her mood: exercise and sunlight.

Mom and Dad, trying to be parents of the year, had insisted on this walk-and-talk. Killing three birds with one stone: sunlight, exercise and persuading her to do something that would ruin her life.

"We think the program will be good for you. A fresh start, but where you can still stay in the area." Mom's voice had taken on that pleading tone that so annoyed Kaitlyn. Why didn't Mom just act like a mom?

"Do you think I'm a weirdo? Do you want me to get teased even worse?" She shouldered past them and stomped ahead, her flip-flops flapping. She could almost hear Mom's effort not to comment on what a stupid choice of footwear she'd made.

So, even though her toes were freezing, she wasn't going to go back inside for socks and shoes. She led the way toward the edge of town where small cinder-block houses gave way to ponds and creeks surrounded by tall golden-dry grasses. Overhead, a flock of geese flew in a raggedy V, honking and calling to one another.

It sounded like the geese were arguing. But at least they had wings and could fly away.

"Tell us what happened to upset you so badly," Dad said, speeding up to walk beside her, his cane sweeping back and forth, "and if there's another way to fix it, we'll try."

"Nothing happened." No way was she telling them about that stupid video. Sophia had somehow gotten the boys to take it down, and she hoped she'd seen the last of it. Hoped not that many of her classmates had seen it, although that was unlikely. Everyone was on their phones 24/7.

The thought of walking into school knowing that half the people there had seen her without a shirt made her stomach heave. She covered the sound with a fake cough and crossed her forearms over her midsection, pressing hard.

"You took an overdose of sleeping pills, Kait!" Her mother sounded impatient. "Something must have happened!"

"It was an accident." Wasn't it?

That was what she'd told the counselor, because she'd realized almost immediately that if she said she'd tried to take her own life, she'd be stuck in that hospital, and counseling, forever.

As it was, she was committed to twice a week individual sessions and weekly family counseling. That was bad enough.

She could barely remember what she'd been thinking before swallowing those pills. She only remembered wanting to escape the ugliness of school and the stress of family problems, the severe shortage of friends.

Going to the behavior support program *would* keep her out of class changes and lunch tables. Or would it? She couldn't remember where the kids from that section of the school ate lunch. She'd tried to ignore them, had considered them strange.

She lifted her face to the cool breeze. Of course, she was now in the "strange" category, too.

If her new counselor heard her say that, she'd flip. Kaitlyn was to work on positive self-talk, remember her strengths, focus on what was going right.

Which, just now, was nothing.

"Can't I do cyberschool?" she asked her parents over her shoulder.

"I don't think that's a good idea." Dad had fallen back to walk with Mom, but now he caught up with her again. His cane found a rut in the road, and she reached out to steady him, but he navigated around it easily. That was Dad— easily managing new challenges, good at everything.

"You'd have to be supervised if you were homeschooled," Mom said, her voice worried, "and I don't see how—"

"Supervised!" Kaitlyn interrupted, staring at her mother. "Why? I'm not a little kid!"

"You tried to take your own life!"

"Stop saying that! I didn't!" She caught a glimpse of herself in the window of a parked car and crossed her arms tightly over her chest. She was wearing an old gray hoodie she'd gotten at Goodwill and her only pair of jeans that currently fit. She'd washed her hair but hadn't curled or straightened it, so it hung down in dampish strings.

No wonder she was being sent to behavior support. She looked like a total freak.

Or like someone who tried to kill herself.

"You did something very risky, at a minimum," Dad said. "So Mom's right. If you were to stay home, we'd need for you to be supervised at all times, and besides the fact that no one has time to do that, it wouldn't be much fun for you. Right?"

She didn't answer; she just grunted.

"Come on." He put an arm around her. "Let's head back into town and go to Goody's."

"This can't be fixed with ice cream!" Mom said. "Besides, one cone from there would take up all my calories for the day."

Kaitlyn had been about to say something along the same lines, but instantly, she shifted gears. "I'll go to Goody's. But I don't want to go to the behavior support thingy."

"Do you want to go back to your regular classes?" Mom was walking along beside her now, head down, kicking at leaves along the sidewalk.

"No." She couldn't. There was no way. It wasn't like she had friends at school, not real ones, but going to the behavior support program would be her social death knell.

Well, technically the video had been that, but going to the "special" program would seal her fate.

"You're not making good decisions," Dad said, tightening his grip on her shoulders just a little, like a hug. "And that's why Mom and I aren't asking you. We're *telling* you you're going to try this behavior support program."

Some tiny part of her felt relieved at Dad's stern, strong tone. And yet... "What do you care? You're leaving," she said.

"No, I'm not." He gave her shoulders one final squeeze. "I'm staying in Pleasant Shores."

Joy bubbled up inside her. "You are? How long?"

"For the foreseeable future. I'll be at the Healing Heroes cottage."

The idea of Dad sticking around made her tight shoulders relax. For three seconds. And then she realized that the kids would make double fun of her for having a blind dad. No way would they forget about it if he was in town, in their face, at the school, every day. "You're volunteering in the behavior support class like Trey did?"

"Nope. I wouldn't do that to you. I'm going to work on a different volunteer gig."

"Doing what?"

"I'm not sure yet, and anyway, this conversation is supposed to be about you, not me."

A truck drove by, and there was a squeal of brakes. "Hey, sexy!" some guy called, and then they squealed off again.

Kaitlyn had no idea who the guy was, but maybe he'd seen her video and recognized her. Or maybe he was yelling at Mom, which happened a lot, too.

"Get his license plate," Dad said, sounding furious.

"I didn't see it and they're gone. Besides…" Mom trailed off, but Kaitlyn took one glance at her and knew exactly what she'd been going to say.

When you looked like they did, you were going to get catcalled. That was life in a 34D body. Mom had talked to her about it in multiple embarrassing conversations over the summer.

What Mom hadn't anticipated was that Kaitlyn would make an idiotic mistake, responding to a dumb boy's plea, and get herself videoed doing it.

Kaitlyn's heart raced and her stomach churned. She moved ahead of her parents again, but they sped up, staying close behind her. She couldn't escape their worry or their stupid plan.

She had nowhere to go.

This feeling was exactly why she'd taken the pills.

"We've already started the paperwork for the behavior support program," Dad said firmly. "We'd like to have you on board and open-minded. But if you're not…well, you're doing it anyway."

Kaitlyn looked at Mom, who was biting her lip. Mom was the weak point. She could be talked out of it. Kaitlyn had done it a million times.

But if Dad was staying in town, that changed everything. She probably was going to have to do what they said.

She pictured walking into school and going to the behavior support classroom rather than following her regular eighth-grade schedule. Would it be totally awful, really? She wouldn't have to worry about getting teased, at least during class time, since it was a small class and closely supervised. Erica, one of the behavior support program's two teachers, was nice.

Maybe it *would* be the best option, even though the thought of being in a special class—not honors, but almost the reverse—made her feel like she'd lost all track of who she was.

"When would I have to start?" she asked drearily.

"Erica said she'd try to talk Principal O'Neil into pushing everything through quickly," Mom said. "You could start as early as Wednesday."

"Fine," Kaitlyn said. "I'll go. But it'll ruin my life."

CHAPTER EIGHT

THE THURSDAY AFTER Kaitlyn came home, Ria was scrubbing toilets. And she didn't even mind.

The paperwork to get Kaitlyn into the behavior support program had taken longer than they had expected, so Kait was to start tomorrow or, more likely, Monday. Erica had met with her to explain how the class worked and get her up to speed, and that was terrific.

Meanwhile, Ria and Drew had been trying to keep Kait supervised, and it wasn't easy. Plus, Kait's mood didn't seem to be improving. She needed to be with other kids, needed to be in school.

Fortunately, Drew had taken over the supervision for today, because, unbeknownst to him, it was a bad day for Ria. The anniversary of her miscarriage. She was just as glad to be cleaning, keeping busy doing the work of one of their cleaning staff who'd called off.

She emerged from a hotel room, bucket and cleaning solution in hand, wearing rubber gloves.

"Hey, Ria."

The deep male voice startled her. "Ted!" What was Ted Taylor doing here?

For one thing, he was looking at her chest. Obviously, the T-shirt she'd worn to clean rooms was a little too old, too thin and too snug.

Ted wasn't being blatant about it; he was just being a

guy. That was what she had tried to explain to Kaitlyn. Men kind of lost their senses around a certain type of female body that both she and Kaitlyn happened to have.

"I'm sorry to just drop in on you." Ted wore a polo shirt and khakis and looked impeccable, as usual. "I tried to call several times and didn't get through. I figured I must have the wrong number."

No, he didn't have the wrong number. Ria had been ignoring his messages. Not so much because she didn't want to talk to him, but because she had been so preoccupied with Kaitlyn.

"I'm sorry about that," Ria said, setting down her bucket and peeling off her rubber gloves. "Things have been busy around here. What can I do for you?"

"Show me the place," he said. "I want to invest in a couple of local businesses, and this little motel is near the top of my list."

Ria frowned. Offhand, she could think of seven or eight much more successful businesses that would be better investments. "Sure, I'll show it to you," she said, "but why would you be interested?"

"I'm not going to lie. I'd like to work with you." He was looking at her with warmth in his eyes.

Ria just didn't get it. "Why?"

"Do you really have to ask?" Still with that long, warm gaze.

She seized the bull by the horns. "I'm not sure the fact that we dated more than fifteen years ago is a good basis for business decisions," she said.

"Oh, that's not the only basis," he said hastily. "You have a great location, and there aren't many small independent hotels here. I have a sense that Pleasant Shores is about to explode, tourism-wise, and investing here would get me in on the ground floor."

"I guess there's no harm in talking to you about it," Ria said, "although I really haven't thought about taking on investors. Come on. I'll show you around."

She figured that would be the end of his interest. Not that the Chesapeake Motor Lodge was a bad place; it just wasn't at all upscale. And Ted, despite his flirting, was reputed to be a shrewd businessman.

As they headed to the far end of the building, Ted looked around, thoughtfully, then turned his attention back to her. "So what made you decide to buy this place?"

Not an easy question to answer. "I needed a source of income after my divorce," she said. "Mom lived here in town, and I figured that if I had my own business, I could spend the time I needed to with the girls and their school activities. Plus, the private school here has a financial aid program for displaced homemakers, which I kind of was."

Remembering those days, the frantic cleanup of the old motel, the late nights developing a website, the days spent cutting down vegetation and doing landscaping... Well, it was no surprise that she had overworked herself and miscarried the baby.

She hadn't wanted another baby, not in her life circumstances. It shamed her, but it was the truth. All the same, she'd never have asked for nor wanted a miscarriage. When she'd had one, it had thrown her into a grief spiral that had lasted weeks.

"See, the layout here is actually ideal." Ted was walking around the far end of the motel, studying the grounds, making notes with his phone. "Private, but with easy parking and access to shops and restaurants. Is there a room I could see?"

"Sure." She pulled out her old-fashioned master key and opened the door of one of the empty rooms. "You'll love the seventies style," she added jokingly.

Wood paneling, heavy red drapes, shag carpeting. All hard to clean and distinctly out of vogue. But the prices at the Motor Lodge were good, and that kept a certain clientele coming back.

"Definitely could use an upgrade," Ted said, flashing her a smile that reminded her why she had gone out with him. He really was a handsome man. "The decor reminds me of my grandmother's place. But the bones seem to be good."

They left the room and walked slowly down one arm of the hotel. Ria waved at Linda and Izzy, two middle-aged women who'd just gotten jobs as pickers at the seafood processing plant. And there was Tommy, in town to visit his sick mother. The next room down, a suite, held a family whose home had been damaged in a recent storm.

"What do you charge for a room, roughly?" he asked.

She gave him a ballpark figure, and he whistled. "With just a little work on this place, you could triple that."

"During the off-season?" She started walking down the sidewalk, slowly.

He strolled beside her. "Off-season doesn't matter if you manage things right. You do discount packages. Target senior citizens who like to fish, couples without kids. Bill it as a romantic getaway, which it could easily be."

"Really, a romantic getaway?" Ria had never actually been on one, but in her imagination, the likes of the Chesapeake Motor Lodge had never appeared.

"Oh sure. People love places like this that are a little remote and off the beaten track. I'm telling you, you could make a killing."

They reached the end of the hotel walkway just as the

last door opened. Mom came out of her suite and did a double take. "Ted Taylor?"

"That's right." He held out a hand. "It's a pleasure to see you again, Mrs. Martin."

"You're probably old enough to call me Julie now," Mom said, her voice cool. She'd never really liked Ted.

What Mom didn't know was that maybe Ted was the best Ria could do. She certainly didn't deserve a man like Drew, not after losing his baby.

Ted and Mom fell back a little, Ted talking earnestly about his investment interest in the motel. Ria led the way around this wing of the building. When she turned the last corner, she stopped.

Sophia and Kaitlyn were carrying boxes to a waiting pickup truck driven by Trey Harrison. Drew stood near the truck bed.

Ria's stomach sank to her toes. Drew hadn't told her he was moving out today. She would've helped. He'd had things shipped from his apartment back in Baltimore and there was a good-sized load to move.

Behind her, Mom and Ted stopped, too. "Need a hand?" Julie asked.

Drew started. "Who's there?"

"Sorry—it's Julie."

"And Mom and some guy," Kaitlyn said.

Drew's eyebrow lifted.

"Kaitlyn, Sophia, this is Ted Taylor," Ria said. "An old friend who's interested in possibly investing in the motel."

Drew waved a hand in Ted's general direction and then went over to the pickup bed. Ria understood the system then: Sophia, Kaitlyn and Trey brought stuff out, and Drew lifted it into the truck. He'd always been a strong man, and that hadn't changed.

She felt like she should have been helping; indeed, Mom went over and climbed up into the pickup bed, rearranging and organizing Drew's few things.

"May I speak to you for a moment?" Ted touched her arm.

Both Mom and Sophia saw it and gave her quizzical looks.

"Sure," she said and followed him down the sidewalk toward the lot where he'd parked.

"Would you be interested in getting together to talk all of this over?" he asked. Like before, his gaze seemed to suggest another meaning, but she didn't know if that were accurate or a ploy.

She had the strange feeling that she should check with Drew before answering, but that was ridiculous. He was moving out and wouldn't care one way or the other. And the motel could use a financial lift. "Sure," she said. "Give me a call, and this time, I'll answer."

KAITLYN PAUSED AT the door of her new classroom at 11:30 a.m. on Monday and immediately realized her mistake.

She'd stalled and delayed, argued that she had to have Sophia to walk in with her, that she couldn't start at the beginning of the day when the halls were crowded, that she had a sore throat.

"Dude, it's almost lunch," Sophia said. "You're gonna have to see everybody anyway." She sounded sincerely sorry it had worked out that way, but also a little absentminded. Something else was going on with Sophia.

But Kaitlyn didn't have time to worry about it, because now she had to face her new life. "Thanks for walking in with me," she said to her sister.

"Hey, it got me out of morning classes." And then Sophia was gone and Kaitlyn walked in alone.

Every face turned her way.

Some of them were familiar. There was Venus Jackson, with whom Kaitlyn had gotten into a physical fight last year—ironically, defending someone else who was being bullied—but now they were sort of friends. At least the closest thing to a friend that Kaitlyn had, which didn't mean much. Beside her was Shane Simpson, a small-built, squirrelly kid who was always in trouble.

A nerdy kid named Rory, who had been mainstreamed into a couple of honors classes with Kaitlyn, sat front and center. He was superbright but didn't have a clue how to navigate the social waters of middle school. He was always saying the wrong thing and getting laughed at, and she could guess that was why he'd left his home school and come to the Academy's behavior support program.

He'd probably been bullied, just like her.

Looking around the classroom of ten or twelve teenagers, she didn't see anyone else who'd been mainstreamed into the honors program. Which meant that she and awkward Rory would probably be teamed up. Yay.

"Ah, come in." Erica Harrison reached for her and half took, half shook her hand, tugging her farther into the classroom. "Everyone's just finishing up their work before lunch. You can take about ten minutes to get settled. We have an empty desk over there, beside Venus, or you can sit up front."

"I'll sit there," Kaitlyn said, nodding toward the desk beside Venus. Then, as she walked back toward it, she wished she'd made a different choice. Two boys in the back were nudging each other and looking at her with sly grins.

Kaitlyn wasn't friends with them, but she knew of them. Everyone did. One, Moses Settler, was regularly in trouble for drugs; with his long, out-of-control hair and red, watery eyes, he looked like he was high right now. The other, big blond Rod Berger, had been a football player until he was kicked off the team.

Kaitlyn's face and neck heated. Maybe—hopefully— they were just general jerks. But with her luck, they'd probably seen the video or at least heard of it.

Erica had stopped to help one of the other students, so Kaitlyn made her way to the desk beside Venus alone.

As soon as she plopped her backpack onto the desk and sat down, Venus leaned toward her. "Why are you in here?" she asked. "You're smart."

Kaitlyn lifted a shoulder, conscious that the classroom was small and that most of the other kids could hear their conversation. "Got in trouble."

"For what?"

Kaitlyn shrugged again. "It's complicated."

"Was it alcohol? Or perhaps a controlled substance?" Venus asked the question in a fake British accent, a weird quirk of hers.

Kaitlyn gave a noncommittal grunt. She liked Venus okay, but the girl was nosy.

"She has emotional problems," Rory contributed from the front of the room.

Kaitlyn glared resentfully at him until he turned back around and faced the front. "My problems aren't your business and your problems aren't my business," she announced to the room in general. She'd never been that assertive in her other classes, but here, she felt like she had nothing to lose.

She also felt that if the boys in the class knew about the video, they'd have said something. Maybe Sophia had, by some miracle, gotten it taken down in time.

Maybe she *could* have a fresh start in this embarrassing classroom. She fooled around with her backpack and started filling out a paper Erica had given her about what she'd covered so far this year in each subject.

"Okay, let's head down to lunch," Erica said a few minutes later, and they all walked in a scraggly group toward the cafeteria.

Did they actually get led around like elementary school kids? That seemed ridiculous, except that maybe, given all the harassment she'd experienced in the halls, it would be a good thing.

Erica was suddenly walking beside her. "Normally," she said, "I head for the teachers' lounge for lunch. But if you're uncomfortable, I can go in and have lunch with you."

A few kids had overheard and looked at her quizzically.

"No, I'm fine," she said. The last thing she needed was to sit with a teacher-slash-babysitter.

"Most of the kids from our class sit together," Erica said. "And they get a little bit of a head start over other students, which is a bonus. Less waiting in line."

"Sure," Kaitlyn said.

Erica turned to the rest of the students. "Take care of our new classmate, everyone, okay?"

"I'll be fine." Kaitlyn forced a smile, and Erica patted her shoulder and turned down the hall toward the teachers' lounge.

Rory actually came up beside her like he was going to walk in as her bodyguard. Terrific for her reputation. "I'm fine," she said to him, and when he looked a little hurt, she added, "Thanks, though."

She walked through the cafeteria line beside Venus, who picked up three pieces of pizza and held out her plate for a scoop of macaroni and cheese. So that was different. Kaitlyn was used to being with girls who ate only salad, and she'd always felt self-conscious getting so much as a sandwich around them. She snagged two pieces of pizza and some chocolate cake. No point in trying to act like a skinny girl now.

"Come on," Venus said. "We've got to get to our table before everyone comes in."

Kaitlyn wondered why, but as she followed Venus through the increasingly crowded cafeteria, she saw the raised eyebrows and heard the whispers. She focused on Venus's hot-pink sweater and didn't look to either side.

As she pulled out a chair, though, the whispering and voices around her coalesced into a chant.

At first, she couldn't hear what they were saying. Then: *Take it off. Take it off.*

Kaitlyn's face burned as she stared at the greasy pizza in front of her, feeling nauseated.

"What are they talking about?" Venus asked, raising her own slice of pizza to her mouth.

"Who knows?" Shane was focusing on something in his lap. It looked like he was playing a video game.

"Is it about you?" Venus persisted. "What've they got on you?"

Kaitlyn shook her head and tried to shrink down lower in her chair. The chant at least wasn't picking up steam; it seemed to be dying out.

"You can't act like you care," Venus advised. "Just tell them to shut up."

Kaitlyn didn't dignify that with an answer. Easy for Venus to say.

Rod, the former football player who'd been in the back of the classroom and had been laughing with drugged-out Moses, now slid out of his seat and walked over to a nearby table of boys.

Oh, great. He'd find out, and the rest of her new class-mates would find out.

Someone yelled "Take it off," following it up with a bad name.

"Shut up!" Shane yelled over his shoulder, and a teacher came toward the boy who'd shouted.

Kaitlyn poked at her chocolate cake. She'd never es-cape bullying and notoriety. She was, after all, at the same school.

She stole a glance around and there Chris Taylor was, looking at her with a burning gaze that had to be fake. She looked away and shoved her food aside, her stomach turning.

Shelby Grayson and one of her friends walked by and stopped. "Hi, Kait," Shelby said, even though normally she wouldn't have given Kaitlyn the time of day. "Are you going to be in the *special* class now?"

Kaitlyn nodded, warily.

"Are you *okay*?" the other girl asked. Her forehead was creased with what looked like genuine concern, but Kaitlyn didn't believe in it. That particular girl had never been mean to Kaitlyn, but she'd also never spoken to her before today.

"She's fine." Venus stood and took a half step toward the girls. She was a good six inches taller than the other two, with a muscular build and a cutting glare. "Y'all be moving along now."

The two girls let out surprised and indelicate snorts. They obviously weren't used to being dismissed, but they did walk away, talking rapidly to each other and shooting venomous glances back at Venus.

"Thanks." Kaitlyn appreciated that Venus had deflected the spotlight from her.

"Girl, what happened to you?" Venus asked. "You know

you're going to have to tell us the story someday. Might as well be now."

Kaitlyn looked up and saw that Moses had now joined Rod in talking to some of the boys who'd been catcalling her. Chris was at the table, too, along with his nerdy, techy friend Kyle and Tyler Pollackson, the incredibly popular guy Sophia was trying to land. All of them kept glancing in Kaitlyn's direction. "The story's going to come out soon enough," she said glumly.

"You might want to put your own spin on it," Rory said. "Spin is everything." Then he went back to the fish-aquarium magazine he'd been reading while eating his lunch.

He wasn't wrong, and Kaitlyn figured she *would* put her own spin on it, once she figured out what that spin was.

She was almost glad to be sitting with the behavior support kids. She felt a little safer. At least she didn't have to walk through the hallway alone, a victim with no protection. The kids in her new class might be weird, with so-called special needs, but they appeared to stick together to some degree.

Moses and Rod headed back to the lunch table, laughing and looking at her.

Ugh. It wouldn't be long until everyone in her new classroom learned about the video. Would they stick by her then, or join the crowd who delighted in bullying her?

CHAPTER NINE

WEDNESDAY MORNING, at eleven o'clock as agreed, Ria stood on the doorstep of Drew's cottage at the beach, arms loaded with supplies. She intended to go in and be civil with her ex-husband, briefly discuss Kaitlyn's therapy and get the spare bedroom set up for the girls to visit.

And leave, without emotional involvement. All the intense feelings she'd been having around Drew were just ridiculous, the residue of their marriage. Apparently, she hadn't worked through it all as thoroughly as she'd thought, and the worries about Kaitlyn had been like a pressure cooker, tightening their bond.

But that was temporary. They would get back to being cordial divorced co-parents, starting today.

She knocked. From inside, Navy gave a sharp bark, and then the door opened.

Drew stood tall, wearing low-slung, faded jeans and an old T-shirt she remembered trying to throw away a few times. His arm muscles bulged out the ripped sleeves. "Ria?" he asked.

She swallowed. "It's me."

He stepped back and held open the door. "Come on in."

The cottage's entryway was small. As soon as she walked in, she could smell Drew's spicy aftershave, feel his warmth. Should she hug him? Kiss his cheek?

Kiss his mouth?

No. She settled for a light touch to his forearm.

He reached out, too. "What are you carrying?" Before she could answer, he was lifting the box and two folded comforters out of her arms. He'd always had good manners, quick to relieve any woman of a burden, to offer his seat, to hold a door open.

How it must rankle that he couldn't see to do those things as frequently as before. Now he was often placed in the position of being the recipient of help.

Navy pushed against her, and she reached down to run her hand over the dog's golden fur. "Should we set up the girls' room first or talk first?"

"Talk while we do it," he said promptly.

Of course. Drew had never much liked to talk. He wasn't communicative, which had been part of their problem.

"I'm just antsy," he volunteered as he led the way up the stairs. "I can't do half the exercise I used to." He led her into the larger of two bedrooms, set the load he was carrying onto the bed and reached down to rub Navy's head. "She's bored, too," he said.

"Do you need help finding a place to exercise? I think there's a gym up the shore, and maybe a ride could be arranged—"

"I've got it covered, but thanks," he interrupted. His voice was a little sharp.

"I'm just trying to help."

"I know. Sorry." He started unfolding one of the comforters. "I have a specialist coming who's going to help me get set up at the gym the police use. And I start my volunteer work next week, I hope."

"That's great." She opened the box she'd brought and started loading flannel sleep pants and tanks into one of the drawers, musing. Normally, Drew wouldn't have explained his tone or his reasons for saying what he did. Somewhere in all of this mess, he seemed to have gotten more communicative.

Had he learned it on his own, through hardship? From counseling? Or from some other woman?

Not her business. She looked out the window to where sunshine danced on the Chesapeake. Gorgeous, and that made her think. "Wait a minute," she said. "You took the small bedroom and gave the girls the master."

"View doesn't do me any good." He said it in a wry, joking tone. "And I'm not a teenage girl, so I don't need a great big bathroom. The hall one's fine."

That was typical of Drew. No, he'd never been one to speak pretty words of love, either to her or to his girls. But he showed it, through actions like leaving the bigger, nicer bedroom for his daughters, even before he knew if they'd want to spend even the occasional night with him.

She dragged her mind away from Drew's kindness and focused on the girls, wondering how often they'd want to stay at Drew's. They still needed to figure out schedules, and she didn't know what to hope for. Didn't want him to be hurt by them avoiding the chance to spend time at his place, and didn't want to be hurt herself if they seemed to prefer sleepovers at their father's to being home with her.

She watched Drew spread a comforter on the second twin bed. His hands were large and competent, smoothing out wrinkles by feel, straightening the corners. Because he couldn't see her watching, she could let her gaze linger.

She remembered how those hands had felt, touching her. Her mouth went dry.

He looked in her direction, eyes narrowed, and suddenly she wondered if he could tell she was staring at him after all.

"So, we should talk about the counselor's recommendations," she said, forcing her voice to sound brisk and impersonal. They'd been to one family counseling appointment earlier this week, and the counselor had spoken to Kait twice more: once in the hospital, and once immediately following the family appointment.

"I'm just glad Dr. Shelton doesn't think Kait's a danger to herself," Drew said. "She's kind of a character. What's she look like, anyway?"

Ria smiled to think of the countercultural woman. "How do you imagine she looks?" she asked, then wondered if that question was insensitive.

But he didn't seem offended. A dimple dented his cheek as he propped his hands on the wide windowsill, then pushed himself up to sit on it. "I'm guessing short gray curly hair and funky glasses," he said.

"Close. She has long gray hair, but it's curly. And her glasses are definitely funky. They have rainbow frames."

He grinned. "One of those big floppy dresses that goes to the floor?"

"Big floppy top," she corrected. "With tights and tall boots."

"I can almost see it," Drew said, laughing. Then he stopped and his brow wrinkled. "I wish I *could* see her. Wish I could see Kait. And you."

Her heart twisted. "Oh, Drew. I do, too." She went toward him, leaned against the window beside him and put a hand on his shoulder. But the feel of his hard muscles beneath her hand sent electricity shooting up her arm to land in her heart.

His head tilted as if he were listening. He reached up and put a hand atop hers. A gull flew past the window, cawing its lonely plea, and sunshine cast diamonds over the waters of the Chesapeake.

At one time, she and Drew would have made good use of a beautiful room, a beautiful view, time alone.

It was all too much for her, too romantic, too tempting. Just too much. She cast about for something to talk about and it didn't take long to find. "Are you still worried about Kait, despite what Dr. Shelton said?"

He frowned, pulled his hand away and nodded. "Yeah."

"Me, too. If there's even the slightest risk..." Ria trailed off. "I just wish there were something we could do. Talk to her, obviously, except she really won't communicate with me."

"Me, either." Drew slid down off the windowsill and started pacing. "The only thing she really expressed during that session was that she didn't like having to see us separately, one-on-one. That she wished it could just be relaxed in the house, like old times."

"Yeah." Guilt bloomed in Ria's chest.

"What do you make of the therapist's recommendation that we try to spend some time together as a family?" Drew shoved his hands into his back pockets and looked in her direction.

"It'll be tough." Ria sighed. He might not experience it this way, but the moments they spent together as a family seemed to stab her, remind her of what she'd lost. What they had all lost. "But if it will help the girls, I'm all in."

He stepped forward and reached out, obviously wanting to touch her but not wanting to invade her space. So she clasped his hand, and again, there was that warm feeling low in her belly. This wasn't going to be easy.

"Look, I can tell it bothers you." He squeezed her hand and then let it go, and again, she was aware that he seemed more communicative, more up-front with his emotions, than he had been before. He spoke again. "Any ideas about when we should get started with that?"

Some part of her, an illogical part, wanted to cry out "Now!" and to pull him into her arms. Just being here today had shown her how foolishly attracted she was.

"Dinner together on Halloween. That's soon enough," she said. "I have to go."

He tilted his head to one side like he was trying to understand her words, what they really meant. And the danger was that he actually could figure it out, because he knew her at a deep level.

"See you later," she said and fled, despite the fact that they had more to discuss about schedules and visitation and Kait. Cowardly, but it was the best she could do.

BACK IN THE DAY, Drew had been considered a good host. In fact, having people over had been one of the things he and Ria had done well together. She'd handle the details of food prep, choosing a menu the guests would like; he'd make sure there was plenty of seating and that everyone knew where to park. During the party, they'd both work to keep everyone's drink filled and make sure no one was standing by themselves.

They had shared the cleaning up beforehand, without much arguing, and washing up afterward had been an occasion to talk over the party and relive its fun moments.

They had been a great team.

The best nights had been the ones when they'd agreed to save the cleanup until the next morning so they could go to bed together. Something about watching Ria sparkle before guests had always made Drew crazy for his wife, and sometimes, that feeling had been returned.

All that had changed with the divorce. Drew had never

invited anyone to his new apartment in the city, unless maybe someone had brought over a six-pack to watch a game. Losing his vision had complicated even that level of getting together.

So how had he gotten roped into hosting a couple of guys he barely knew for dinner at a cottage that was completely unfamiliar?

Having Trey Harrison, whom he'd met only a couple of times, and Earl Greene, the police chief who organized the Healing Heroes program, over for pizza and beer was hardly the social event of the year, but without his sight, everything took twice as long: finding the game on TV, cleaning up, ordering pizza...

Stop feeling sorry for yourself.

As if she'd heard Drew's thoughts, Navy gave a little whine in response. She had been following Drew around as he straightened up the place.

He heard a car door slam shut outside, then another. Trey and Earl, not the pizza guy. Earl was bringing over paperwork for the Healing Heroes program, because Drew needed help navigating it: the state services for the blind had provided a technology tutor, but Drew wasn't proficient yet, and he needed to get this paperwork done immediately if he were to start work.

Accepting help. It was one of the hardest things he'd had to learn how to do.

He met them at the door and opened it. Navy barked, then barked again. She'd met Trey, but not Earl Greene.

"Come on in," he said, and Earl introduced himself, shaking Drew's hand with his own weathered one. Navy sniffed them briefly and then ran into the living room. Seconds later she was back, squeaking her favorite rubber chicken toy.

"Navy's glad to get company," Drew said, "but if you start throwing her toys for her, she'll never let you stop." He held out a hand. "Take your coats?"

"Actually…" Trey started, then stopped.

"What's up?"

"I should've cleared this with you beforehand. My dog, King, is in my car. Former K-9 dog, high energy, so I like to bring him with me when I can. What do you think about me bringing him in?"

"Do it."

"Think he'll get along with Navy? It's no problem to keep him in my car."

"Navy will be glad of the company." Drew was a dog lover; you pretty much had to be, working as a K-9 officer. "Let me harness Navy. If they meet outside, she'll do fine. She likes other dogs." For just a moment, Drew flashed back to the monthly K-9 team trainings, where he and several other officers and their dogs had gone through various exercises, keeping their skills sharp. Afterward, they'd always let the dogs run together. Navy hadn't gotten to have that experience in a while. She probably missed it.

Drew missed it, too.

Sure enough, the two dogs got along well. So they all stayed outside, letting them play, until the pizza guy came.

Then they settled in the cottage's living room with pizza and beers. Thursday night football played at low volume in the background because it wasn't a game any of them cared much about.

"Great pizza," Earl said around a mouthful.

Drew pulled another steaming piece from the box, breaking the long strings of mozzarella with his fingers. "Least I can do, considering you're letting me live here. It's basically your cottage, right?"

"No," Earl said. "I just help run the volunteer side of it and help pick out the officers. Julie's been bugging me to get someone into the cottage for the past month."

"You love every minute arguing with Julie," Trey said.

"Hey, hey," Earl said, rueful laughter in his voice. "My relationship with Julie is strictly professional."

"Uh-huh. Whatever you say."

So that was how the ball rolled. Drew had wondered whether Julie had started to date again and was glad to know that the answer was yes. It couldn't be easy to be single in such a small town, and someone like Julie, beautiful and dynamic, was a prize.

After his third slice, Drew checked on the dogs. Navy lay beside him, and he could hear King panting from where Trey was sitting.

"How's King handling retirement?" Drew asked Trey.

"He's starting a second career," Trey said. "Search and rescue. He needs to work."

"Yeah, I get that." He gestured toward Navy. "Her, too."

"Any chance she could be retrained as a guide for you?" Earl asked.

Drew had actually had that thought. "I doubt it. Navy is mostly gentle as a lamb, but she's trained to attack at command and hold a suspect, so I'm pretty sure that guide-dog training schools wouldn't have her. Not to mention that she's way beyond the puppy stage."

"One of my uncles got an older dog as a guide," Earl said.

"I need to do more research on it," Drew said. He'd thought of trying to get a guide dog at one point, but he could never give up Navy, and he didn't think she'd react well to sharing Drew with another dog.

The game got exciting, so they turned up the TV and

watched part of a quarter, polishing off the pizza and a six-pack between them. Not exactly heavy drinkers.

"Doing okay with the vision loss?" Trey asked gruffly when a commercial came on.

Drew let out a snort. "Nope. Hate it." He did hate it, but he didn't usually complain. Both his family and his police work had gotten rid of that side of him, or so he'd thought. "Need to work on my attitude."

"Your attitude can't be worse than mine was when I got disabled and came here," Trey said.

"Truer words were never spoken." Earl let out a low laugh, and Trey joined in. "When I first told this one he'd be working with at-risk teenagers, the look on his face... My, my."

"I got into it with the principal of the school," Trey said. "Almost caused the program to be shut down."

"Until you helped get it funded for the future." Earl's tone was approving. "You made up for any early mistakes with that move." He paused, then added, "Drew, your work's gonna be different, but challenging in its own way. Ever done any interviewing that wasn't police related?"

"Not really. Look, I don't know that I'm going to be much use, given..." He waved a hand at his eyes.

"You don't need to see to do an interview," Earl said. "Mary thinks it'll be better to have the guys interviewed in their own environment, which means you have to get down to the docks. But once there, it'll be all about recording interviews, following the direction they go, asking the right questions."

He made it sound easy, but Drew still hesitated. Navigating any new environment was difficult when you couldn't see where you were going or see people's facial expressions, read their cues.

"You'll need to be aware of their culture a little bit," Earl said. "Learn about it, take account of their sensitivities and their pride. Most of these people have lived on the shore a long time, and fishing is what their families do. Sometimes tourists look at them as quaint and take their pictures, and that irritates them to no end. They're some of the hardest-working people I know, with a skill set that's dying out."

"I could take you down there and show you around," Trey said, "but it might be better if your daughter Kaitlyn did."

"Kaitlyn? Why?"

"She has some friends among the watermen," Earl said. "I see her down there pretty often."

"Wait a minute." Drew shook his head. Had he heard that right? "She's hanging out at the docks?"

"It's not dangerous," Earl said. "There's other teenagers there. It's just a little unusual she'd connect with them, since she's new in town and they've been here for decades. But that's commendable in a young girl. Most of them have no time for the older folks, or those different from themselves."

"I'm sure she's not there when the bar starts getting wild," Trey added.

The *bar*? He was definitely talking to Ria about this.

"Anyway," Earl said, "she would be a good in, since she knows some of the folks. Might get you past your outsider status a little more quickly."

Drew reached down to pet Navy, buying himself some time to think. He wasn't sure he could do this job, or do it well, but he didn't really have a choice; doing volunteer work was a condition of staying in the cottage. And he *had* to stay. His daughter needed him.

Drew was a churchgoer, but he wasn't the type who thought God reached down from heaven and moved people around like pawns on a chessboard. Nonetheless, the way this was coming together had the mark of some kind of divine plan. If he could spend time with Kait, and if she could legitimately feel like she was helping him…it might be just what the doctor ordered.

"I've been wanting to do more with Kait," Drew said slowly. "Is it okay if she comes on some of the interviews?"

"Sure thing. We don't have funding to pay her, but as long as you put in your twenty hours per week, we don't care if you have an assistant or not." Earl paused, then chuckled. "Just don't go falling in love on the job like this one did."

"Hey now." Trey just sounded happy. "My job had me spending every day with a beautiful woman. He's going to be working with a bunch of old watermen. And besides…" Trey trailed off.

Something about Trey's tone caught Drew's attention. "Besides, what?"

There was a little silence. Then Trey said, "I got the feeling you are still interested in Ria. Or rather, my wife got that feeling, when we had the meeting about Kaitlyn."

Great. It was obvious. "It's not going anywhere," he said. "It never was."

"Why not? Ria's great. And, I mean, you got married, so you must have loved each other at some point."

Must have loved each other at some point…yeah. He had loved her, but he wasn't convinced she'd ever returned the feeling. She'd assured him she did, but words weren't the same as true, heartfelt emotions.

"Sorry if it's not my business," Trey said. "Newly married guy, looking for wisdom to make it last. That's all."

"Just…it helps if you get married for the right reasons. Not because you have to."

The two other men were silent for a minute.

"That's tough," Earl said finally, "but it doesn't mean it can't work. Lots of good marriages got started that way, back in the old times."

"Sure." He'd been willing to make it work, had tried the best he knew how. But he'd always figured Ria regretted that she hadn't gone forward with Ted Taylor.

Which now she might have the opportunity to do.

Footsteps trotted down from upstairs.

"Who's that?" Drew called sharply.

"It's Kait, Dad. Just getting something to drink."

Drew hadn't even known she was here, and now he felt uneasy. He and Ria had agreed from the start that the girls shouldn't know how their marriage had gotten started.

How much had Kait heard? Would she even know what it meant, saying they'd gotten married because they had to? It didn't seem like young people did that anymore.

The men focused on the game for a little while longer. Kaitlyn went back upstairs. Soon after that, the other two men said they needed to leave.

As Drew ushered them out the door, Earl tugged him aside. "If you *do* still like Ria," he said, "you need to make a move. I've seen Ted Taylor around the motel a few times."

Drew's fists clenched, but what was he supposed to do? How could he compete with someone like Ted Taylor, especially now?

CHAPTER TEN

ON HALLOWEEN, Ria pulled baked chicken and rice out of the oven, set it atop the stove and brushed a stray lock of hair back from her sweaty face.

She didn't want to be in Drew's cottage, which used to be her mother's house, cooking a family dinner for him and the girls. It stirred up way too many memories. But she was doing it. For Kaitlyn.

Being around Drew was exquisitely painful. She couldn't stop staring at him. He was so handsome, and all the challenges he'd faced had made him more communicative, more willing to engage with others. Oddly enough, she was even more drawn to him now.

She piled roasted vegetables into a serving bowl. "Kait! Sophia! Come help me get this on the table," she called. Drew hunted for napkins, and Navy watched the floor for tidbits accidentally dropped, and it felt like old times.

And that felt so very good. Too good. Having her family back together where they could take care of and love one another was a dream come true.

But it was a dream from which she'd have to awaken, she thought as they all trooped into the little dining area carrying dishes and platters and serving spoons.

As they seated themselves, Drew lifted his head and sniffed. "Oh, man, I've missed your cooking," he said. "Chicken and rice, roasted vegetables, and…is that corn bread?"

"Yep." Sophia set the corn bread right in front of him. "Inhale and weep." She slid into the chair at Drew's left, and Kait took the one to his right, leaving the end of the little table for Ria.

"Let's have a blessing before we eat," he said, and Sophia made a little face at Kaitlyn, who wrinkled her nose back. Both girls were in a phase of teenage rebellion about going to church. He reached for the girls' hands, and Ria did, too. Thus circled, they all bowed their heads. "Thank you for bringing us all together, Father," he said. "Bless this food to our use and us to thy service. Amen."

"Amen," they all murmured.

Ria felt a little teary. They hadn't prayed together at every meal, especially in later years, but it had been a good part of their family life early on.

They passed dishes around, and everyone loaded their plates. Ria felt a satisfaction she hadn't experienced in a while, watching her family dig in to the food she'd prepared.

"Mom, are you trying to make us fat?" Kaitlyn asked, complaining, but not in a serious voice. She actually sounded almost happy, and that made the challenges of a family dinner altogether worthwhile.

Kaitlyn seemed to be doing okay in the behavior support program. She'd talked about a couple of kids she was getting to know, and there had been no phone calls from the school. When Ria had called Erica and asked her how Kait's first week had gone, Erica had assured her that Kait seemed to be fitting in and was doing her work.

Drew tilted his head back more than she'd seen him do before, apparently seeing his food well enough to know where everything was. He cut his chicken and ate, more slowly than he had in the past, but without spilling anything.

"This is good, Mom. Thanks for cooking a real dinner."
Sophia smiled at her.

The compliment burned, though, because it made Ria
aware of how often she'd relied on pizza and takeout re-
cently. It didn't seem as important to cook for her and the
girls, especially since they—or at least, Sophia—were on
the go so much.

But that was a fallacy. She needed to do better.

"How come you're twisting your head around, Dad?"
Kaitlyn put her fork down and studied her father. "Can
you see?"

He smiled at her. "I wish, baby girl. I have a little vision at the sides and bottom, but not much at the center.
Just some blurry shapes."

"What *is* it that happened?"

Ria put a hand on Kait's arm. She was glad Kaitlyn was
taking an interest, and Ria was curious, too; on the other
hand, she didn't know if Drew was ready to talk about it yet.

He swallowed a bite of food and wiped his mouth. "Traumatic optic neuropathy," he said. "And even though I can't
see, I know that's making Sophia's eyes glaze over."

"How'd you guess, Dad?" Sophia helped herself to another piece of corn bread, cut it open and piled on butter.
Oh, for the metabolism of a teenager. Ria was eating her
small piece of corn bread dry.

"I know your love of science," he joked. "But your mom
and Kait might like to know. I had a traumatic brain injury,
closed, and it caused damage to my optic nerve." He lifted
a shoulder. "It stinks, but in a way, I was lucky. A lot of
people have a lot more issues from TBIs."

"TBI... *Oh*. Traumatic brain injuries," Kaitlyn said.
"One of the kids in my class had one. He was in a coma
and had to, like, retrain his memory."

"Exactly," Drew said. "I didn't have any real cognitive

symptoms. Just some headaches and dizziness. And the vision loss."

"Will it come back?" Sophia asked. "Your vision, I mean."

He shrugged. "Not sure yet. Some might. I have an appointment coming up that should give me a lot more information."

Ria's heart twisted with concern for him, but she kept her mouth shut. Drew was managing things well, and the positive attitude he'd always brought to life was in evidence here, as well. Whatever news he got from the doctors, he'd handle it.

"Enough about me and my issues," Drew said. "Right now, I just want to finish this fabulous meal."

"Don't worry. Soph and I will stick by you," Kaitlyn said in a matter-of-fact voice. "Like we stuck by Mom when she got so sick, when we first had the motel."

Ria's senses sprang to attention. *No, don't say any more.*

"What happened?" Drew asked.

Sophia and Kaitlyn glanced at each other, frowning like they were trying to remember. "Mom got real sick and had to spend, like, two weeks in bed," Kaitlyn said finally. "But Grandma took care of us and said we needed to help Mom cheer up, and we did."

Oh, Lord, would he guess what had happened?

She felt that she ought to find the calming words that would ease Drew's suspicions without rousing the girls to realize that she was trying to be secretive. But her mind was a blank. She couldn't think of anything to say.

"How about what I found out the other day?" Kaitlyn said casually. "I heard you two *had* to get married." She put air quotes around the "had."

Ria froze.

Color rose into Drew's cheeks. He put down his fork.

"It was the best thing I ever did, marrying your mother," he said with dignity.

"Wait," Sophia said. "What do you mean, you had to get married?"

Kaitlyn gave her a meaningful look. "What do you think it means?"

"But my birthday is… Wait a minute. When did you two get married?"

They'd never celebrated their anniversary much, for this very reason.

"I already calculated it out," Kaitlyn said. "They got married seven months before you were born."

"Wow," Sophia said, looking from Ria to Drew and back again. "Just wow."

"Honey…" Ria reached for Sophia's hand. "Your dad's right. It was a big blessing."

"Why'd you get divorced, then?" Kaitlyn said, her voice snippy.

Sophia went over to the drawer where they'd all stowed their cell phones. "Hey, Kait, we have to get ready for that party. You promised you'd at least try it. Come on."

It was clear the two girls wanted to talk about the family news they'd discovered. Well, fine. Ria wanted to talk to Drew about it. Strangle him, really.

ONCE THE GIRLS were upstairs, Drew held up a hand. "I know, I know. I'm sorry. It came out, for some reason, when I was talking to Trey and Earl the other night. I didn't know Kait was home."

"But we've always tried to keep that from them. The last thing we need is another issue making Sophia feel guilty or bad."

"There's no reason at all she should feel bad," Drew said

firmly. "Any baby is a blessing, and I don't regret marrying you and having her for one second."

Ria tried to process that. He didn't regret marrying her. That was something.

But on the other hand, of course he was happy they'd married, because he was that rare type of man who loved infants and little kids. He'd loved every minute of the girls' baby years.

If he found out about her miscarriage…

As if on cue, he tilted his head and leaned a little toward her. "What happened when you got sick, back when you bought the motel? I didn't know about that."

"Just…just a bad case of the flu," she said. Which was no lie; she'd developed the flu concurrently with the miscarriage.

"Got you down, did it?"

"What…what do you mean?"

"The girls needing to cheer you up. That doesn't sound like you."

She sucked in a breath. "It's tough being sick," she said. "Anyway, do you think we need to do any processing about how they know why we got married now?"

"Probably a subject for family counseling." He sighed. "There's no shortage of them, it seems."

"I wish she hadn't found out," Ria fretted.

"I'm glad she did," Drew said. "Of course, I wouldn't have told her on purpose. But secrets are toxic."

The words hit Ria like a hammer blow. *Secrets are toxic.*

She'd read that, heard it said by people who had major family problems. She'd never thought she would fit into that category herself.

But here she was, trying to keep multiple secrets…from the girls, from Drew.

Footsteps clattered down the staircase, and then Sophia and Kaitlyn came into the room in their costumes.

Ria sucked in a breath.

"What is it?" Drew asked immediately.

"They look…" Ria paused. "Well, Kaitlyn looks great. She's a…doctor, right?" Kait wore green scrubs and a sterile mask over her face.

"Yep. Easy costume." Unasked, she went over to Drew and showed him her toy stethoscope and doctor's bag.

"And I'm a nurse." Sophia winked at Ria.

Sophia was indeed clad in a white nurse costume, which Ria could only identify by the red cross on her perky nurse cap. Her short skirt, bare midriff and high heels—well, no actual health professional would be caught dead in the getup.

The overall look might very well cause a few heart attacks.

Should she call Sophia out? It really wasn't an appropriate outfit. On the other hand, she'd seen some teen costumes on social media, and sexy seemed to be the theme. By comparison, Sophia's costume was almost discreet.

Which didn't mean she should let her daughter go out that way. "I'm not sure—"

The doorbell rang, and Navy let out a short bark. Ria opened the door to a crowd of trick-or-treaters and immediately forgot everything but how cute they were. "Come in for a minute. We have the big chocolate bars." She'd always gone all out for Halloween. This year, since they were at Drew's place, she hadn't done her usual extensive decorations, but she'd roped the girls in to carving a huge pumpkin, which now graced Drew's front porch.

The kids filed in and showed their costumes, a mix of traditional princesses and superheroes plus one kid dressed as a box of tissues. She and the girls oohed and aahed over the costumes and described them to Drew. As soon as that group left, another pair came to the front porch, and Ria recognized the Thornton twins. They were dressed as a waitress and chef, and between them was a cardboard table with a covered platter. "Trick or treat! Can we serve you dinner?" the twins chorused, and when she and the girls agreed, they swept the lid off the platter...only to reveal their little brother's curly head grinning up at them.

They all jumped and shrieked, and then they had to examine the costume to see how the little brother was walking along underneath the table. Ria explained it to Drew, who'd taken on the role of handing out candy. Of course, he gave extra to the twins and their brother for such a creative costume.

More kids came, and in between, they laughed about costumes the girls had worn as kids. Even Kaitlyn loosened up and smiled.

"We should go to the party," Sophia said finally, during a lull. "I promised Courtncy we'd come."

Drew reached out an open hand and gripped Sophia's arm, lightly. "Hold on. Will this bc okay for both of you, especially Kait? No bullies?"

"It's an all-girls party," Sophia assured them. "Nice girls."

Ria found the all-girls part a little hard to believe, given Sophia's costume. But then again, girls often dressed up for each other as much as for boys.

"Be back here by eleven," Drew said. It was his second night of having the girls at his place, and he seemed to have settled into his custodial role with enthusiasm.

"We will, Dad," they chorused, and then they were gone.

The trick-or-treaters thinned out, and in between, Drew and Ria cleaned up: she carried dishes to the sink, and he loaded them into the dishwasher or put them into a sink full of soapy water, mostly by feel.

"Last dish," she said, handing him the empty serving plate for the corn bread, which had gotten devoured.

He put it into the dishwasher and then set the thing running, and she marveled at how he could perform household tasks as well as any sighted person.

"That was fun tonight," he said. "Brought back a lot of good memories. Glass of wine?"

Ria hesitated. Having a glass of wine together after cleaning up the kitchen was a good memory, too, something they'd done a lot in the early years of their marriage and then as young parents.

The trouble was, it seemed so romantic.

He was waiting for her reply, his hand on the wine bottle he'd pulled out of the fridge.

His brow was raised, and there was the tiniest trace of a dimple in his cheek, already bristled with his heavy beard even though she knew he shaved every morning.

She should go home. She should just leave.

But the thought of her empty house didn't beckon in the same way her handsome ex-husband did. "Sure," she said, her voice coming out a little breathless. "Just one glass."

In the living room, there was a moment of silence between them. Ria wondered if they were going to talk—about something serious or something mundane?

"Want to watch a movie?" Drew asked, surprising her.

"Can you?"

"Yep," he said. "Especially one of the scary Halloween ones I've seen a million times. Can you find one?" He fumbled around for the remote and handed it to her, then sat down on the couch.

"I can find one," she said, "but you know I don't like scary movies."

"I'll protect you," he said, his voice a low rumble that

danced along her nerve endings. Her palms broke out in a sweat that made it hard to hold the remote. She clicked on the first show she saw connected to Halloween and then sat down, a proper arm's length away from Drew.

As the show's music came on, a corner of Drew's mouth quirked up. "Charlie Brown? Really?"

"It's Halloween," she said. "And it's not scary."

"Do you remember…?" they both said at the same time, and then laughed.

"You first," Drew said.

"I was just thinking of the Halloween when Kait got scared of the jack-o'-lantern, and you had to take it away and donate it to a neighbor family," Ria said.

"I remember! They were happy to get it since they didn't have one, but someone smashed it late that night."

"And Kait cried," Ria remembered, chuckling. "I guess she's always been the emotional one."

"I was thinking of the first Halloween we spent together," Drew said.

"What? Oh." Ria's mouth went dry.

They'd been married only a month. They'd gone to a party, dressed as a pirate and a serving wench, and Ria didn't know which one of them had gotten more jealous. The girls had been all over Drew, handsome and rakish, and the guys had kept trying to dance with her, mostly, it seemed, so they could look down her tightly laced bodice and make crude jokes.

She and Drew had sneaked out early, gone home and made passionate love.

Drew's arm reached along the back of the couch, found her shoulder and gave a little tug. "You don't have to sit way over there."

Ria blew out a breath, not sure how to answer. She desperately wanted to slide over next to her warm, handsome ex. She also wanted to jump up and run out of the cottage toward home.

He didn't push; he just let his hand slide up into her hair, caressing gently.

"Drew, I don't think—"

"Don't think."

She froze, and he did, too.

Did he remember? He'd said that very thing the night they'd made love on the beach. The night she'd lost her virginity; the night Sophia had been conceived.

"Last time you said that, it got me in a world of trouble," she tried to joke.

"I'm an idiot." Drew straightened, pulling his hand back to his side. "I shouldn't have said anything of the sort, then or now." He hesitated, then added, "But like I told you before, I don't regret the outcome. Do you?"

She didn't answer; she couldn't. Instead, she picked up her wineglass and took a couple of gulps, then set it down. The last thing she needed was to get plastered at Drew's place. To start thinking that she wanted him back.

She wanted someone who could love and accept her as she was, flaws and all. With Drew, there was too much baggage, too much insecurity, too much guilt. "I should go," she said. "Thanks for having us over, Drew. The girls really enjoyed it. I could tell."

"Sure." He sounded dejected, but that wasn't her problem, was it? He'd come on to her, in a mild way, and though she didn't take it seriously, she knew that leaving was the wisest move.

Getting up and walking out the door, though, was one of the longest, hardest journeys of her life.

CHAPTER ELEVEN

THE TROUBLE STARTED as soon as Drew and Kaitlyn headed for the waterfront, Navy walking along beside them. Drew was in a bad mood to begin with. Last night with the family had been great, just great. He had thought, or at least hoped, that he and Ria could continue the evening, just the two of them. Lately, his body responded to her every move. Finding the discipline to keep his hands off her took up way too much of his energy.

Asking her to sit with him, flirting with her, it had all come so naturally last night.

Natural to him, maybe, but not to her. She had run away as if he had a horrible disease.

And that shouldn't be a surprise. They had always come from different worlds. He had always felt a little bit inadequate. That hadn't changed since the divorce.

"How often do you come down here?" he asked Kaitlyn now. He was concerned about his daughter for all kinds of reasons, but one of them was her apparent familiarity with the waterfront. He'd never known a dock area that wasn't seedy and dangerous, no matter what Earl Greene thought about this one. For his young daughter to be hanging out there didn't seem right.

"A few times a week."

Don't criticize and judge. Part of the point of starting

this new volunteer job was to spend positive time with his daughter. "What do you like about it?"

"I like that no one else from school comes down here." She paused, then added, "A few of the dock kids go to my school, but they're not really a part of things. They don't give me a hard time."

Drew frowned. Kaitlyn seemed to have accepted that the majority of kids were going to give her a hard time. Why? She was a beautiful, smart, good-hearted girl. He just didn't get it.

"This way." She slowed way down and then grabbed his arm, stopping him. "Look out—the road is sort of rocky."

Drew used his cane to navigate the small bumps and dips in the road, but it wasn't easy.

"Take my arm," she ordered, then paused. "I know, I know, I'm supposed to wait until you ask for help. Mom keeps drilling that into us. So do you want to hold on to me? And here, I can take Navy's leash."

"Thanks." He took her elbow, wishing he didn't have to depend on a fourteen-year-old to walk down the street. "I'll get better at this," he promised Kaitlyn. "I'm meeting a new orientation and mobility specialist later this week."

"Sure you will, Dad." Her voice held doubt, covered over with a too-sweet, encouraging tone that was *not* Kait's style at all.

He wasn't much more enthusiastic about the O&M specialist than Kaitlyn, but for a different reason. His vision was improving a little, and he kept hoping he wouldn't have to entirely learn to navigate the world as a blind person. Hoped his blindness would just go away, though the odds of that happening were slim. His field of vision was getting wider to include perception of peripheral movement, but none of it was very clear. He saw blurry shapes, but not enough to distinguish landmarks or curbs. In bright sunlight things got a little clearer, but even then, he couldn't rely on his vision. He was trying to resign himself to the fact that this might be as good as it got.

Seagulls squawked but there was no sound of other people.

Good. He needed all the time he could find to get used to the thought of meeting a bunch of new people, trying to work with them, when he couldn't see. He felt at a huge disadvantage.

There were so many things that could go wrong, including the downright embarrassing way that people sometimes walked away without him realizing it. There he would be, talking to the air. He remembered doing that himself, sometimes, when talking to someone with a visual impairment. He hadn't realized how rude it was, or how alone and isolated it would make the blind person feel.

He blew out a breath. The last thing he needed was to focus on his insecurities, so he cast around for another topic of discussion. It wasn't hard to find. "I'm not sure I like you spending time down here at the docks," he said.

"It's fine, Dad. Hey, are you and Mom getting back together?"

That was an obvious conversational dodge, but it worked. "Why do you ask?"

He felt her shrug. "Last night was nice."

"It was. And we'll spend more time like that." Even though it might kill him to be around Ria, knowing he could only get so close and no closer.

"If you guys are fine spending time together," she said, "then why not…?"

She wanted to know, obviously, why they didn't just get back together. "It's complicated," he said, because he couldn't explain. Couldn't tell Kait that her mother just didn't love him enough.

The smell of brackish water and a fishy odor drifted to his nostrils, and he heard some distant shouts and then some conversation, along with the rhythmic lapping of the water against the shore. The Chesapeake didn't have big waves, but it could get pretty choppy.

"Hey, Juan. Sunny." Kaitlyn was greeting people now, but she didn't pause to introduce Drew. "We're going to meet Captain Eli first," she said. "If he likes you, and if Bisky likes you, everyone else will fall into line."

That analysis must be part of the waterman culture Earl Greene had mentioned. He guessed it was helpful that Kaitlyn knew something about it. No doubt her middle school social radar helped her detect the subtleties of any situation. "I'm not sure I like how you know everything about everyone at the docks. How much time do you spend here?"

"Oh, Dad, I'm fine." Then her pace quickened. "Come on. There he is."

Unprepared for her speedup, Drew stumbled and nearly fell. *Great, just great. Way to impress a bunch of working guys.* His face heated as he regained his balance and held Kaitlyn's arm a little tighter.

She slowed down, stifling a sigh. A minute later, she came to a stop. "Captain Eli, I'd like you to meet my dad."

Drew wanted to give the man a good look in the eye, and to inspect him, as well. He didn't know the man's age, or how he looked at Kaitlyn. He straightened his shoulders and held out his hand. "Drew Martin," he said, and when the other man's calloused hand gripped his, he squeezed hard.

The captain's grip was firm, but he didn't respond with a test of strength. "We like your girl," he said mildly.

"Thanks. Rough place for her to spend time."

"Dad!" Kaitlyn sounded embarrassed.

He could feel the captain shift his position, and when he spoke, his voice was less friendly. "We're not any rougher than anyone else down here, especially when there's a young lady present. We do work hard, though."

Footsteps approached on the wooden dock and Kaitlyn said, "Hey, Mitch."

"Kait's dad," the captain said. "Look out—he's a strong man. He'll squeeze your hand off."

Drew felt his face heat as sweat dripped down his back. He couldn't tell whether the joke was friendly or mocking. He shook the other man's hand, consciously trying not to overdo it. This just stank. Here he was amid strange men with his daughter, and he couldn't know how they were looking at her, couldn't know if she was safe.

"Dad's going to do some interviews. It's his new job. Miss Mary and Chief Greene set it up."

"Oh, the project for the new museum," said Mitch.

"I heard about that," the captain said.

"Yeah," Drew replied. "So I'll be spending time here and Kait won't, after today."

"Dad!"

"I just don't think this is a safe place for you," he said to her, not caring that the other men heard, actually intending it.

"Might be safer for her than for you, if you come in and talk down our way of life," Mitch said and stomped off in what sounded like heavy boots.

"Don't have time to debate about whether the waterfront is more dangerous than some city," the captain said. "I have work to do." Then he, too, stomped off.

"Dad!" Kait was almost crying. "You were so rude to them."

"Just letting them know you have someone who cares about you," he said.

"They were here for me this summer when you weren't!"

Ouch. This was going all wrong. "Look, Kait, I want to make that up to you. And part of that is doing what I'm supposed to do as your father. Protecting you from dangers you don't even know are here."

"You don't even know about the dangers there are now. It's nothing to do with these people. The kids at my school are worse than them any day." She stomped her foot, that vibration reverberating down the dock. "And you know what? If you're so tough, find your own way back home." She thrust Navy's leash into his hand.

Then she, too, stomped away from him.

Shaken, Drew made his way back to land, slowly. Once, he nearly went off the edge of the dock, and would have if not for Navy's nudging him back to the center.

He tried to get his bearings, to remember exactly what way they'd come. He got started on what he thought was the right road and walked along slowly, like a ninety-year-old, listening for cars, feeling for obstacles with his cane.

What a day's work. He now had a poor setup for his job. His daughter was furious with him. And for all he knew, he was walking in the wrong direction, getting deeper and deeper into the fishermen's world, where he had just made some enemies.

"Need a hand?" The voice was deep, but melodic. He was pretty sure the speaker was a woman, but not 100 percent.

And, yeah, it was easier to take directions from a woman than from another man. "If you could direct me back toward town, I'd appreciate it," Drew said.

"Let me walk you partway there," the woman said. "I'm Bisky."

The one who Kaitlyn had said was the other important person to know. Maybe he could do a better job with her. Mend some bridges.

"Drew Martin," he said. "Pleased to meet you. I appreciate your help."

"Not a problem," she said. "I saw Kaitlyn running off. I have a young daughter myself, just Kaitlyn's age, so I know how hard it is to please them."

He could tell she was tall, almost as tall as he was. "Do you work the waters here?" he asked.

"Since I was ten years old. Lived here my whole life."

"I'm going to be taking some oral histories for a museum they're building," he said. "Maybe I could talk with you when you have a spare hour."

"I don't have a whole lot of those, but we can figure something out. I like Kaitlyn. I'd like to help out her dad."

So she was making it clear that he was getting an in with her only because of his daughter. Well, he guessed he deserved it. "Do you think the waterfront is a safe place for a young girl like Kaitlyn to spend time?"

"Yep. My daughter's here every day of the week." She slowed. "Okay, here we are at the edge of downtown. About half a football field up, you'll make a left and head all the way down that road, and it'll take you to the cottage."

"You know where I'm heading?" Drew asked.

"Honey," she said, "you haven't spent much time in a small town, have you?" She laughed, loud and long. "See you around the docks, Drew Martin. Bring your daughter."

He heard her walk away and then headed in the direction she'd indicated, Navy at his side. This new job, as well as rebuilding his relationship with his daughter, was going to be a lot more complicated than he had expected. But at least he had somewhat of an ally.

RIA SAT IN the passenger seat of the Tesla, listening to Ted Taylor drone on about all the car's features and wishing she were anyplace else.

Dusk was closing in around them, and after a long day of working, she would much rather be at home curled up on the couch with her girls and some takeout.

But instead, she was having dinner with Ted. A "business dinner," though he had dressed up in expensive preppy clothes and brought her flowers. Not very businesslike.

"I'm just as glad DiGiorno's wasn't open," Ted said, finally running out of Tesla features to extol. "Gives us a chance to take a nice drive up the coast and get out of town, see some new sights."

"That's true," she said politely. "The sunset is pretty." She turned to look out the window as they drove through Pleasant Shores' downtown. When she saw a familiar silhouette walking in the dusk, though, she froze, then gripped Ted's arm. "Stop the car!"

"Stops on a dime," he said, and indeed, the car halted silently.

She climbed out and rushed to the side of the road. "Drew, it's Ria! Why are you walking alone at this time of the evening?"

"Heading home from the docks," he said. "I'm fine."

Maybe he was, between his white cane and Navy, who was walking beside him. "You probably are, but your dark clothes make it hard to see you in this light. I thought Kaitlyn would be with you."

He blew out a sigh. "I did, too," he admitted. "But we had a disagreement, and she took off."

"Whoa. I could strangle her. Do you…?" For the first time, she considered that Drew might not welcome knowing that she was out with Ted, nor accepting a ride home in Ted's vehicle. Still, his safety was the most important thing. "Can we give you a ride home?"

He shifted to face her head-on, and Navy settled at his side. "Who's we?"

"I, um, I have a business dinner with Ted Taylor."

He let out an inelegant snort. "Uh-huh. Sure you do."

Even though Ria herself had thought the same thing, it annoyed her that Drew assumed she was covering up a different kind of meeting. "I'm just concerned."

"Thanks for that, but I'm fine." He turned to go, but now Ted was out of the car and headed their way.

"Hey, Martin. Can we run you home?"

Drew stopped, turned in Ted's direction and glowered. "No, thank you."

"Are you sure?" Ria asked. How did you navigate a city on your own when you were blind?

"No need to infantilize the disabled," he said. "Nothing to see here. I'm just an ordinary guy walking home from my new job, and I would appreciate being left in peace to do it."

He spun and started walking, and Ria had to admit he seemed to be doing just fine. A strong, solitary, competent figure.

With enough pride to fill some big buckets. And a complete unwillingness to accept help.

At least, help from his ex-wife and her date.

"See you later," Ria said, too quietly for him to hear, and watched him as he faded into the deepening dusk.

"Do you want me to follow him, make sure he's safe? The Tesla is quiet." Ted sounded proud, and Ria felt like strangling him. He was using Drew's blindness as just another reason to brag on his car. Or maybe she was just being oversensitive. Regardless, she knew Drew would be infuriated at the notion of being followed.

"No, I'm sure he's fine. Let's just head on up to dinner."

Even though the restaurant was lovely, Ria barely tasted her seafood, ignored her wine despite its expense and couldn't even focus on the brownie magic cheesecake.

That right there was the evidence that she was upset. Worried about Drew—whether he'd gotten home, whether the fact that she was out with Ted had bothered him. She deeply wanted to call him and check on both issues, even as she tried to pay attention to Ted.

She had made an effort to keep the discussion on business throughout the whole dinner, but Ted had seemed equally dedicated to learning more about her personal life. The result had been a pretty uncomfortable evening, and Ria was glad it was almost over.

"Gosh, it's rough that Drew is blind," Ted said now. "He can't earn a living anymore, I guess."

His words jolted her into an automatic defense of Drew. "Why not? Plenty of blind people earn a living every day."

"A few do," Ted corrected. "Most people with disabilities are chronically underemployed. It's a sad statistic, but true."

The notion of Drew working at some job that didn't use his abilities made Ria's stomach churn. He had always devoted himself to his work, investing highly in his identity as a policeman and public servant. The thought of him now doing something way beneath his skill level was horrifying to her, mostly because she knew how horrifying it would be to him.

"I have the feeling that Drew will land on his feet, whether his vision improves or not," she said to Ted. It was true, she realized. Whatever Drew's issues, he was competent. Good at everything.

"Are you…?" Ted paused. "Are you still attached to him?"

She met his eyes and then stared at the table, the rich chocolate dessert melting on her plate. "I shouldn't be, but I am, a little bit."

"That's okay. It makes sense."

She looked up at Ted, touched by the kindness in his voice.

"In fact," he said, "it speaks well of you, that you don't let go easily. It's awfully hard to get over a divorce. I know. It took me several years to get over my wife."

"I didn't even know you were married." She felt guilty that she hadn't probed into Ted's past the way that he had probed into hers.

"I don't talk about it much. Letting a marriage die feels like a failure, and I'm not eager to brag about it. But I do understand." He reached out and took her hand, holding it lightly with his own soft one.

"It does feel like a failure," she said, "especially since it's had a bad effect on our girls."

He nodded, his head tilted to one side, his brow creased. "Divorce is hard on children. Even if the children are practically grown up, like your girls."

"Thanks for understanding." She extricated her hand from his. "And for being so easy to talk to."

"It's my pleasure, and I really mean that. Eat your dessert."

"Oh, I had such a good big meal, and I'm really not that hungry. Besides, I shouldn't."

"You are not worried about your weight, are you?"

Ria frowned. Why would he say that? But then again,

Ted was just a friend, like a girlfriend. "I always worry about my weight. Comes with the territory of having a dad who's very weight conscious."

"Speaking of your dad," Ted said, "I'm pretty sure that's him over by the wall."

Ria turned and saw her father at a table with a woman she didn't know. Not his new wife. "Hmm, yes. Yes, it is."

"Do you want to go over and say hello after dinner?"

"I'm not sure he would welcome that." As she watched her father, defensive anger rose up in her. Not that she adored Dad's new wife or even knew her that well, but she did know the woman was at home with a new baby. So what was Dad doing in a town up the shore, gazing at another woman, leaning in, touching her hand?

"Sounds like there's a story there," Ted said.

"Not a very original one. Dad likes women who are tiny and adoring, with all their attention on him. Which pretty much means he can't have a relationship that lasts longer than a few months."

"But were your parents married for a long time?"

She nodded slowly. "They were," she said, "but I'm not sure how loyal and committed Dad was, especially during the last few years."

"That must've been hard for you. I'm glad you stayed strong and compassionate through all the issues you've had." He was looking at her with warm admiration. "You are an incredibly beautiful woman, but you don't act like you know it. You're not vain at all."

"I'm the opposite of vain," she said, laughing a little. "I never feel like I look good enough." Certainly, she hadn't felt pretty enough for Drew.

Ted raised a hand to the waiter and made a signing gesture on his palm.

Ria went to the ladies' room, avoiding the area where her father sat. She couldn't believe the man. How could he leave his beautiful young wife home alone with the baby while he ran around with someone new?

She wondered whether he had run around on her mother.

She wondered—just for a minute—whether Drew had run around on her. But she was pretty sure not. Drew was an honorable man, focused on doing the right thing.

She loved that about him, except that it made him somewhat intolerant of other people who didn't do the right thing.

Like when his ex-wife didn't take good enough care of herself to keep the baby they had conceived together.

Outside the restaurant, Ted opened her door for her, and then, before she could climb into the Tesla, he wrapped his arms around her and pulled her to him. "I can take this slow," he said, "but I would really, really like to get to know you better."

"I don't think so, Ted." Firmly, she pushed his arms away and took a step back. "I'm really not ready for that."

"I'm a patient man. And I have a genuine business interest in the Chesapeake Motor Lodge. So I hope you won't mind if I stay in touch."

She smiled at him, grateful he wasn't angry. "Of course. Thank you for understanding."

They drove back to Pleasant Shores in a companionable silence, but Ria's mind was racing. It seemed that Drew had ruined her for other men.

Thanks a lot, Drew.

CHAPTER TWELVE

"YOU SURE YOU'RE not too hungover to do this?" Drew asked Ria the next day as he led Navy to her car. He knew the words came out as sarcastic, and he didn't care. He was still fuming about her condescending offer last night: to take time out from her date and give him a ride home.

"Of course I'm not hungover. When have you ever known me to drink too much?"

"I don't know anything about you anymore." He felt small and petty, picking at her like this, but he was all tangled up inside.

He needed to figure out how to be a man despite being unable to do some of the things that had always defined manhood to him, like driving. Needed to find a definition of masculinity different from what he'd grown up on, what had been pounded into him by his father.

It was tough when Ria was going out with a man who had no apparent problems, who was sighted, who drove an expensive car, who was wealthy.

Drew couldn't even drive his own dog to the vet.

"Look, I don't know what your attitude is all about. But I agreed to drive Navy to the vet and I still want to. I love her, too." Ria took the leash from him and guided Navy into the back seat, then got into the driver's seat while Drew climbed into the passenger side. "Is she still sick?" Ria asked as she started the car.

"She's worse." He reached a hand back to stroke Navy's muzzle. "She didn't even touch her breakfast this morning."

"That's not like her."

"No, it isn't." Fear that there was something really wrong with his dog scared him enough that he kept quiet through most of the drive to the vet. Inside, they got into an exam room pretty quickly after Navy was weighed.

She had lost five pounds.

Doctor Ben, the vet, sounded young and laid-back, but he also seemed to know a lot of recent information about animals. They'd gotten his name from Trey, who used this vet for King. So the man was at least familiar with former police dogs.

He didn't mess around, but ordered blood drawn for tests and had his technicians analyze the stool and urine samples right away. Then he felt what seemed like every inch of Navy's body while Drew held her head and petted her and talked to her, keeping her calm.

The vet examined her teeth, eyes and ears, and talked with Drew about the symptoms that had brought them in.

"I don't think she's in any pain," Drew said. "She's just not right. She's sleeping all the time, and she's not eating. She doesn't get excited about going outside. It's like she's depressed."

"She could be, in a manner of speaking." The veterinarian remained kneeling on the floor, petting Navy. "We don't understand enough about dogs' emotions to know if they actually feel depression, but in a lot of cases, it seems like they do. They can become withdrawn and inactive. Their eating and sleeping habits can change, and they can lose interest in activities they used to enjoy."

"That describes Navy to a T." Drew frowned. "I know she has to miss her police work, but the thing is, she didn't get this way until a couple of weeks after we moved here to

Pleasant Shores. She seemed plenty energetic when I first lost my vision and had to take her off duty."

"Hmm." The doctor was quiet a minute, and Drew liked the way he kept stroking Navy, scratching her ears. He was obviously a dog lover. "The most common triggers of dog depression, if you want to call it that, are losing an owner or losing another pet in the family. But it can also be caused by a move. And it's possible she's picking up on the emotions of people around her."

"Which would be me," Drew said bleakly. Moving to Pleasant Shores had definitely thrown him into more turmoil, but if that had made Navy sick, it would be hard to forgive himself. "What can I do?"

"A few things." The vet rose up into a chair, so Drew moved also to sit beside Ria. He appreciated how she had let him handle it, not speaking up or trying to take over. He noticed that, when it was possible, she let him be in charge. She wasn't one of those people who acted like those with a disability were incompetent or stupid.

"Normally," the vet said, "I would just suggest a little more exercise and a few more play sessions than usual. Of course, all of this is contingent on her test results coming back negative. But if it really is psychological, a little more exercise might not be enough for a dog who's used to something intense like canine police work. Have you ever considered agility classes or other dog sports?"

Drew shook his head. "That's a world I'm not real familiar with." He remembered, vaguely, watching a couple of dog shows with the girls over the years. But truthfully, it had seemed silly to him, compared with the important work dogs could do.

"Well, and would your vision be enough to run an obstacle course with your dog?"

"No." He had to admit that now. "No, probably not." It was galling, but the longer he was here without substantial improvement to his vision, the more likely it became that this was going to be it. That he wouldn't improve much more.

"How about you?" the vet said, clearly talking to Ria. "Could you work with the dog?"

There was a pause, and Drew spoke up to fill it. "She just drove me here. She's not living with the dog, and she's not responsible for her."

There was silence in the room, broken only by Navy's panting. Drew's spirits sank. Of course, he was glad the vet didn't think there was anything seriously and physically wrong with Navy, but the fact remained that she wasn't happy and wasn't eating. That would leave her open to illness and would drain her strength.

"We do have two daughters," Ria said. "Maybe they can help with Navy. Is it possible to do agility work or other dog sports when you're under eighteen?"

"It's usually required to have a parent there, but sure. A lot of young people handle dogs. They're often very good at training, because they have the time and energy we adults tend to run short on."

They talked a little longer and then left the office with assurances that if any of the tests came back showing something dangerous, the office would call them right away. They got Navy back into the car and both climbed in, but Ria didn't start it up.

"I hate this," Drew said.

"Yeah, that's obvious, but…" Ria paused.

"Just say it."

"It's just that you can't let yourself get too blue, because it's affecting others around you. Look, I feel sad you've lost most of your vision, too, and that you and Navy can't do police work. Really sad. But I know you can cope with it. You're a strong person. You'll land on your feet."

He turned his face away. "I don't need a pep talk on being a man."

"It's nothing to do with being a man, Drew! You've always had a messed-up notion of what makes a man, anyway. Your concept of gender roles is completely archaic!"

"And I'm sure Ted Taylor is real progressive about gender. Maybe he'll even let you drive his Tesla."

She made some sort of sound and started the car, squealing out of the parking lot and spitting gravel. Leaving Drew to wonder: Was his concept of masculinity really archaic? Or was Ria dating someone else because he was right, because he wasn't enough of a man for her?

ONE OF THE things Kaitlyn liked about being in the behavior support program was that they didn't have to sit in the classroom all day, every day. Service projects in the community were the norm, at least once or twice a week.

Today, a rare warm day in November, their whole class was heading for the waterfront.

Kaitlyn hadn't been there since Dad had made such a botch of things, and she worried he'd ruined the place for her. But as they got close, as she smelled the salty, brackish water and heard the lapping of the bay against the pilings, her shoulders relaxed for what felt like the first time in a week. She threw off her worries about school, which still felt like a dangerous place. And she shoved aside thoughts of the counseling that had been forced on her. She sort of liked her new counselor in the individual sessions she'd had, but spilling her guts to a strange adult was stressful. And the family sessions were excruciating.

The sunshine, weak and golden, slanted onto the bay, making it into a blanket of glittering diamonds. She could hear a few voices from the docks and crab shacks, although most of the fishermen were out for the day.

The rest of her body relaxed, even the muscles in her face. She loved it here so much.

She walked along beside Venus, who was talking to another girl in the class. Kaitlyn had pretty quickly realized that the behavior support program was just another classroom, and the kids there were just kids. It was no big deal to be there, not some bunch of weirdos or freaky activities for special kids. In some ways, it was better than the regular school because she could work at her own pace, rather than wait for the rest of the class to figure out the basics. Erica was a great teacher, keeping order by giving them a lot of responsibility, surprisingly, more than in the regular school. The other teacher for behavior support wasn't as cool, but he wasn't bad.

Today, everyone was doing different tasks. The main thing was a shore cleanup: of litter and anything else that could hurt fish. Rory and Kaitlyn were supposed to take water samples for their honors science class. Then they'd use their data to write a proposal for one of the nonprofits working to improve the health of the bay. Erica seemed to think it might really make a difference.

"Have fun with Rory," Venus said in a low voice filled with laughter. She veered off toward the group that was collecting gloves and trash bags to do the shore cleanup.

Rory headed right for the water, eager to get started, apparently. Kaitlyn took an extra moment to look around and enjoy just being here.

"Didn't think you were ever coming back," came a voice from one of the piers, and Kaitlyn looked up to see Sunny, Bisky's daughter.

"Yeah, I stayed away for a few days after my dad was sort of a jerk. I'm sorry."

"Mom said she helped him get headed in the right direction toward home," Sunny said. "How'd he go blind? Mom said he didn't seem that used to his white cane."

Guilt nudged at Kaitlyn's stomach. She'd been a brat for leaving her father alone in an unfamiliar place, with no means of finding his way back home. "He's a cop. Was a cop. Got a head injury in the line of duty and lost his vision."

"Bummer." They were quiet for a minute, watching the group of kids spreading out along the shoreline to pick up trash.

Kaitlyn considered how nice Sunny was being, and also the fact that she was outside the usual social hierarchy of the school. "So, hey…did you hear anything about that video of me?"

"Yeah." Sunny nodded.

"Do you think people have forgotten about it yet?"

Sunny's nose wrinkled. "I heard something about it a week ago, I think. Not since then. But it's not like I'm part of the popular crowd. Who knows what they talk about."

"Who'd you hear about it from?"

"Shelby Grayson," Sunny said. "No big surprise. She's always looking for attention. Hey, is your dad's dog a guide dog?"

Kaitlyn shook her head. "Nope. She was a K-9 officer until Dad got injured. Why?"

Sunny shrugged. "I like dogs," she said. "We used to raise puppies for one of the guide-dog schools."

"Do you know how to train dogs to be guide dogs?"

Sunny held out a flat palm and tipped it from side to side. "Not really. We just did real preliminary training with the pups. I like working with dogs, though. When one of our pups washed out, we got her back for a while, and I taught her all kinds of tricks."

"That's cool." Kaitlyn hesitated. Sunny was being friend-lier than she ever had been before, maybe because there was no one else here and she was bored. "Would you want to help me train Navy? I mean, I know you're busy, so it's fine if you don't have time."

"Would your dad let you come down here to do it?"

Kait rolled her eyes and looked up at the sky. "He doesn't have to know."

Sunny looked skeptical. "He's been down here most days this past week for a few hours," she said. "Doing his interviews. He'd probably find out."

"Like Venus says, it's better to ask forgiveness than permission." She tried to mimic Venus's fake British accent, and Sunny snorted.

"Kaitlyn," came Erica's voice. "Don't let Rory do all the work for your science project."

Kaitlyn waved acknowledgment. "I'm going," she said. And then to Sunny: "I'll see if I can bring Navy down one day after school. When are you here?"

"When am I not here?" Sunny gave a wry smile.

"I'll try to bring her tomorrow." As Kaitlyn walked down the little road and then cut down to the water, she realized she was walking faster than normal and smiling. It would be fun to try to train Navy with some new tricks. Fun to surprise Dad with something she'd accomplished.

Fun to have plans with a friend, if Sunny actually became a friend.

She got some sample bottles from Rory and headed over to one of the tide pools. The sun warmed her back, and she lifted her face to the cool breeze off the bay.

"Hey, Kaitlyn." Rod Berger beckoned to her from a picnic table where he was sitting with Moses. "Got something to show you."

"Not interested." With those two, it could be anything from a dead fish to a picture from a porno magazine. Whatever it was, Kaitlyn already knew she didn't want to see it.

They came over to her, and that was when Kaitlyn realized that she was out of sight of Erica and the rest of the class. She could scream and someone could hear her—in fact, Sunny was repairing a crab pot a couple of docks down—but she still felt uncomfortable and isolated as the two boys crowded her toward the water.

Rod pulled out his phone. "Great-looking picture of you," he said. He held up a still of her starting to take off her sweater, a half smile on her face. She looked like she was into it, and she remembered clearly that she'd forced the expression, but in the picture, it looked real.

Heat rose through her chest and neck to her face. "Did you screenshot that?"

"It's online. It's out there."

"Heard there are more where that came from," Moses added with his trademark slurry voice.

Kaitlyn felt like lying down and groaning. She thought she was getting free of the bullies in her new environment, free of everything that had made her lose it before.

But if someone started releasing photographs of her... "Get out of here," she said, and when the boys didn't move, she gave Moses a sharp shove and glared at Rod. "I took self-defense," she said. "I know just where to kick you."

The two boys backed away, hands raised, giggling.

Kaitlyn turned away like she didn't care and went back to collecting her samples. But her mind was racing. Were more pictures going to come out? And if so, what would that do to her possible friendship with Sunny and the students in her new class?

CHAPTER THIRTEEN

DREW MIGHT HAVE gotten over enough of his masculinity issues to be okay with Ria's driving him. But as she gunned the car's motor over the bumpy, rutted road, he couldn't help thinking, *Oh, man, I could have done this better.*

It was Friday morning, just three days after they'd taken Navy to the vet and argued about Drew's attitude.

"This road is awful," she complained. "Are you sure this is the right way?"

"We should come to a fork in another thirty seconds," he said. He had memorized the detailed directions beforehand. "You'll veer to the left."

One more big jolt made his head bump against the ceiling of the car.

"There's the fork!" she cried as she steered left. "You were right!"

"In just a quarter of a mile, you should see a trailhead sign on the right." He wasn't sure this was a good idea, but he found he was looking forward to it. He needed to talk to Ria, and Navy needed the exercise. And, yeah, he wanted to prove to her, and himself, that he could let her be in charge. Not that it was easy.

"There's the trailhead sign. And a parking area. Let me just pull up…" The car stopped, and then she turned it off. "Whew. Not an easy drive. But I hope it's worth it."

"It will be," he said with more confidence than he felt

inside. He got out, opened the rear passenger door and hooked on Navy's leash. He could feel the dog's perked ears and slight quiver, could hear her panting. She was glad to be here, at least.

"Do we have water for her?" Ria asked.

Drew tapped his backpack. "Water for her and for us." He didn't say it, but he'd also brought a little food and a blanket and a bottle of wine.

Why he'd done that, he didn't know, except it made him feel like a man again, in charge of an excursion. And, yeah, he wanted to beat out Ted, overcome his advantage in planning and executing a date with Ria.

A molten hot feeling rushed through him at the thought of Ria with Ted, dining at a fine restaurant, riding in Ted's soundless, expensive car. Ted might be wealthy and from the most elegant of homes, but Drew knew what he wanted, and it was exactly the same thing any other red-blooded man wanted when he was around a woman like Ria. And Drew didn't want him to have it.

A wave of possessiveness crashed through his body. Ria was *his*.

"Drew, are you okay?"

"Yeah. Why?" His voice came out thick and heavy.

"You seem kind of mad."

"Sorry." He took a slow breath in, let it out. "What's it look like?" he asked her as they set off down the trail.

"There's still some green and some color in the leaves," she said. "It's a nice wide trail in this spot. The sun is dappling the ground, real pretty, and there are big ferns. And what looks like a hawk overhead."

A stream murmured beside them. He breathed in, and the sharp scent of pine filled his nostrils. A breeze caressed his face. Navy tugged at her lead, and he could feel her snuffling through the dead leaves. He held Ria's elbow, but he didn't like the dependence, didn't want her to think he'd always be that way. "A lot of blind people hike with hiking poles," he said, nearly choking on the word *blind*. But he was trying to use it. Trying to get used to it. "I'm not there yet, and I think the rocks would muck up my cane, but I sure would like to be able to do this independently."

"Is it so bad, holding on to me?"

Her question hung in the air for a second as Drew recovered from his surprise. He gave her arm a little squeeze. "Actually...it feels good to hold on to you."

He heard her sharp little intake of breath, something he probably wouldn't have noticed before he'd lost his sight. It wasn't that his other senses had miraculously gotten sharper, like a lot of people thought. He focused on smell and sound and touch more, that was all. Just as he was more alert to the sound of Navy panting, the crunching of dry pine needles beneath their feet, he was also more alert to the sounds Ria made and the way her soft skin felt beneath his fingertips. And to her scent, the smell of honeysuckle, but with a little musk, like a moonlit summer night.

Navy barked joyously. "Should we let her off the lead?" Ria asked.

"She has a fantastic recall. So, yes." He reached down and unhooked her, and she took off. To test it, he gave her return command, and she rushed back to him. "See?" he said to Ria, and then added "Okay" to Navy, giving her permission to dash off again.

"She looks really, really happy, Drew. This was a good idea."

It *had* been a good idea. Drew had always liked to hike. Now, without his sight, he was more conscious of the sun baking on his shoulders, the fresh pine air and the chirps and whistles of birds.

"Do you remember the hikes we used to take when Sophia was a baby?" Ria asked. So she was thinking along the same lines as him. Hikes they had enjoyed together in the past.

"Those were good times," Drew said. "We should never have stopped hiking together."

She was quiet for a moment. Then: "So…we should talk about Kaitlyn. The weekly check-in, like the counselor recommended."

Okay, so she didn't want to delve into their past. "To me," he said, "she seems to be doing better, not that she's sharing a whole lot of her feelings with me." He slowed down to find his footing on a rocky stretch of ground.

Beside him, Ria slowed, too. "Yeah, she doesn't talk that much to me, either. But she seems happier when she comes home from school. She says the behavior support classroom isn't as bad as she thought, and I know she's made at least one friend, a girl named Venus."

They reached a wide, smooth stretch of trail and by unspoken agreement picked up the pace. "I found out that she has another friend down at the docks," Drew said. "Daughter of a woman named Bisky."

"Yes, I think that's Sunny. I've met her. Seems like a nice girl."

Something tight in his shoulders loosened up a little. "So her social life is better." That, he knew, was the most important thing for a girl Kaitlyn's age. "What about academics?"

"That's good, too. Erica says she's catching up with her studies, and that she works independently real well."

Gratitude washed over him. "We're so lucky. When I think about what could have happened…"

"I know…but, Drew?" Ria's voice had gone uncharacteristically hesitant. "I…I really think she needs you to stay here in town for a while. Are you going to be able to do that?"

"Yes." When it came to his kids, there was no question about his priorities. He'd mixed that up a little when he'd first lost his sight, but no more. "I'm staying at least three months. That's the agreement on the cottage and with the volunteer gig."

Navy rushed back at them, barking, and practically crashed into Drew's legs. He reached down, felt her coat full of burrs and laughed. He would have some brushing to do tonight, but it was fine. She was happy and that made all the difference.

"Aw, Navy, you like it here, don't you?" Ria's tone was tender and warm.

He remembered that tone when it had been turned on him, and he enjoyed it. Too much. So he kept walking, causing her to do the same. Navy brushed back and forth against his legs a few times and then rushed off, crunching through leaves. A cool breeze stirred, making music through pine needles above.

"We're coming to something," said Ria. Drew heard the light lap of water against the shore just as Ria said, "Drew, it's beautiful!"

A primitive sense of pride rose in him. He had caused that lilt of pleasure in her voice by finding this place and getting her to come here.

Then she squeezed his shoulder. "I'm sorry. I shouldn't talk about how beautiful it is when you can't see it."

"I can't see it, but I can feel it." And it was true. He smelled the fragrance of the water as it came to them on a light gust of wind; he heard the rustling in the trees. His foot found a thick stick and he picked it up and threw it into the water, and a splash indicated that Navy had followed it in.

"The water's so blue today," she said. "Remember how it changes colors?"

"Based on the sky," he said, smiling.

"There are a couple of sailboats way off to the left," she added, "and a big log sticking out into the water to the right."

"See any fish?" he asked.

She leaned forward. "No, they're hiding."

Navy jumped at them with a little bark, and Drew felt the end of the wet stick poke his thigh. He reached down and tugged it away from her, then tossed it out into the bay again.

"That's it, girl. Get it!" Ria said, and a moment later the dog returned to shore and brought the stick and then shook, splashing water all over them.

"Navy!" he scolded, not meaning it. "Be nice. Go shake off in the woods."

"There's a little picnic table here," Ria said. "Or there's a big downed tree where we could sit."

"Picnic table." He knew she'd be more comfortable there. "I have a blanket in case it's dirty."

"Perfect. It's five steps forward and five to the left."

He got to the table, slid off his backpack and felt her reach to help him unpack it.

Frogs chirped, and overhead, leaves rustled. Their hands made contact, the slightest touch.

It set Drew on fire.

He turned toward her and slid an arm across her shoulders. He could feel her start to relax and move closer. He also felt the moment when she stiffened and pulled back.

His desire for her made him incautious. "Ree. Sweet Ree."

"Drew…" She shook her shoulders as if she was trying to relax them.

"It's just… I'm drawn to you still. Can we explore that?"

"I don't… We still have the same issues." She pulled farther away.

The move felt familiar. She had started to pull away from him, sometimes, after Sophia was born. After Kaitlyn's birth, it had been more common, and by the end of their marriage, he'd barely been allowed to touch her.

He let his grip on her arm slide down to where he was holding her hand, and he squeezed it. "You're an amazing woman, Ria." His thumb moved across her wrist, and he felt her pulse quicken. Heard the hitch of her breath.

He ought to listen to her words, not to her body. But she hadn't said no, not exactly.

He moved until he was directly in front of her and took her other hand, loosely. "Do you know what I want?"

"I am… I'm not sure." Her voice was breathless, and he could tell that she did know exactly what he wanted. Maybe she even wanted it, too.

There was only one way to find out. He slid a hand slowly up her arm, past her shoulder, and let it tangle in her hair. Moved a little closer. "This okay?" He didn't want to do something she didn't want, no way.

She made a tiny sound in her throat.

He inched closer, until their breath mingled. "Was that a yes?"

He felt her nod and lowered his lips to hers.

The feel of her mouth, familiar and yet new, sent shock waves through his body. His sweet, complicated Ria. His wife, still, in his heart.

Because he knew her so well, he felt the tightness of

her muscles. Disappointment spread through him. If he was reading the signals right, she didn't want this to happen. He lifted his head, reluctantly. Stood for a minute with her circled in his arms, a couple of inches' buffer between them. Even that distance was hard for him to maintain, but he knew what was right, and it wasn't right to push himself on her.

She let out a little sigh, then nestled in closer, lifted her hands to his face and pulled him down to kiss her again. This time, she kissed him back, and every rational thought flew away.

Replacing it was desire that had been pent up for way too long. He pulled her tight against him and deepened the kiss, and instead of the rebuff he half expected, she responded eagerly. Relief and rightness mingled in with the wanting.

She tasted of peppermint and smelled like home, and she was in his arms. Heaven.

RIA CLUNG TO DREW, knees weak from the intensity of his kiss. He was firm and gentle, stroking her cheek and making little approving noises, and it was enough like making love that her body turned to liquid heat.

Had he ever kissed her like this before?

He was so confident, so powerful, yet so aware of her every movement, in touch with each reaction. She didn't want it to stop, and when he lifted his head, she couldn't help the small sound of protest that came out of her throat.

"Wait," he said, tilting his head back. "I can see you a little. I want to see you."

She smiled and bounced a little and tried to catch her breath. "That's so wonderful." She stood on tiptoes and pecked his mouth again.

"You're as gorgeous as always." He ran his hands down

from the sides of her breasts to the curve of her waist to her hips. "More than seeing you, I can feel how beautiful you are." His hands slid to her back and he pulled her close against him.

His hard body, pressed to hers, stole her breath and sent heat straight to the core of her. Dimly, she was aware of the cool breeze and the birdsong and Navy leaning against the sides of their legs…but only dimly, because Drew's energy was so intense that it nearly overpowered her. She wrapped her arms around him and clung to his hard, muscular back.

He moved against her, the feel of him exotic and yet as familiar as her own heart. He lifted his head. "I want you," he said hoarsely. "I want you so bad."

His words shot to the heart of her, torching a fire banked long ago. She sucked in air. "We're outside, and it's cold."

"Wouldn't bother me." He stepped forward, making her step back, and she felt the picnic table behind her. He lifted her effortlessly, sat her on it and moved between her knees.

"Drew…"

"Shh. I know." He kissed her again, light, tender touches along her jawbone, her neck, the very top of her shoulder. And then he pulled her close, so that the side of her face rested against his chest. "It's not the time or the place, but, babe…" He took a deep breath and let it out. "We'd be so good together. We always were."

Her own breathing was coming back under control now. She opened her eyes and stared out at the bay, immense and beautiful.

They should talk about this, the problem of their desire for each other, like rational adults.

But talking would ruin it, and she wanted to hold on to it, relive it, keep it apart from the real world of children and money problems and secrets.

Navy let out a yelp and jumped up to put her front paws on the picnic table beside them. At the same moment, they both reached out a hand to pet her.

"She always did get jealous," Drew commented, smiling. "Remember?"

"I remember." She remembered hushing Navy, not wanting to wake up the girls, and tiptoeing back to the bedroom. Sometimes, when Navy was new to them, Ria had even bought special chew treats she knew would last a long time, to give them an hour of privacy.

Unfortunately, she also remembered times when she'd been just as glad to let Navy interrupt them, because she was feeling self-conscious about her weight. And with those memories, more rushed in: their arguments, Drew's neglect of the girls over the summer and her own terrible secret.

She slid sideways, escaping Drew's hold on her. "What kind of food did you bring, anyway?" she asked, keeping her voice deliberately distant and bright.

Letting him know that their moment, whatever it had been, was over.

CHAPTER FOURTEEN

SATURDAY STARTED OUT to be a great day.

When Kaitlyn texted Sunny about whether she wanted to take Sophia's place and do a few hours of cleaning at the motel for pay, she hadn't known whether she and Sunny were close enough, whether Sunny would get insulted at being asked to do something menial like cleaning motel rooms. They'd only exchanged phone numbers because they'd talked about getting together to train Navy.

But Sunny had texted back immediately: YES! I'm broke.

She'd arrived on her bike half an hour later and got off at the room where Mom was giving Kaitlyn instructions she didn't need.

"Remember, no rag that touches the toilet gets used anywhere else."

"Toilet rags are special," Kaitlyn said to Sunny. "That's one of Mom's prime rules."

"I agree that toilet rags should be separate from anything else in the universe. When I go to people's houses, I'm worried they won't know that rule."

Mom's face broke into a smile. "We're going to get along fine."

Kaitlyn took Sunny's arm and pulled her into the to-be-cleaned room. "We'll text if we have questions."

"Open the window when you're using the strong cleaner," Mom called in.

"We will." Kaitlyn rolled her eyes at Sunny, who grinned back.

Quickly, Kaitlyn discovered that Sunny was a hard worker. She had to be, given her mom and her work at the docks. Kaitlyn had spent a lot of time cleaning motel rooms in the past year and a half, so she knew it was best to just get the job done and done right. They worked well together.

Truthfully, Sunny was better at cleaning than Sophia would have been, any day. Especially when Sophia was in a rotten mood, like she'd been this morning. Kaitlyn didn't even believe her claim of being sick, not really; at the most, she was probably on her period.

But whatever. "I'm glad you could come," she said to Sunny as they made up a bed with clean sheets.

"Me, too. That's good pay your mom is offering." And it was true; it was more than minimum wage. Mom understood that asking teenagers to work for her required spending a little cash, and she was willing. In some ways, a few at least, Mom rocked.

"So how's that new class you're in?" Sunny asked. "They wanted to put me in it, last year, but Mom kicked up a big enough fuss that they didn't."

"Why'd they want to put you in?" Then Kaitlyn reflected that she didn't want Sunny to know why *she'd* gotten put in the class. She opened her mouth to retract the question.

But Sunny was already answering. "Fighting and skipping school," she said, shrugging. "No big deal. I stopped, mostly."

"What were you fighting about?" Even though she was a dock kid, Sunny didn't seem like the kind of girl anyone would harass.

"Stupid stuff. That little twerp Kyle Sprang started spreading rumors I'd slept with him. When I shot him down in front of a bunch of people, he claimed he'd dumped me because I smelled like a fish boat."

Kaitlyn's eyes widened. "That's awful!"

Sunny shrugged, then grinned. "He messed with the wrong dock kid," she said.

"What did you do?"

"I told him if he didn't shut up, I'd tell everyone he was this big." She held her forefinger and thumb three inches apart. "Man, was he mad. But he didn't want my story to spread, so he stopped saying anything about us sleeping together."

Kaitlyn stared at her. "You're a genius."

"Yeah, that's why I'm cleaning toilets." Sunny held up a hand. "I'm not complaining, believe me. This got me out of sorting and culling, *and* it pays."

They finished that room and moved on to the next, talking about school and Navy and the kids in Kaitlyn's new classroom. Sunny asked her about her family, especially Dad. "I wish he wasn't blind," Kaitlyn said. "I mean, of course I wish that for him. But he used to be, like, this big mean-looking cop, and no one would mess with me once they saw him. Now…nobody's afraid of him."

"That stinks." Sunny squatted down to extract a used tissue from the floor under a desk. "But he seems like a pretty good guy."

"Yeah. He's just trying to figure it all out, and he's, like, oversensitive. That's why he was kinda rude to the captain."

"Eli will get over it. If he even noticed."

"Is your dad around, like, part of your life?" Kaitlyn asked. "Sorry if that's a rude question," she added quickly.

Sunny waved a hand. "Not rude. I don't know my dad."

"Oh." Kaitlyn didn't know whether to express sympathy or ask more questions.

Sunny grabbed the vacuum, then paused. "Mom's a little... Well, she's not exactly traditional. None of us, not me and not my older brothers, know our dads. None of them stuck around."

"That's awful!" Kaitlyn's heart hurt for the family. Plus, she was a little shocked because it sounded like Bisky's kids all had different dads. "Your mom seems so strong. I wouldn't think she'd *let* men treat her bad."

Sunny laughed. "She wouldn't. She doesn't *want* them to stick around." She turned on the vacuum cleaner and started pushing it vigorously around the room.

Kaitlyn pondered that. Mostly, she'd seen boys dumping girls, or men leaving women. Or at least, women who were wrecked about a relationship ending, like Mom after the divorce. To think that women could happily leave men behind, and go on proud and happy like Bisky, was kind of mind-blowing.

Kaitlyn was heading into the bathroom—two separate rags and buckets in hand—when her phone pinged with the tone that meant a social media message. She didn't get too many of those these days, so she stopped, pulled out her phone and tapped the notification.

You shouldn't have blocked me. Love, TomDickandHarry.

Her heart started pounding. How had he gotten to her when she'd deleted her account and started a new, private one?

Your dad's getting some print photos in the mail today.

Kaitlyn's breath whooshed out of her, and then she was panting. "I gotta go to my dad's," she called over the noise of the vacuum cleaner. "Now."

"What's wrong?" Sunny stopped the vacuum cleaner.

Kaitlyn's phone pinged again.

I have the digital ones ready to go.

Kaitlyn was breathing so hard she thought she might faint. "Somebody sent bad pictures to my dad."

Sunny came over and took the phone out of Kaitlyn's hand. "What pictures? And anyway, he can't see them, right?"

"I have to go get them before he finds them and shows them to someone." She grabbed her coat. "And his vision's coming back some. He might be able to see them."

"Wait up. I'm coming, too. We have to lock the room and tell your mom we're taking a break."

"There's no time!"

"There's time." Sunny handed the phone back to Kaitlyn. "Text her."

With shaking hands, Kaitlyn texted something to her mother, she barely knew what, and then they were running to Dad's cottage.

What images did TomDickandHarry have? They could only be stills from the video, like the one Moses and Rod had shown her down at the docks; there was no other time she'd done anything that would be remotely interesting to a guy like that. And who *was* he, anyway?

She ticked through possibilities in her mind as she ran. It couldn't be Chris. While he'd been the one to ask her to take off her shirt, he wasn't shifty and cruel, or at least, she didn't think so. Tyler and his other popular friends… it could definitely be one of them, but who? Would Tyler himself do it? Was he TomDickandHarry?

But Sophia was dating him, sort of. Would he really do something so awful to his girlfriend's sister?

And then she thought of Moses and Rod, and the picture they'd tried to show her down at the docks. Had it been them all along?

Kaitlyn's lungs burned by the time they got there, and images of Dad's disappointed face kept flashing through her mind. She couldn't let him see how badly she'd screwed up. For Mom to see it would be bad enough, but Mom already knew Kaitlyn was far from perfect.

Dad still thought she was his little princess, and though it was stupid, she wanted it to remain that way.

The mail at Dad's cottage came through a slot in the door and landed on the floor. Thank heavens she had a key. Thank heavens he didn't seem to be home.

She unlocked the door and saw the mail scattered over the floor, and her tight shoulders relaxed a little. Navy rushed into the entryway to see what was going on, letting out one sharp bark. Then she stretched, back end in the air, front half forward, and gave a yawn that came out like a little groan.

While Sunny fussed over the dog, Kaitlyn fumbled through the mail until she spotted it: a big manila envelope with Dad's name and address in block letters. No return address. "This has to be it," she said, holding it up for Sunny to see.

Sunny looked up from rubbing Navy's belly. "No postage. Dude must have stuck it through the door himself."

"What a complete, total jerk." Kaitlyn was catching her breath now. Relief washed over her. They'd gotten here in time. Dad hadn't had a chance to see it, or show it to someone who could describe it to him.

"Aren't you going to open it?"

"Yeah, I guess." She sat down on the floor in the entryway, leaned against Navy and ripped open the envelope.

There was an eight-by-ten photo of her in the midst of taking off her shirt. The same one Rod and Moses had shown her, and it made her cringe. Instinctively she held it where Sunny couldn't see it.

A note was paper-clipped on. "If you don't want your parents to see this, come back and finish the job. We like you better than your sister."

Confusion made Kaitlyn dizzy. What did they mean? What did Sophia have to do with it?

"Kait?" The voice came from upstairs, then the sound of rapid footfalls. Uh-oh. Dad was here, and he was coming down. "Is that you, honey?"

He came around the corner as Kaitlyn attempted to stuff the envelope under her shirt.

"Hi, Mr. Martin," Sunny said, stepping in front of Kaitlyn. "I'm Kait's friend Sunny. You met my mom before?"

Thank you, Kaitlyn tried to project to Sunny.

"It's nice to see you," he said, reaching out a hand, which Sunny clasped and shook vigorously. "What are you girls up to today?" He tilted his head back. "Is that the mail?"

"Um, yeah." Kaitlyn quickly grabbed up the flyers and circulars and handed them to him.

"Anything look interesting?"

"No," she said, too quickly. "I mean, probably not. It's just ads."

"We wanted to see if we could train Navy a little," Sunny said.

"Or at least play with her," Kaitlyn added, knowing Dad wanted to keep her active. They'd talked about taking her to some agility classes up the shore, but so far, Dad hadn't signed Navy up.

The manila envelope chose that minute to fall out of her shirt and onto the floor. Dad spotted it, or heard it, she wasn't sure which, and held out his hand. "More mail?"

Kaitlyn froze, looking at Sunny.

"No, that's my notes about dog training," Sunny said, taking the packet from Kaitlyn. "Is it okay with you if we take Navy down to the beach for a little while? It's not that cold out."

"Navy would love it. The more activity she gets, the better she feels."

"Great!" Sunny clicked her tongue to Navy. "Where's her leash?"

Dad pointed her toward the hook on the wall and helped her get Navy's harness on, while Kaitlyn stood by with her skin hot, feeling dizzy. She'd come so close to being caught.

"We'll be back in an hour. C'mon, Kait!" Sunny took her arm and practically dragged her toward the door.

Outside, they walked down the path to the beach.

"You saved my butt. Thanks," Kait said to Sunny.

"I'm good with adults. And dogs," Sunny added, putting her hands on Navy's back and rubbing down her sides, causing the dog to tip back her head with what looked like a big smile.

"Did you see the note?" she asked Sunny.

Sunny nodded. "What did they mean, *finish the job*? Finish taking off your clothes?"

Kaitlyn's heart sank. "That's probably exactly what it means." She bit her lip, then knelt to pet Navy, too, needing the comfort. "What am I going to do?"

Sunny's brow wrinkled and she lifted a hand, palm up. "We'll think of something." Her voice didn't sound certain.

Kaitlyn was drawing a blank, too, but she knew she had to take action and stop this jerk. It would kill Mom and Dad to find out.

SUNDAY AFTERNOON, the day after Kaitlyn and her friend ditched their cleaning job at the motel—which actually made Ria happy, because it meant Kait was making friends—Ria opened the door of her house and welcomed in her mom; Erica and her sister, Amber; and Mary. Another car was pulling in the driveway, and a tall woman got out and headed toward them.

Ria had realized that the girls were spending the afternoon and evening at Drew's. That meant there was no one to eat the big pot of minestrone she'd made.

Nothing to stop her from ruminating on the fact that she and Drew had kissed so sweetly, so intensely, that she'd relived it in her mind, over and over.

She'd looked out the window at dark skies and a cold, steady drizzle, built a fire in the fireplace and called her woman friends. A little hitch of hesitation and she'd called Sunny's mom, too, and invited her. It was good to know the families of your kids' friends. Surprisingly, the woman, known as Bisky, had said yes.

Everyone brought something: salad, bread, dessert, wine. They all crowded into the steamy, fragrant kitchen together and soon sat down at Ria's big kitchen table. They ate and talked and laughed, getting louder as the wine flowed.

Ria rejected offers to help with the dishes. "Let's go sit by the fire for coffee and dessert," she said, so they all went into the den. She was glad of the big wraparound couch she'd splurged on, as everyone nestled in. The fireplace radiated warmth, and gathered here, the cold outdoors seemed safely distant.

"How's your sweet Kaitlyn doing?" Mary asked.

Ria laughed. "*Sweet* wouldn't be my word to describe her, most days," she said.

Bisky let out a snort of agreement. "Teenage girls. I got combat pay when I was in Iraq, but I swear I need it more now." She looked at Erica. "You teach over at the school, right? I don't know how you deal with them every day."

"They're better with me than with their parents, at that age," Erica said. "As for Kaitlyn, she seems to be doing pretty well in the classroom. Gets along with the other kids, and wow, is she ever smart."

Ria and Julie exchanged little glances of pride. They'd both always thought Kait had a wonderful mind.

"I'm glad Kait's become friends with your daughter," Ria said to Bisky. "She's a lovely girl. Good manners and a terrific work ethic."

Bisky smiled. "Thanks. I'm proud of her."

Amber emerged from the kitchen carrying big slices of the chocolate turtle cheesecake she'd brought. As she handed plates to Julie and Mary, Erica jumped up to help her.

Amber waved Erica back to her seat. "Sit down," she said. "I'm doing well, remember?"

Erica bit her lip. "Of course you are," she said and sank back onto the couch. But her eyes followed her sister as she returned to the kitchen, and Ria saw her mom and Mary exchange glances. Amber had fought a major battle with cancer and had been skinny and frail when the sisters had come to the island. She seemed to be doing much better now, with an energetic walk, blooming cheeks and a head of short, thick hair. But it seemed Erica didn't feel completely confident of her health yet.

Amber emerged again and held out a plate to Ria.

Ria studied the gooey chocolate and the caramel topping, then forced herself to look away. "That's okay. I'm full." And she didn't want to gain an ounce, just in case she and Drew...

"No one's too full for cheesecake," Mom protested.

"Hear, hear," Bisky said, forking up a big bite.

Mary reached out, took the plate Amber was waving in front of Ria's nose and set it down on the coffee table. "Don't force food on the poor woman. Let her make her own decisions."

"You're right," Amber said. "Sorry. If it's for you and for your health, then do what you need to do."

"On the other hand," Bisky said, "if you're trying to lose weight to impress a man, forget about it."

The others nodded approvingly. Although six-foot-tall Bisky earned her living on the water, with a career much different from those of these in-town business owners and teachers, she seemed to fit right in.

"Ria has no need to watch her weight for a man," Mom said. "She's got someone hanging on her every word and eager to spend every minute with her."

"Ooh, who's that?" Amber looked up from her cheese-cake with interest. "There are, like, zero attractive single men in this town."

Erica raised her eyebrows. "Thought you weren't inter-ested in dating."

"I wasn't. But a lady's allowed to change her mind. Who's hitting on you?" she asked Ria. Then she added, "I prom-ise, I won't poach."

"It's her husband. Ex-husband," Mom corrected herself. "Drew's still crazy about you, from everything I've seen."

Ria looked down, her insides churning in a half-pleasant, half-sickening way. She'd relived her kiss with Drew so many times since their hike. It had been amazing, had shown her that the spark between them hadn't died at all; instead, it seemed to have grown to a higher flame.

But they'd had plenty of attraction when they'd gotten together and in the early years of their marriage, and it hadn't made for a successful relationship. She'd worried constantly about her weight, and although he'd never said one contrary word to her, she'd been sure Drew noticed and disliked it, as well. She'd seen pictures of his former girlfriends, and most were model thin.

"Drew's hot," Amber said.

Ria's head jerked around to look at the woman, and Amber held up a hand. "Remember, I don't poach. He's all yours."

"Well, he's not *mine*. We're divorced. And the twenty pounds I've gained in the past couple of years..." She shrugged. "Let's just say it doesn't make me super interested in a relationship."

"A good man will want you to be happy and love you as you are," Bisky said.

"Drew's a good man," Mom said.

"He is," Ria admitted. "But he's a man, and men care about looks."

"Well," Erica said, and the rest of them turned toward the thoughtful sound of her voice. "Trey overlooked a lot I thought was a deal breaker. The fact I couldn't have kids," she explained, looking at Bisky, probably the only one who didn't know Erica's story.

"And it didn't strain him a bit to do it," Amber said. "He still looks at you like you're some kind of goddess."

Erica blushed and shook her head, but with a smile on her face.

"Still," Ria said, "you're skinny. Men care about weight." She hesitated, then added, "Look at my dad." Then she bit her lip. She didn't want to hurt Mom by bringing up the problems that had led to the divorce. And she certainly wasn't going to tell her mother that Dad seemed to be cheating on his new wife.

Amber set down her empty plate and propped her feet

on the ottoman. "Skinny isn't all it's cracked up to be," she said, looking into the fire.

Her words struck Ria hard. Amber, about Ria's age and the mother of a teenager just like her, had nearly died and wasn't out of the woods yet. How foolish it was to worry about a few extra pounds in comparison to what Amber had been through. She picked up the plate of dessert from the coffee table—it had been calling her name anyway—and took a decadent, delicious bite, savoring the way the salty caramel contrasted with rich, creamy chocolate.

After a little more desultory chat, Amber stood up, and immediately Erica did, too. "I'm sorry to cut out early," Amber said. "Still working on my endurance."

"And I have papers to grade before tomorrow," Erica said. "Thanks so much for this. What a treat."

Ria hugged them both, saw them out, then returned to find her mother, Mary and Bisky discussing Amber's health.

"She's doing much better," Mom was saying. "Starting to think about how to live the rest of her life, what her future might hold."

"That's good," Mary said briskly. "We none of us know how much time we have left. We need to live life to the fullest."

"Speaking of full, I'm way too much so," Ria said. Without really noticing, she'd eaten the entire slice of cheesecake, using way more calories than her diet called for. "I should never have eaten that cake."

"Stop it," Bisky said. "You deserve a little treat every now and then. We all do."

Ria didn't answer that. Bisky had way more confidence than she'd ever have.

"Sometimes," Mary said slowly, "I think we'd all be

better off if we stopped thinking about how we looked to others, what they thought, and just focused on keeping ourselves happy."

"Easy for you to say," Mom said. "You're tiny by nature. And gorgeous, too. Most of us have to struggle if we want to look good."

"That's if you care what men think," Bisky said. "And you know what? You'd be surprised. Most guys aren't as worried about size as you'd figure. I mean, look at me. I'm big enough to beat the tar out of three-quarters of the men in the USA, and yet…nobody seems to mind." She smiled a little.

Curiosity struck Ria. Did Bisky date? But still… "Most men are visual," she said. She knew she was repeating herself, being anti-feminist and self-defeating, but she also felt she could be honest among these women. "And they care how you look. And what's pretty to most guys is skinny."

Bisky shrugged. "Stick with that viewpoint if it makes you happy," she said.

"It doesn't make me happy, but it's true." Ria knew it was so.

"Then you can't win, can you?" Mary asked. "And what are you teaching your girls?"

"Kaitlyn is starting to worry about weight," Mom said and sighed. "It's a shame. You were the same way, at her age," she added, looking at Ria.

Guilt washed over Ria. Was she teaching a poor body image to Kaitlyn? She'd never said one word to Kait about her weight—not just because Kaitlyn looked perfect to her, but because she knew it was wrong. But meanwhile, she was always harping on her own weight in front of the girls. Teaching, and teaching the wrong thing, by example.

Ugh. Would she ever get this motherhood thing right?

CHAPTER FIFTEEN

"You gotta be the man of the family!" His father's parting words on the phone echoed in Drew's ears as he made his way through town.

And Drew wanted that. Now that he'd gotten closer with Ria, he *really* wanted that. He thought about her all the time, remembering her warm eyes, her lush lips and body, the little sighs she always let out when she felt pleasure.

Problem was, he'd already showed, clearly, that he wasn't good at relationships. Just basically defective. Now, in addition to his character inadequacies, he had a major disability. And he didn't have a job.

Well, not a real job. Although he had to admit he was starting to enjoy his interviews with the watermen. After a rocky start, a couple of them had begun to open up to him. Especially Bisky, who was meeting him today in front of Goody's, where they had agreed to do an interview in more comfort than they could find down at the chilly, windy docks.

He was curious about how she held her own in such a male-dominated world, and he wanted to interview her about her life on the water. But he also wanted to pick her brain. What did she think about a blind guy in a relationship? From her point of view as a woman, did something like that even seem feasible?

"Hey, Martin." Bisky greeted him in the same friendly way she greeted the men she worked with. She also touched his arm when she reached him, which he appreciated. It was good to know where the people around you were actually standing, and he wasn't yet real good at sensing it, like those who'd been without vision for a longer time than he. From his work with his new orientation and mobility specialist, he was learning more about the subculture of the visually impaired, and on his better days, he actually found it interesting: the young people who made videos and used their social media prowess to advocate for disability awareness, but also those who'd lost their vision as older adults and were learning to cope, just as he was. There were so many different types of visual impairments and so many styles of coping. The more he learned, the less alone he felt.

They went inside, and immediately the lunchtime smells surrounded them. Goody's had a very limited menu, but what they sold was good: crab-cake sandwiches, burgers and giant vegetarian hoagies, all with crispy, greasy French fries on the side. Goody's didn't even stock sodas, forcing everyone to drink milkshakes with their lunch; it was that or water.

Having tasted Goody's milkshakes, Drew was pretty sure that no one ever chose water.

They both ordered crab-cake sandwiches and then Bisky found a table by the window. It was bright over here, and Drew found he could see more blurry shapes than ever before.

Hope rose up in him. Maybe he'd... But no. He wasn't going to go there, to that la-la land where he regained his vision and lived happily ever after. His doctors thought he'd regain minimal sight, at best. Not enough to drive. Not enough to be a cop.

The little dining room was half-full, from the sounds of it. Lots of murmured conversations, good lunch smells, the occasional sharp laugh or high giggle. Goody's was a happy place.

At least, it felt this way now. He could only imagine the change that would take place when those nasty middle and high school kids started to fill it up. His fists clenched, remembering the teasing that Kaitlyn had endured, teasing that might have been a part of her decision to take a handful of pills.

Their food arrived, and Drew welcomed the distraction of the hot, spicy crab cake on a homemade yeast roll. He dunked his fries in ketchup and sucked down a large chocolate milkshake. He'd have to hit the gym hard after this lunch, but it was worth it.

He could tell from the sounds across the table that Bisky was enjoying her lunch, too, even though she didn't say much. Maybe it was because she spent so much time with men, but she was a comfortable person, easy to be quiet with.

She could talk, though, too, and once they'd eaten their fill, he started asking her questions about life on the water. How long had she been working it, how long her family had been here in Pleasant Shores, what she looked forward to in the future, since the Chesapeake Bay was changing so fast. Since taking on the oral history project and talking with some of the watermen, Drew had listened to a couple of audiobooks about the bay's history and ecosystems. Complicated stuff, lots of science involved, but he was enjoying it.

She talked about all of it, including the erosion that was eating away at the shores of this area and especially of the islands out in the bay. "Put that together with the fact that my kids aren't real interested in crabbing and oystering, and I'll probably be the last generation of my family to work the water."

"It's a loss, isn't it?"

"I don't know." She sounded philosophical about the

whole thing. "Would I like my kids to take over the business, live the same life my grandparents did? Sure, but things change. And we can't know the future." Her voice lowered a few notes. "Speaking of, what's *your* future? You going to stay in Pleasant Shores? Remarry your wife and help raise your girls?"

The question came out of left field, but Drew supposed he deserved it after asking her so many personal things. "There are a few issues standing in the way of that."

"Such as?"

"Such as I barely have a job, I'm still adjusting to being legally blind, and I wasn't the best husband and father even when I had my vision and some money."

"You're there," Bisky said, raising her voice a little over the increasing noise of conversation and laughter. "You're available for your kids. That's worth something."

He lifted a shoulder and shook his head. "I can't take care of them, not the way I used to. Can't protect them."

"Seems to me you're pretty protective," she said. "Anyway, that's not what we want you men for. Macho stuff, it's overrated. Hey, there's…" She paused. "Never mind."

Something had come into her voice. "What is it?"

After a beat of silence, she sighed. "Your ex-wife is here."

"Ria?" His heart did a little dance and he couldn't keep the happiness out of his voice. "Where?"

"With someone else," she said.

Drew's happiness rushed out of him like air from a punctured balloon. "Wait—don't tell me. Blond guy? Rich looking, wearing a suit?"

"Yeah."

Drew's head dropped and he sighed. "Can they see us?"

"Do you *want* them to see us?"

"I don't know." Drew scraped a hand over his face. He

wanted to teleport home without having to walk by his wife and her lunch date.

Bisky scooted her chair. "There. You're kind of behind a potted plant and now I'm blocking the rest of you, too. Just until you decide whether you want to try to make her jealous or not."

That surprised him. "I don't want to make her jealous. I'm not playing games."

Bisky laughed. "Don't you know that love is always a game?" she said. "It might be interesting to see how she reacts if she sees us together."

"Thanks, but no. That's not my style."

Just then, he heard the rich peal of Ria's laugh, accompanied by a baritone version, certainly Ted's.

Heat rose in Drew's chest and adrenaline clenched his fists. Another man was making his woman laugh.

And he couldn't be that type of caveman; it was the twenty-first century. Drew fumbled for his cane as a huge sense of inadequacy came over him.

It wasn't going to work between him and Ria. He wasn't enough for her, couldn't give her enough. Ria deserved so much more than he could offer.

He needed to make sure he didn't rouse the girls' hopes that they could be a family again, because they couldn't.

For his own mental health, he needed to douse his own hopes, too.

He stood and snapped open his cane. "Thanks for the interview," he said to Bisky. "Are you walking out now?"

"Sure," she said. "Take my arm if you want to."

He didn't want to and started to walk toward the door, but his leg banged into a chair, knocking it over. He could see, just barely, that Bisky righted it. What he couldn't see, but could imagine just fine, was that everyone was looking at the clumsy blind man. Including his ex-wife and her new squeeze.

He took Bisky's arm and kept his face expressionless while emotions churned inside him. How could he compete with a man like Ted when he couldn't even get across the room without a woman's help?

THE DAY AFTER meeting with Ted at Goody's, Ria pulled into Drew's driveway and turned to her extremely cranky daughter. "You can—" But Kaitlyn was already out of the car and slamming the door.

Their mother-daughter outing had been a complete bust.

Ria climbed out of the car, back aching, mentally exhausted. It had seemed like a good idea, spending the afternoon bonding with her daughter. There had been an early dismissal from school, and Kaitlyn needed new clothes. Initially, Kaitlyn had been enthusiastic.

But within half an hour, she'd gotten sulky and uncooperative, not wanting to try anything on, not wanting to take a walk together, wanting to go back to Pleasant Shores and to Drew's place.

Ria's gut twisted as she watched her daughter's head-down rush away from her. She wanted so badly to help Kait, and it just wasn't happening. She was making things worse.

If only it had been a bright, sunny day to improve Kait's mood, instead of gloomy November weather. If only the Chesapeake would sparkle, rather than toss gray waves at the shore.

Kait was almost at the door of Drew's cottage when he came out and intercepted her, reaching out and gripping her by the forearms. "What's wrong?"

"Mom's wrong!" Kait gestured back toward Ria. "She wants me to walk, like, ten miles on a horrible day and wear nun clothes to cover up how fat I am! Make her stop, Dad!" She broke away from him and rushed into the house.

Drew stood on the steps, facing Ria's direction, arms crossed. If she hadn't known him so well, she'd have thought he was flexing his muscles for her benefit, but he wasn't like that. He wasn't vain; in fact, he had no idea how good-looking he was.

She took a deep breath, trying to quell her automatic visceral reaction to him. "Hey, I'm here," she said to orient him. "Sorry to bring her over in an upset state."

"What happened?" His tone was cool.

She thought of the friendly way he'd walked with Bisky yesterday, holding her arm. Was he moving on?

She stifled her feelings about that. "I just wanted to take a walk with Kaitlyn, do some shopping," she explained.

"Why does she think you think she's fat?"

Ria blew out a sigh and sat down on Drew's front step. "Because I screwed up. Talked about my step goal on my pedometer, which she interpreted as me saying she needed more exercise because she's fat. Which she's not, of course. She's beautiful."

"Is that all?" He sat down beside her, but a good arm's distance away.

"No." Her stomach clenched with the shame of making such a bad mother-choice. "I also talked about how to dress to de-emphasize…" She trailed off, then decided she might as well finish the thought. "To de-emphasize her chest." Her face heated as she said the words, remembering how Drew always loved it when she wore clothes that showed a little cleavage.

Drew frowned. "The counselor said not to mention her weight at all."

"I didn't! It's just that she was complaining about how

her chest is all that boys look at, and I sometimes have the same issue, so I thought…" She trailed off as Drew went rigid. "I did some bad parenting today. Thank heavens she has you to turn to."

"I'll do what I can."

"I will, too," she promised. "As soon as she's speaking to me again. I mean it, Drew. I'm so glad you're here to help with her. I grate on her nerves like squeaky chalk."

"Does Ted Taylor look at your chest?" he asked, his voice tight.

"What?" She tilted her head, studying him.

"Does he look at your chest? When you're out on your lunch dates." Then he waved a hand. "Never mind. I know the answer to that question."

Ria did, too. She'd caught Ted looking a few times, more than she remembered him doing when they were dating before. Of course, she'd gotten more voluptuous. Maybe looking at her chest was hard to avoid.

"It was business," she said uneasily. "Our lunch date was just business. Ted's probably going to invest in my motel." Except that he wanted a lot of involvement in the running of it, which she didn't think was a good idea.

"Uh-huh." He blew out a disgusted breath, obviously not believing her.

"If you want to be that way…why were *you* out with Bisky Turner?"

Surprise showed in the quick twist of his head in her direction. "You saw us?"

"Goody's is a small place."

"I'm interviewing her for my job. And that's all."

Relief washed over her, and she impulsively reached out and took Drew's hand.

He squeezed it and tugged her closer. "You're perfect as

you are, you know," he said with that telltale little growl in his voice. "Don't ever feel self-conscious about the looks God gave you."

This was bad. His touch, the sound of his voice were sending warmth through her entire body. She tried to pull her hand away. "We shouldn't..."

He held it captive, squeezed it. "We shouldn't have started a fire if we didn't want it to burn," he said.

"That's true," she whispered. "But I still don't think it's a good idea." Because if they got close again, they'd still have the same problems they'd had before.

Because you *have problems*, a little voice in her head said, and she knew it was true. She couldn't trust a handsome man like Drew not to run around the way her father had, couldn't trust him not to judge her body as it changed throughout all the stages of a woman's life.

Besides, if he knew about her miscarriage, he'd hate her for causing that, too.

But would he? She wondered. Drew had become more accepting than he used to be.

She thought of the women she'd shared a meal with on Sunday, how they'd talked about body image. Every one of them seemed to have a healthier one than she did.

That negative way of looking at herself had affected her marriage, for sure. Now it was affecting her mothering, as well. And if she didn't work on it, she'd continue to mess up in both areas. "I have to go," she said, standing and pulling her hand from Drew's, hurrying away before he could say or do anything to try to keep her here.

She had some self-examination to do.

CHAPTER SIXTEEN

ON WEDNESDAY MORNING, Kaitlyn walked toward the school, for once feeling okay and safe. How could she not, with Venus on one side of her and Sunny on the other?

The sun was finally peeking out and the wind had died down, so there was a slight possibility of a good hair day. Kaitlyn had gotten over her mother's annoying behavior after Mom had made an awkward apology. And then there'd been an even more awkward conversation with her father about how all bodies were beautiful.

They meant well, and they cared, but ugh.

"I have a good feeling about today," Sunny said. "We're gonna figure out who sent those pictures. Easy."

"How?" Venus asked, frowning.

"Trust me. We're going to nudge our suspects until they rat themselves out."

"I kind of think someone who's good with computers. I mean, someone edited down that video into stills, high-quality ones. They even…" She hesitated.

"What?" the other two girls said simultaneously. They must have heard something in her voice.

"They doctored them," she said. "I took them home and looked, and they made me even bigger than I already am."

"How is that even possible?" Venus gave a sideways glance at Kait's chest.

"Shut up!" Kaitlyn's face heated. If only she could be a cute, moderate B cup like Sophia.

"Wish you'd throw some of your endowments my way," Venus said. "I'm still flat as a tortilla, and looking at how my mom's built, I'll probably stay that way."

"It's not always easy having Kaitlyn's figure," Sunny lectured. "It can make boys interested for the wrong reasons."

The two of them talked so *normally* about bodies. Not like Mom, who was all tied up in knots about it. "Anyway," Kaitlyn said, "in addition to Chris and maybe Tyler, we think Kyle Sprang could be involved, right? So you know the drill by now."

Both girls nodded, because this was the third time they'd gone through it, casually discussing loaded topics with their targets, eliminating suspects each time.

They walked into the school and down the hall three abreast, Kaitlyn in the middle, Venus on one side and Sunny on the other. Today was an all-school assembly—about bullying, ironically enough—which Kaitlyn usually hated. School assemblies were a chance for kids to yell stuff, catcall and make mean remarks, because they were outside of their normal school routine.

But with her friends flanking her, she felt protected.

"There they are," Venus said, nodding in the direction of Chris, who was finding a seat next to popular Tyler Pollackson. Ugh. Normally, Kaitlyn would have sat as far away from them as possible.

Her heart pounded as they found seats directly behind Kyle, Chris and Tyler. "So, Tyler," Venus said, leaning forward, "what do you think about the topic of today's assembly?"

He frowned back at her, obviously surprised to have been spoken to by a mere mortal. "What is it?"

"Cyberbullying," she said patiently. "You know, like posting inappropriate photos of people to make them feel bad."

Did Chris and Tyler look a little uneasy? It was hard to tell.

"It'll be boring just like all assemblies," Chris said and glanced over at Tyler, his forehead wrinkling. Then he reached into his pocket. He pulled out a contraband Juul and took a hit.

Tyler laughed, and then Chris did, too. Obviously, doing something against the rules—making their *own* rules—made them feel in control again.

Hearing their cocky laughter made Kaitlyn's stomach hurt, and she wished she was sitting anywhere else. But Sunny and Venus didn't seem to feel any of the same fears.

"How come you're vaping, Chris?" Venus asked. "Nervous about the assembly?"

"No." Chris sneered back at them, and Kaitlyn wondered why she'd ever thought he was cute or would make a good boyfriend.

"Feeling guilty?" Sunny asked. "Done any cyberbullying lately?"

Chris shifted in his seat. "Shut up! Why are you even talking to us?"

"Dude! She's still hot for you!" Tyler guffawed loud enough for a bunch of kids nearby to turn around and look at him.

He seemed to notice the attention, and he smiled even bigger and spoke even louder. "Maybe next time you can do a *real* photography session."

Kaitlyn's gut clenched.

Sunny nudged her. "He knows," she whispered. "Maybe he put the pictures in your dad's door."

Several teachers headed in their direction, probably

drawn by the sound of Tyler's big mouth, just as Chris took another hit on his Juul.

One of the really old teachers sniffed the air. "Is that marijuana I smell?"

"What did you just put back in your pocket?" the other teacher asked Chris.

Chris opened his mouth and put on an innocent expression. Then, after looking at the teachers' stern faces, he stood and pulled out the pipe. "It's a vape pipe! It's not drugs!"

"I'll take that," one of the teachers said, neatly lifting the Juul out of Chris's hand. "And since it's against the rules to vape on school property, I'll take *you* down to the office." She frowned at Tyler. "Are you involved in this?"

Tyler lifted his hands, palms up. "Not me. I don't believe in vaping."

From the other side of him, Kyle, so scrawny that he hadn't even been visible before, let out a laugh.

Chris glared at them both as he was led away.

After the assembly, Kaitlyn, Sunny and Venus eased out of their seats and hurried to the back of the auditorium. There was no security guard at the main doors of the school, so they took a chance, sneaked outside and high-fived each other. "We got to Chris, and we got him in trouble."

"He totally looked guilty."

"He definitely was involved in the video, not an innocent victim. Now he'll be afraid of us."

But Kaitlyn wasn't so sure. They'd gotten Chris in trouble for vaping, and they'd gotten a hint that he felt uncomfortable about cyberbullying. But knowing he'd likely been involved in the video, not just a dupe like she was, didn't make anything better. Now she knew he was the jerk she'd suspected he was, but she also knew he'd be really angry about getting in trouble.

WEDNESDAY AFTERNOON, Drew walked down toward the docks with his father beside him.

It was an unexpected visit. When Dad had called last night, he'd sounded like something was wrong. For his father to display any emotion at all was rare, so Drew had agreed to the visit even though he had an interview to conduct that afternoon.

Dad hadn't wanted to talk the minute he'd walked in the door, and Drew knew from experience that there was no point in rushing him. So after making him a sandwich, Drew had invited him along for the interview. Everyone had been okay with Kaitlyn coming along for the interviews, and bringing his father shouldn't be much different.

Actually, bringing Kait along on his interviews hadn't happened as often as Drew would have liked. Then again, that was because she was making friends and doing things with kids her own age, which was all for the good.

Thinking about Kait, and worrying about Dad judging him, made Drew less sure of his route, so he stopped on the next street corner, getting his bearings. "Is this Main?" he asked.

"How would I know?"

Drew consciously relaxed his jaw. "Look at the street sign."

"Main Street…yeah." Dad's voice was tight. "Thought you said you knew the way."

Of course. Dad *hated* not knowing the way and always refused to ask for help. "I do know the way. It just takes a little time. We'll go to the right." He nudged his father, felt the sidewalk before him and walked on.

"If this vision thing doesn't get better," Dad said, "what are you going to do for work? *Can* you work?"

A familiar tension settled into Drew's shoulders. His dad's demanding, never-satisfied voice was something he and his brothers had grown up with. It had caused Drew, as the oldest, to strive constantly to follow in his father's police footsteps and to be the best cadet at the academy, the best cop on the beat.

Unfortunately, Dad had also pitted him and his brothers against each other, or tried to, and although they all lived in the Baltimore area, they weren't close.

Striving to please his father had gotten Drew exactly nowhere. Now that a police career was closed to him, there was no way he could please Dad.

Unfortunately, when you'd tried to impress someone for your entire life, you couldn't drop the desire all that easily. Drew focused hard on the route and managed to get to the interview site without asking any more questions and without taking Dad's arm, which would have been uncomfortable for both of them.

An hour later, they emerged from the seafood company's headquarters, where crabbers and oystermen came to sell their day's catch. They'd arranged to meet a longtime marine police officer there, and he'd shared a lot of stories—of enforcing catch limits, of course, but also of nabbing poachers and apprehending boaters who were under the influence. He hadn't minded Dad's presence at all, once he'd learned Dad was a former cop, and Drew felt like his dad had enjoyed being here and meeting the officer, as well.

"Nice guy," Drew said as they headed back to the road.

"Uh-huh," Dad said gruffly. "Is that all you do, interview people?"

His father's words hammered at him, taking away the pleasure he got from his new job. He sighed and didn't answer. "Want to get a beer before you drive home? Or a couple, and you can spend the night at my place." He didn't expect his dad to say yes, but on the other hand, Dad hadn't yet brought up whatever was bothering him.

"Sure. Need to talk to you."

Here it was. "There's a little dive bar down at the end of the pier road, I think. You'll have to help me find it. Place called Tiny's."

It was a mark of his father's upset state that he asked a passerby where Tiny's was, and they quickly made their way to the bar. Inside, the smell of cigarette smoke and beer made it clear that news of the statewide smoking ban hadn't reached this far down the peninsula. Voices echoed, indicating that at least a few tables were occupied, all men, from the sounds of it.

They sat at the bar and ordered drafts. "So, what's up?" Drew asked.

"Your brothers, that's what." Dad sounded disgusted enough that, when the bartender brought their beers, Drew started a tab. This wasn't going to be a one-beer afternoon.

"What did Mike do now?" Mike, Drew's middle brother, never kept a job or a relationship longer than a few months.

Dad gave a snort. "He's broke again. Begging your mother for money."

"No big surprise."

Another frustrated noise. "I keep telling her to cut him off, but I caught her taking her stash out of the cookie jar right before he was coming over."

Drew couldn't help smiling, thinking of the old apple-shaped cookie jar. "Mom's always been a soft touch."

"Yeah, well, that's why I've always kept an eye on her cookie-jar money."

Mom enjoyed earning a little extra by doing odd jobs—helping neighbors with their taxes, babysitting, pitching in as a cook at big catered events. In a marriage where Dad was the breadwinner and the boss, it represented a little independence. "She's earned that money, and she ought to spend it however she wants."

"Giving money to your brother is like throwing it in the garbage," Dad grumbled. "Ready for another?"

Drew had barely sipped his beer, so he shook his head and waited while the bartender refilled Dad's glass. Looked like Dad was definitely staying over tonight.

"How's Steve doing?" Drew asked.

Dad was quiet for a minute, taking a long draw, and then he thumped his glass down on the bar. Drew tensed. What bad news was Dad stalling about?

Dad leaned close to Drew. "He's..." Dad paused, straightened and took another big chug of beer.

Dread washed over Drew. He hadn't seen his youngest brother, Stevie, in months. If he was sick or had been in an accident... "Just tell me."

Dad leaned close and lowered his voice. "Turns out he's...he's gay."

Relief made Drew's breath whoosh out in relief. Stevie was okay. Then he processed what Dad had said and his eyebrows lifted. "Really?"

"So he says." Dad's voice was glum.

Drew thought of his six-foot-three youngest brother, now a nurse. The idea of him being gay had never occurred to Drew, probably because Stevie had excelled in sports and hadn't hesitated to fight, especially to defend some younger or smaller kid.

Just because Stevie didn't fit the stereotype, Drew had assumed he was straight. Not too smart. Come to think of it, he hadn't heard of Stevie bringing home any girls lately, and Mom would definitely have told him; she wanted more grandchildren and had given up on getting them through Mike and Drew.

"Why didn't he say anything before now?" he asked his father as his perceptions about his brother did a turnaround.

"Who knows why he never spoke up." Dad's mug banged down again. "Guess he was too chicken."

"Get you another?" the bartender asked, and Dad grunted in the affirmative.

Drew waited until the man had brought the drink and, from the sound of clanking glasses, moved down the bar. "What did you say when Stevie told you?"

"He didn't tell me. He told your mother, and she told me. I haven't spoken to him." He paused. "That's why I came. Could you talk to him, maybe? Straighten him out?"

Drew blew out a breath that was half laughing, half not. "I don't think that's how it works."

"How would *you* know?" Dad asked. "You're not... That's not why you left Ria, is it?"

"No!" Drew propped his forehead on his hand for a few seconds. "No, I'm straight. But I can't make Stevie be that way. It's probably... Being gay is probably just part of who he is." Sadness came over him, thinking of the younger brother he rarely saw, who'd kept a vital part of his identity secret from the family for all these years.

Dad pounded a fist on the bar. "Where did I go wrong, raising a son who's a...a pansy?" He was silent for a minute, then growled in a near whisper, "Mom says he has a boyfriend."

Any idea that Stevie was just looking for attention bit the dust. "Wow."

"I just... I just don't know what to do."

It was the sort of admission his father had never made before. He'd always been in control, always the gruff, stern cop dad.

Drew wasn't all that enlightened about LGBTQ issues, but it looked like he was elected to nudge Dad in the right direction. "For one thing, you don't call him a pansy," he said. "And...if you want to be a good father to him, you invite him and his partner over for dinner."

"I'm not doing that!" Dad's voice was louder now, and

Drew signaled the bartender and held up a couple of bills. "If this gets out down at Julio's…"

Julio's was where all the retired cops went to drink their morning coffee and talk over what they'd heard on the police scanner the night before.

"I'm sure there are people at Julio's who have gay family members. Maybe even are gay themselves."

"Not a chance," Dad said. "Not a chance." But there was the tiniest bit of doubt in his voice. "At least you're more like me, or you will be if you get your family back and head it up right."

"And get my sight back, and get back into police work?" Drew shook his head. "Not gonna happen."

"You're not keeping up this…this *interviewing* stuff, are you?"

"It's a temporary, part-time job, so no. But I like it."

Dad made another one of his famous disgusted sounds.

It stung, but Drew ignored the feeling. "I have to figure out what to do about my career. The department has a social worker who can help."

"A social worker." There was a sneer in Dad's voice. "What are my sons coming to? I was always so proud."

"There's nothing wrong with… Wait. You were proud?" It was news to Drew. Dad had always been the one to yell at them, maintain discipline. Words of love and pride had come from Mom.

"Thought I was bringing up three boys who'd grow up to be like me." Dad was slurring now, very rare for him, as were these disclosures. "That's all I wanted. For my boys to grow up and follow in my footsteps."

It wasn't the moment to say it, but all of a sudden, Drew didn't want to follow in his father's footsteps, not as badly, not anymore.

Now that he was blind, he'd started to see things a whole lot differently.

CHAPTER SEVENTEEN

FRIDAY NIGHT, Ria finished her virtuous solo dinner of salad with chicken strips, looked in the snack cupboard and decided against dessert, and headed into the TV room. What should she do with a night to herself?

The girls had told her about their evening plans only this afternoon. Kaitlyn was sleeping over at Sunny's place, and Sophia was going to a party at a girlfriend's that might turn into a sleepover.

Usually, one or the other of them was home in the evening. And it was usually Kaitlyn. Ria tried not to plan activities for herself when she knew Kait would be home, because there was a chance Kait would need to talk, would get hungry, would in some way need her mom.

It was actually a very good sign that she didn't need Ria quite as much in the past couple of weeks. Her counseling sessions seemed to be helping, even the family ones she claimed to hate. More important, she was finally starting to make friends. Wednesday after school, both Bisky's daughter, Sunny, and a girl from the behavior support class, Venus, had come over to hang out with Kaitlyn, and Ria had nearly jumped for joy when she'd heard the three of them laughing and playing music and talking a mile a minute. Venus and Sunny had ended up staying for dinner, and they were both lovely girls—strong, independent, exactly right for Kait.

Ria felt guardedly optimistic about Kait's state of mind. She just needed to get better at figuring out what to do with herself when she had a night at home alone.

She was flipping channels when the doorbell rang.

Dark had fallen, and she wasn't expecting anyone, so she peeked out the venetian blinds. Her heart leaped and she hurried toward the door but stopped herself halfway there. She took a slow, calming breath, then walked the rest of the way to the front door at a leisurely pace and opened it.

"Hi, Drew," she said with at least a semblance of calm in her voice. "Hi, Navy. You came to see me, did you?"

Navy wagged her tail hard and panted.

Drew held up his toolbox, eyebrow raised. "Heard you had a slow drain, ma'am?"

He was joking around like he used to do long ago, and hearing the fun in his voice did something to her. She held the door open. "Come on in," she said. "Sounds like the girls have been complaining."

He smiled. "Easier to complain to Dad than to figure out how to give you a hand themselves," he said. "And I hope you don't mind that I brought Navy along. She's been doing better, but I want her to have as much exercise and attention as possible. Plus, she looked all sad when I started to leave without her."

"And you're a soft touch." Had the girls told Drew about her need for handyman help to get him to come over? Were they trying to push the two of them back together?

No matter. She welcomed his presence for all kinds of reasons she didn't feel like examining. "The slow drain is just the tip of the iceberg, if you're serious."

He came in, slipped off his coat and hung it at the end of the banister before she could take it from him. Then he kicked off his work boots. "I'm serious about helping you with repairs," he said, "but you'll have to be my partner."

I want to be your partner. "Sure," she said, trying to get used to the fact that he'd come over. What did it mean? Why had he come, really? "Would you like something to drink?"

"Not now," he said. "Maybe later."

Wait—he was planning to be here later? Ria's body flushed warm. "It's the drain in the main bathroom," she said, going for a businesslike tone. "I'm sure it's clogged because of all our hair, but I can't get the stopper out to clean it out."

"Uh-huh. You have to disconnect the pivot rod underneath."

"Oh… Never heard of that, but I believe you." She led the way to the bathroom, Navy tagging along behind, and opened the cupboard beneath the sink. "Just wait a sec while I clean out all the stuff under here."

She grabbed bottles of shampoo and stacks of rags and set it all down beside the bathtub. "Okay, it's empty. Do you do this or do I?"

"Let me see if I can do it by feel." He knelt and felt around the pipes, then lay down on his back so he could reach in. "Hand me my pliers, will you?"

She did, and flashed back to when they'd first been married, living in a tiny fixer-upper in Baltimore. This was how they'd spent a lot of Friday nights, working on the house. Usually, Drew did most of the work and she was his helper, grabbing rags or wrenches, cleaning up spatters of paint.

It had brought them close together, and usually those nights had ended up passionate. She flushed, remembering.

"Can't find those pliers?" he asked.

She forced her mind back to the present. Rummaged in

his toolbox, found a small pair of pliers and handed them to him.

He worked at whatever he was unscrewing for a few minutes, his muscles stretching the sleeves of his shirt.

Ria rubbed damp hands down the sides of her jeans and then clenched them into fists. She wanted to move closer, be closer, and there was a part of her that felt it was her right. In many ways, she still felt like his wife.

She also had the feeling he wouldn't mind.

"Got it. Let me slide the pivot rod through and… There. Try pulling up the drain stopper."

She did, and it came up immediately. "Oh, how disgusting," she said, jolted out of her romantic fantasies. She grabbed a couple of the rags and cleaned off the gunk she could see, then ran for paper towels and a chopstick to swab out the inside of the drain.

"Somehow, I'm glad I can't see what you're seeing," he said as he sat down on the edge of the tub to wait for her.

She pulled up clumps of long hair out of the sink drain. "Aren't you glad you don't have to deal with the hair of three women all around your house and clogging up your drains?"

He said something under his breath.

"What?" Had he said what she thought he'd said?

"I miss it."

"Our hair all over the bathroom?"

One corner of his mouth turned up. "Yeah. I miss everything."

"Oh…" She let out a breath as she said the word. Her whole chest warmed.

He cleared his throat. "Something else I've been wanting to say. I was wrong, pushing you into what we did on the beach all those years ago. It seems like way too little and way too late, but I'm sorry."

Her hands stilled and she stared at him. "You mean… the first time we…?" Absurd that she couldn't bring herself to say what they'd done.

"Yeah. I mean, I could never regret having Sophia. But I shouldn't have pushed like I did. I didn't get it, how important it is to have, what do the kids call it…"

"Consent?" she asked, amazed he was even aware of the issue. Not that Drew was sexist—he was a true gentleman toward women—but he wasn't exactly the type of man who listened to NPR.

"Yeah. Consent. I was way too aggressive. A jerk."

"You may not remember," she said, "but you definitely had consent." She swallowed as memories of his hands, his scent, his male intensity, came back to her. She'd never experienced anything like it before, and it had shocked and overwhelmed her. And she'd loved it. "I was all in," she said.

"I thought so, but… I've always felt bad."

"Water under the bridge, anyway."

"Well, but it's not, because it colored everything that came after. You felt like you had to marry me, like you didn't have a choice."

"You felt the same," she pointed out. "You felt obligated, too. Were you ready to get married at that point?"

"Probably not," he admitted. "But I wanted to anyway. Done with that drain?"

"Uh-huh." She watched while he slid under the sink again, instructed her how to lower the drain plug and re-hooked up whatever needed hooking up down there.

She couldn't believe he'd brought up the circumstances of their rapid marriage. In all their years together, they'd barely talked about it. Drew had never been a big communicator, and she hadn't either, she guessed. She'd always felt lucky to be his wife, but also like she wasn't entitled to the honor, like she'd gotten it unfairly. That hadn't been something she'd known how to put into words.

He stood up and washed his hands at the sink, then turned in her direction. "Next?"

She felt her lips curve into a smile, unable to tame down her delight that he wanted to spend more time with her, to help her. "Well…if you're sure, I bought some weather stripping to try to stop the breeze from blowing through the dining room windows, but I got the nail-on kind and I don't know how to put it up."

"Lead on," he said and followed her to the dining room.

"Sit down," she said. "You can have a beer while I find the materials." She handed him a bottle, her face flushing a little when she realized she'd bought his favorite brand at the store last week. Had she been subconsciously planning to have him over? Should she dig up something else for him to drink so he wouldn't know that?

In the end, she opened his favorite beer, set it in front of him and hurried off to get the weather stripping.

By the time she got back and explained to him what she'd bought, she'd cooled down a little. She listened to his explanation, cut the weather stripping to size, then held it while he nailed it in place.

"What we were talking about before," she said, picking up the conversation where they'd left off. It was a knack most married people had, she supposed—keeping a conversation going all day, in between the chores of daily life. "Your parents always acted like I trapped you into marriage."

"Maybe they felt that way at first." He whacked the last

nail into place. "But they realized pretty quickly that it was a trap I entered willingly. And then you gave them grand-children—probably the only ones they'll have."

Ria felt a pang, thinking of the miscarriage. They'd be heartbroken if they knew.

So would Drew.

"Pretty quickly, my folks came to love you."

She smiled. "I love them, too, especially your mom. I miss seeing and hearing about them."

He leaned back against the wall and raised an eyebrow. "Want to hear about Dad's visit Wednesday, and how he got drunk and had to stay over?"

She stared. Drew's dad wasn't normally a big drinker. "He *did*?"

Drew nodded. "We went to Tiny's, down at the water-front, and I had a hard time getting him back to my place. He was stumbling all over."

Ria sank down on the edge of a chair. "I've only seen him a little tipsy, and that was on holidays. Was some-thing wrong?"

Drew's handsome face went serious. "Yeah. He's upset because Stevie told Mom he's gay."

Ria nodded, thinking of Drew's youngest brother. "Yeah. I figured."

Drew's face jerked toward her. "You *did*? Why didn't you tell me?"

Ria let out a snort. "Because I didn't think you could handle it, of course!"

"Really? I'm not like that." His forehead wrinkled. "Am I?"

Ria shrugged. "You were always pretty invested in how macho you Martin men were. Not that a gay guy can't be macho. If anyone can, it's Stevie."

"Yeah." Drew shook his head. "Apparently he has a boy-friend."

"Oh, that's great!" She'd always thought Stevie seemed lonely. "Are your folks…? Does your dad accept it at all?"

"I'm sure Mom's fine. Dad…well, he wanted me to talk to Stevie and, quote, straighten him out." He chuckled. "I told him it didn't work like that and that he should ask Stevie and his partner to dinner."

"Good for you." Ria couldn't keep the surprise out of her voice. She'd never have accused Drew of outright homo-phobia, but she'd also never have guessed he'd be quick to accept a gay brother. "Do you think he'll do it?"

"I don't know. It's hard to picture."

"Hey, you know what?" Ria smiled as an idea took shape in her head. "We could invite them to dinner here, and have your folks over, too." And then she flushed. It wasn't like they were married, that they should be hosting his fam-ily together.

But being here at the house, talking in this twilight set-ting, she felt like they *were* married. Only better, because Drew was changing. He seemed easier to talk to, somehow. A little warmer.

"Yeah. I'd like to see Stevie, meet his partner." He spoke slowly, like he was thinking it through as he talked. "Stevie's family, and I should make more of an effort to understand him."

"He'd like that. He's always looked up to you so much."

"Really?" He looked in her direction, shaking his head. "You saw a lot of things I didn't." It looked like he was going to say more, but then he straightened. "Any more projects?"

"Of course," she said promptly. When you were a home-owner, there was an endless list of them, and since she had the motel to manage, she rarely had time for repairs in her own actual house. "There's a sticky drawer in my dresser that's driving me crazy."

He smiled. "Are you still using the girls' old one?"

"Sure am." He'd always made fun of her for the cartoonish daisies stenciled on it, a look the girls had long outgrown. But she liked how it reminded her of those early, carefree days. "It's perfectly functional and it would be—"

"A waste to throw it out and get a new one," he finished in unison with her. "I know, I know."

"Up the stairs and to the right," she said. "Banister's on the left."

She followed him, trying not to think about the suggestive situation of going upstairs together. Still, by the time they reached the bedroom, she felt a little breathless. *Stop it*, she told herself and led him directly to the dresser, showing him the drawer in question. "It sticks every time I go to pull it out," she explained, demonstrating, pleased that her voice sounded normal. "And then again when I push it in."

His hand was over hers, and when she went to pull away, he grasped it for just a second. She looked at his face, so she saw the slight flush that crossed it. "Do you have some of that canning wax?" he asked. "Or even a candle. That's all this needs."

"Um, sure. Let me grab some." She welcomed the chance to get away from him, to cool down, and yet when she grabbed her box of Gulf Wax, her feet carried her back upstairs rapidly. It was like she couldn't stand to be away from him when she knew he was in her house.

He'd pulled out the offending drawer. "Okay if I dump your stuff out?" he asked.

"Of course!" She watched while he did it and then put the wax block into his hand. He rubbed it slowly along the drawer slides and then handed it back to her. "Try that."

She put the drawer back in, and when it slid perfectly, she clapped. "Thank you! That's going to get rid of a daily annoyance, and the girls will be glad not to hear me complain about it every day." She piled the clothes back into the drawer while Drew sat on the edge of the bed, patient in a way he'd never been before.

She slid the drawer in and turned and looked at him, instantly flooded with memories of all the good times they'd had in that very bed, the same one they'd had in their first apartment. Frugality and all that.

Driven by feelings she barely understood, she sat down beside him, wrapped her arms around him and rested her head on his shoulder. "Thanks for helping me," she said, hearing the huskiness in her own voice, drawing in that special Drew-scent from his neck.

He froze.

She went still, too, heat flooding her face. Why had she been so forward? What was she thinking?

But she *wasn't* thinking, and that was the problem. She was feeling.

She let her arms fall away and lifted her head. "Sorry. I—"

He wrapped his arms around her, brushed her hair back with a big hand and pressed his lips to hers.

There it was, that male certainty he'd always had, and it intoxicated her as he deepened the kiss. It was Drew, it was the same, and yet it was all new.

He lifted his head and she let out a little sigh of regret, but he was only adjusting her, pulling her into his lap. "Do you like this as much as I do?" he breathed into her neck, punctuating his question with a light nip that shot her heart rate so high she thought she might pass out.

She nodded, because she couldn't speak.

"Let's lie down for a little bit," he said, sliding and tugging until they lay face-to-face. He kissed her nose, her forehead, her cheeks in a reverent, caring way. Then he tugged her close so that they were pressed against each other head to toe, and her insides melted.

They hugged and kissed some more, and then both of them were breathing hard.

His hand went to the bottom of her shirt.

She wanted him to touch her. She wanted her husband to touch her. Because even though legally they'd divorced, neither her body nor her heart had accepted the decree.

His hand slid beneath her shirt to her stomach, and she felt that icky little qualm: he'd feel that her stomach wasn't flat.

It doesn't matter. There are all types of bodies.

She didn't completely believe it, but she was starting to. She leaned in to kiss him, moving her body to allow him access.

Abruptly, he withdrew his hand and pulled away, rolling over to lie flat on his back, breathing hard. "Sorry. I shouldn't have done that."

"It's okay, Drew." She felt cold in the places he'd stopped touching.

"No. That's what got us in trouble the first time."

It was taking her brain some time to catch up with her body. "Huh?"

"I'm not making love to you again unless we're married," he said. "What if you got pregnant again? Which you probably would, knowing how we are together." He shook his head. "I'd love to have another child with you, even at this late date, but not unless we're a married couple."

Every word he said dripped cold reality onto Ria. What if she got pregnant again?

Unbeknownst to him, she *had* gotten pregnant, the very last time they'd made love.

And then she'd lost the baby through her own negligence.

She rolled away from him and sat up on the edge of the bed, taking deep breaths. "You're right. I'm sorry. We shouldn't have... You should go."

"Right. Sure." He sat up, too, adjusted himself and pulled her close for a hard, fast kiss. "But know that I'm thinking about this, Ree. About us."

She was thinking, too. She was thinking about the secret that stood between them, and wondering if it was time to tell the truth.

THAT SUNDAY NIGHT, in Ria's kitchen, Drew put his plate away after eating way too much homemade pizza. "You're an amazing cook," he said to her.

"Yeah, Mom, you're an excellent cook when you cook." Kaitlyn's tone indicated that she was only half complaining. "She hasn't made pizza since...since forever," she added, trailing off.

"Since they got divorced," Sophia said. She sounded unusually annoyed.

"Well, I appreciate it now." He reached for Ria's hand.

The feel of her hand brought their home-repair evening back into his mind, and his body snapped to attention. He really wanted her, and it had taken superhuman effort not to go to full-on seduction. After all, she was his wife.

But she wasn't. Not anymore. And things needed to be resolved before they took any steps toward a physical relationship.

He realized he was still holding her hand, his thumb rolling over its softness, and dropped it.

"Family game night wouldn't be right without pizza." Ria sounded a little breathless.

Kait cleared her throat.

"Family game night is stupid," Sophia muttered.

Drew caught the awkward vibes and figured they were due to the hand-holding. He and Ria had better not build curiosity into the girls until they had figured this out, figured out if they could possibly get back together, if he could be a decent family man, if Ria even trusted him enough to try.

"Speaking of games," he said, "bring it. I'm going to crush you guys."

He remembered all the times they'd played cards or Monopoly as a family. He'd taught the girls to be competitive, not to cry when they lost. They'd had a lot of fun together, talking and laughing, jokingly trash-talking one another. Those were good memories.

"Monopoly or Scrabble?" Ria asked.

"How about…?" He trailed off as a realization slammed into him. He couldn't play regular board games; he was blind. Without even trying to, he had built an expectation he now was unable to meet. In addition to his own disappointment—because he loved family game night—he felt like a failure.

If he'd have planned in advance, he could have at least pulled out the low-vision playing cards they'd given out in the rehab program.

"I vote for Scrabble. Let's play Scrabble," Kait said. Her voice had risen to the same tone she'd had as a younger child.

"Dad can't play Scrabble, dummy." Sophia's voice was sharp.

"Oh ye of little faith." He heard Ria push back her chair, and he tipped his head back to see the blur of her walking over to the shelf and pulling something off.

"Check this out." She sounded triumphant as she thumped a box down onto the table.

There was a pause while the girls studied the box.

Then: "Braille Scrabble?" Kait said.

"Dad can't read braille." That was Sophia again.

"Hey, I'm trying to learn a little." He reached for his older daughter's arm and gave it a squeeze. She wasn't herself tonight.

"It's not just braille," Ria explained, opening the box and pulling out the pieces, handing them around. "There's braille writing on each piece, but there are also raised letters you can trace. They're printed large, for people who have some vision. But here's the really cool thing." She pulled something else out and thumped it onto the table, too. "It's a Scrabble board with a grid, so the letters don't get knocked out of place as easily."

"So it's tailor-made for klutzy Kait." Sophia gave a little laugh.

He heard the sound of a light slap. "Shut up. So I knocked the board over a couple of times. I was little."

Drew ran his hands over the raised grid of the Scrabble board. He felt notations in certain squares. As the way it worked dawned on him, he felt a grin spread across his face. "So this is a triple word score," he said, touching one square, "and this is a double word score, right?"

"You got it," Ria said. "He's not even going to have much of a learning curve here, girls. We're doomed."

As he heard her joking tone and ran his fingers over the Scrabble tiles with their raised letters and braille cues—maybe he could develop his braille skills a little from using them—Drew's heart swelled with a different kind of love for Ria. He'd never stopped loving her as the mother of his children, and the moment he'd come to Pleasant Shores, he'd realized he was still attracted to her.

But this was something different. That she had anticipated the issue with his blindness and taken the time, had the foresight, to order their family's favorite game in a format he could still use… That was true thoughtfulness. Ria didn't call attention to her own quiet acts of kindness. It was just part of who she was.

Love for her swelled his heart.

They started to play. Drew was slow at first, but he got the hang of feeling the letters and visualizing word possibilities in his mind pretty quickly. The first time he was able to form a thirty-point word using a triple word block, he pumped his arm in the air. "Yes!" he crowed. "Step aside, ladies. The Scrabble King is back."

"You've just been dethroned." Kait was clicking tiles onto the board, and both Ria and Sophia groaned. Kaitlyn took his hand and showed him what she had built right beside him, raising her points above his.

Ria got a call from the motel—an employee had called in sick, so she'd have to take over the late shift in a couple of hours. Then Kaitlyn got a call from Venus and a text from Sunny. "We need to put these phones away," Ria said, and Kaitlyn agreed, and they both tossed their phones in a basket Ria kept in the dining room for that purpose.

And then they were all just laughing and competing, and he felt like Ria was flirting with him a little bit, which warmed him, opened up possibilities.

Kait was involved in the game and happy, and he spontaneously reached out and squeezed her hand. "I'm glad you're doing better, kiddo," he said.

"Don't think you can soften me like that," she joked, but

she squeezed his hand back, showing him that she understood what he had meant.

He'd missed being surrounded by the laughter and chatter of his family. He wanted it back.

But there was something missing: the sound of Sophia's voice. Usually, she was as enthusiastic as the rest of them, but she'd been quiet tonight. Too quiet. Cranky and sad sounding when she did speak.

He reached for her hand. "What's wrong, Sophia?"

She didn't answer, but he heard her suck in a hitched, broken breath. Something wet dropped onto their clasped hands.

"Hey, you're crying," Kait said.

Ria put her hand on top of Sophia's and Drew's. "What's wrong, honey?"

"Yeah, it's great that Kait is all better," she said, her voice bitter. "But…"

"But what?" Ria asked. "What's making you so upset, sweetie?"

"I…I think…" She broke off. "I can't even say it."

"What is it?" Drew could hear the fear and worry in her voice, and his lighthearted mood drained away, replaced by concern. "You can tell us."

"I think…I'm pregnant."

"What?" Ria said. "Are you sure? How late are you?"

"I took a pregnancy test." Sophia blew her nose. "So I guess I'm sure."

"You're kidding me," Kaitlyn said. "I thought… Never mind."

Rage and fear warred in Drew's chest, making it hard to speak. Hard to even breathe. Finally, accompanied by the sound of Sophia's quiet sobs, he got the words out: "Who did that to you?"

"Yeah, Soph. Who was it?" Kaitlyn asked.

They were all quiet, waiting for her answer.

Finally, she spoke. "I can't say."

"Honey, you have to say!" That was Ria, her voice choked.

Grasping Sophia's shoulder with one hand, Drew reached his other hand across the table and found Kaitlyn's arm. He wanted to hold on to all of them. "I'm going to get to the bottom of this," he promised.

"That's not going to fix anything, Dad!" Kaitlyn said.

"I'm not some mystery to solve!" There was the sound of Sophia's chair pushing back, then footsteps rushing out of the room and up the stairs.

Drew pulled in a breath and let it out slowly, trying to think. *Don't use your impulses. Use your training.* It had been drilled into him during police academy, and the concept had never let him down.

Though it was his immediate impulse, seeking revenge on whoever had gotten Sophia pregnant wasn't what he should do. Especially since he didn't know the whole story.

A thought rocked him: he was once that young person who'd gotten a girl pregnant without benefit of marriage. All of a sudden, he could see why Ria's dad had hated him.

Ria was crying, and when Drew pushed back his chair and walked over to try to comfort her, he realized that Kaitlyn had gotten there first. She stood behind Ria's seated form, her arms wrapped around her mother. "We'll be okay, Mom. She'll be okay."

Drew closed his eyes. He was changing, changing from his dad's approach to things, but the trouble was, he had no idea how to deal with his daughter's pregnancy if he wasn't going to act like a caveman dad. "What do we do?" he asked the huddled forms of Kait and Ria.

"You stay with Mom. I'll talk to her." Kait put his hands on Ria and then turned away.

"Kait—are *you* okay?"

"I'm fine. Better than you two." She patted him on the arm. "I'll make sure she's okay. Give me a few minutes with her."

"All right," he said, "but we'll be up. We need to have a talk."

"Okay," Kaitlyn said, and her footsteps raced across the dining room and up the stairs.

In the midst of his distress, he was proud that Kait was a sensible, loving girl. But this had to be killing Ria. He could hear her breathing hard, and when he reached out to touch her face, it was drenched with tears.

Tugging over a chair, he sat down heavily beside Ria, put an arm around her and pulled her to him. It was a mark of how upset she was that she allowed him to hold her.

He wasn't crying on the outside, but inside was a different story. Sophia. His sweet young daughter, only seventeen now, so vulnerable. "We didn't pay her enough attention, with all of Kait's problems," he said, guilt and regret rising up inside him.

Ria nodded against his chest, still crying.

"We'll find a way to help her," he promised.

They'd made a mistake, but they were going to fix it. Somehow, together, they were going to help Sophia cope with this devastating change to her life.

CHAPTER EIGHTEEN

KAITLYN THREW OPEN the door of her sister's room and marched in. Sophia lay facedown on her bed, her shoulders shaking a little.

She put her hand on her sister's shoulder and tugged. "Sit up."

Sophia rolled onto her side. "Leave me alone."

"We've got to get out of the house," Kaitlyn insisted, still tugging at her sister's arm. "Come on. You're coming over to the motel with me."

"Mom and Dad hate me for what I did." Sophia propped herself on her elbow, kind of gasping out the words.

She was so dramatic, although if any situation warranted drama, this one did. "They're freaked out, but they don't hate you. No one does."

"I just want to sleep." Sophia flopped back down on the bed. Her phone buzzed, and she lifted her head, looked at it, then flopped back down.

Kaitlyn stood and tugged her into a sitting position. "Look, if you don't come with me, they're going to come up here and have a talk with you. Is that what you want?"

Sophia shook her head.

"Then come on. I bought you some time, but we can't stay here. We've got to go to the lobby."

"Why?" Sophia rubbed at her eyes with the sheet, carefully getting rid of the raccoon-eye effect of her soggy makeup. Only Sophia could make an all-out crying jag look pretty.

"Because somebody has to work the desk and it can't be Mom. She's a wreck." Kaitlyn tugged Sophia to her feet. "She won't even go over there when she's so upset, and Dad will stay with her."

Sophia frowned, then nodded. "Okay."

"Get your phone. Do you want your coat, or should we just run over fast?"

"I need a coat for the b-b-baby," Sophia said, her voice rising into a sob again.

"Get a grip!" Kaitlyn put both hands on her head. Was she the only one in this family with any sense? "The baby is the size of a paper clip, at the most, and it's way inside you. It won't get cold." She took her sister's hand and pulled her down the stairs.

Mom and Dad were still in the dining room. Dad was comforting Mom, who, just as Kaitlyn had predicted, seemed to be in about the same bad shape that Sophia was in. "We'll be over in the lobby working the desk," Kait said loud enough for them to hear, then hurried Sophia out of the house before either of them could question it.

She wanted to help the family by taking this shift at the motel desk. But she also wanted to escape Mom and Dad's cluelessness and get Sophia alone, so she could figure out just what was going on with her.

They ran across the lawn and the parking lot and burst into the lobby just as Clarence, one of their part-time desk clerks, stood up and stretched. "I was just wondering when the next shift would come in," he said, his bushy white eyebrows lifting. "I've got a date with a bottle."

"Terrific. You enjoy that." What kind of old dude talked about drinking in front of teenagers?

The lobby was decorated with pumpkins and fall leaves in an old-fashioned way that seemed kind of excessive. Kaitlyn had heard Mom talking to creepy old Ted Taylor about updating everything, but Kaitlyn doubted it would happen. Everyone liked the motel just fine the way it was, despite, or maybe because of, decorations like the googly-eyed turkey made out of gourds.

The radio was set on an all-Elvis, all-the-time station, another thing the guests enjoyed. If anything, Kaitlyn thought they ought to go tackier, serving peanut butter sandwiches and showing Elvis movies. But no one had ever asked her.

She went behind the tall desk and checked the computer to make sure old Clarence hadn't messed it up. Sophia flopped into one of the overstuffed chairs.

"So who's the dad?" Kaitlyn asked. "Is it Tyler?"

Sophia looked at her for a minute, looked away, then nodded.

Worry for her sister spread through Kaitlyn's chest. "I thought you didn't want to have sex."

"I didn't." Sophia's lower lip stuck out. "And you shouldn't do it just because I did. It's not exactly fun."

Kaitlyn leaned forward, propping her elbows on the desk. "If you didn't want to, did he…?" She frowned and studied her sister, who still wasn't looking at her. "Did he force it?"

"No."

"Okay, but…" There was something, Kaitlyn could tell. Boys could be such jerks. "Why'd you do it, then?"

Sophia shrugged, still looking away. "I don't want to talk about it."

That was her right, but Kaitlyn was still worried. "Did you tell him about the baby?"

Sophia nodded.

"Well, what did he say?"

"He said…" Her voice choked up and she started to cry again.

Kaitlyn grabbed a box of tissues from behind the desk and took it out to her sister, perching on the edge of the chair beside Sophia. "What did he say?"

"He said it's not his, and if I say it is, he'll post all kinds of trash about me on Frock."

Kaitlyn clenched her fist and pounded it into her other hand. "Man, I'd like to kill him." Even more, she'd like to find a way to get enough dirt on Tyler that he'd never dare to post a bad thing about a girl again.

"He already did post some stuff, hinting at me being nasty, and I'm getting hassled." Sophia's voice was bleak.

Yeah. Kaitlyn *really* wanted to get some leverage on Tyler, and she was going to find a way to do it.

Meanwhile, she put an arm around Sophia. "Whatever they're saying about you, you can handle it. I did." And she realized with some surprise that it was true. Yes, people made fun of her some, teased her, but it wasn't the devastating thing she'd thought it would be at first. She had a life and it was a decent one, completely separate from the mess that social media could be.

"And when I'm nine months pregnant…" Sophia dropped her face into her hands. "I won't be cute anymore! I won't be skinny!"

Kaitlyn's worry started to fade. If Sophia had moved on to thinking about her pregnancy appearance, she'd be okay. "You'll be cute. You'll wear all kinds of great maternity clothes, and you'll probably stay really tiny for the whole time, and everyone will think you're adorable. You'll get all kinds of attention."

"Do you think so?" Sophia's voice still sounded shaky.

"Yep. I know so." Kaitlyn handed her the tissue box, and Sophia blew her nose with a loud honk.

The bells on the door jingled, and one of their long-term guests, old Mr. Patterson, came in wearing his bedroom slippers. "Do you have change for a dollar?" he asked.

"I do," Kaitlyn said, and she opened the register and started counting out quarters. "What are you going to buy at this time of night?"

"Just a Coca-Cola," he said.

"They're two dollars," she reminded him. "You don't need quarters—you need dollar bills. Or a credit card."

"Are you sure? That's ridiculous." He frowned.

"You know what? I think we might have some Coke back here in the fridge." She got him a can.

He put the quarters she had just given him back into her hand. She thought about telling him it was on the house, but she didn't want to get him in the habit of free soft drinks if Mom wasn't willing to follow up on it. No point in giving him a reason to be unhappy with the motel. They needed every long-term paying guest they could get.

After he had wandered back outside, and she watched to make sure he was going in the right direction toward his room, she came back in to find Sophia on her phone.

"He posted something on his Frock account."

Kaitlyn looked over her shoulder. "Wait. Tyler isn't TomDickandHarry, is he?"

"No, but I think he follows him. Or maybe he's part of that account and shares it with some other guys. Look, just leave it alone. I'll deal with it."

"You're not going to see him again, are you?"

"No way. I told him to get lost. He may be incredibly hot, but you should see his house, Kait."

"Fancy?"

"Yeah, but…his mom is…" She trailed off.

"Mean?"

Sophia shook her head. "It's not that. It's just… Tyler's brothers treat her like crap. And apparently, that's nothing compared to how the dad treated her when he was around." Sophia gave a shiver. "And their dog is chained up in the backyard, and they never give him any attention. It's not right. There's something not right about that house."

"Sounds awful. Is that where you…?"

"Yeah, when no one was home. And I'm never going back there. He's disgusting."

Kaitlyn studied her sister, wondering at what a contradiction she was, and then a horrible thought occurred to her. "You know…the threats against me have mostly stopped. You didn't sleep with him to make them quit hassling me, did you?"

Sophia looked away.

Kaitlyn knelt in front of Sophia, grabbed her hands and tugged until Sophia looked her in the eyes. "Tell me the truth!" Kaitlyn's heart pounded.

Sophia nodded. "Okay. Yeah. I did. And they *did* stop bothering you, right? It worked."

Love for her sister surged in her chest, alongside horror at what Sophia had done. "Yeah, but… Oh, man, Soph. I don't want you to have to pay this price."

Sophia shrugged. "It wasn't a big deal," she said with a bravado that was obviously fake. Then her chin quivered. "It's just… I didn't think I'd get pregnant." Her face scrunched up again like she was going to burst into tears.

Kaitlyn was reeling, but she wanted to forestall that. Sophia needed to calm down, not get worked up again. "I mean, there *is* an upside to you being pregnant," she said. "It's sorta cool that I'm going to be an aunt."

Sophia giggled a little at that, but her forehead was still wrinkled. She had a lot to deal with, for sure.

Another guest called the desk, needing help to get back into his room because he had lost his key. Kaitlyn told Sophia to watch the desk and jogged down the road to open his room for him. On the way back, she noticed a bunch of empty pizza boxes outside an overnight guest's room. As she ran them to the dumpster, she thought about what she'd just learned.

Determination grew in her. Somehow, she was going to find a way to make sure Tyler and his friends could never do anything like that again. She didn't know how, not yet, but she was going to figure it out. Between her, Sunny and Venus, she was pretty sure they could form some kind of devious, amazing plan. Maybe Sophia would want to be involved, too.

Sophia had made a huge sacrifice for her, and she was paying the price. Now it was Kaitlyn's turn to return the favor.

ON MONDAY MORNING, Ria stood in the kitchen sautéing vegetables for an omelet. Rain streaked down the windows, and at the cracked spot, she could feel the cold air from outside.

Another spot for her and Drew to weatherproof.

She'd already cut up fruit, and biscuits were baking in the oven. She beat six eggs with a whisk, looked at the bowl, then cracked a couple more and threw them in.

She was probably overdoing it. She wasn't even hungry. Normally, she made do with half an English muffin and some coffee.

But after Sophia's bombshell revelation last night, she knew she needed her strength. And the girls needed it even more.

She heard steps on the stairs, and Kaitlyn burst into the

kitchen. "Hi, Mom," she said, coming over and giving Ria a side-arm hug while looking over her shoulder at what was on the stove.

The easy affection shocked Ria, in a good way. She hugged Kaitlyn back. "Where's your sister?"

"She doesn't want to go to school today."

Ria handed Kaitlyn the bowl of eggs. "You've seen me make an omelet. Now it's your turn. I'll go and get her down here."

"Good luck with that." Kaitlyn poked at the vegetables in the skillet doubtfully and then poured the eggs on top of them.

Oh well. So it would be a different kind of omelet.

Upstairs, she pushed open the door of Sophia's room and went to her oldest daughter's bed. Sophia lay with her back to the door, hunched over. Sympathy overcame Ria, making her chest ache, until a second look told Ria that Sophia was looking at her phone. Not asleep.

"Up and at 'em," Ria said, shaking Sophia's shoulder. "Get dressed and come downstairs. I want you to have a good breakfast."

"Mom! I don't want to go to school, and after last night, I would think—"

Ria held up a hand to stop the flow of words. "No, uh-uh. You're going to have nine months of 'I don't wanna,' and you're not staying home the whole time." She felt more empathy for Sophia than the girl would ever know, having been in a similar situation herself. But she and Drew had talked last night, and they had decided that tough love would be what Sophia needed. Treating her like she was fragile, acting like this was a disaster, wouldn't do Sophia any good and would just heighten what was already a sizable tendency toward drama.

And their plan started now. Drew had even offered to come over and make sure that Sophia got to school, but she had told him she was pretty sure she could make that happen herself.

"You don't know how embarrassing this is," Sophia moaned. "What if I throw up in school? What if it already shows?" She lifted the covers and ran a hand over her stomach, flat in a skintight tank top. "Does it show?"

"Not yet."

"But it *will*!" Sophia dissolved into sobs.

Ria was sorely tempted to say what her own father had said to her, that since she had let it happen, she needed to suck it up and take the consequences. That had been harsh, but there was truth in it.

"Look, honey," she said, "I'm sorry I've been so focused on Kaitlyn that I haven't paid enough attention to you. I had no idea you were even in a relationship."

"I'm not," Sophia said and sniffed. "Not anymore."

"Oh, honey." She rubbed Sophia's arm. That was something Ria had never had to deal with. From the moment Drew had learned of her pregnancy, he had taken responsibility, talking immediately about marriage, wanting to go to all the doctor's appointments with her, hovering over her until she was driven crazy by it. But it had been lovely, too, an indication of his character. Had made her feel cherished. Ultimately, it was why she'd agreed to marry him.

If Sophia's young man was treating her badly, Ria would have his head on a platter. And she knew she'd have to get in line behind Drew.

On the other hand, if the relationship was a bad one, then good riddance to him.

There was time in the coming weeks to talk about what had led Sophia into having sex, let alone having sex with a boy who wasn't a good person. Last night, they'd ascertained that she had been a willing partner. There were no charges to be filed, only discussions about choices, and those talks could wait.

Ria felt inadequate, as she so often did, facing this complicated, unexpected, delicate piece of parenting. But she was also starting to realize that she had problem-solving skills, and that Drew would help. They would get through this like everything else.

"We have a lot to talk about, honey," she said. There was a basket of wrinkled but clean clothes at the foot of the bed, and she pulled it toward her and started folding clothes while she talked. "First off, medical care. That's the priority. And then we do need to talk about the father—"

"I don't want to talk about that."

"We *will* talk about it, but not this morning. We'll also talk about whether you want to parent the baby or place it for adoption." There was another choice Sophia could make, but Ria was pretty sure Sophia wouldn't consider ending the pregnancy, just as she hadn't herself. "Whatever you decide, Dad and I will help you all the way. Kait will, too."

Sophia peeked out from where she had her head buried in her arms, just like she'd done when she was a young girl. The lines on her face softened. She looked relieved.

Ironically, now that she was pregnant, Sophia seemed even more a little kid who needed her parents.

"But first, throw on some clothes and come downstairs. We've got to get you to school."

She made sure Sophia had swung her feet to the floor and then went downstairs to finish fixing breakfast.

She reached the kitchen just in time to save the biscuits from burning and shooed Kaitlyn to the table while she dished up three plates. A little butter on the biscuits—okay, a lot of butter—strong coffee for her and fruit juice for the girls, and they were ready to go.

Sophia walked into the room and slid into her chair, and they all dug in.

Ria looked around the warm kitchen and then focused on each of her beautiful girls. Despite their issues, they were good kids, good people. Taking the time to have breakfast together helped her focus on her love for them and made the three of them feel like more of a family.

That thought made her glance at the one empty chair at the table. They'd be even more of a family if Drew were here.

Sophia took a couple of bites and then threw down her spoon. "I'm not that hungry, and I don't want to gain weight," Sophia said. "I already feel totally bloated."

"It's normal and healthy to gain weight when you're pregnant," Ria said, which felt a little surreal, but she figured they were going to be having a lot of surreal conversations over the next nine months. "You have to take care of yourself and eat healthy foods. If you don't, you might risk miscarriage."

"I *want* to miscarry." Sophia looked at her and lifted her chin.

"No, you don't, believe me."

Kaitlyn's head snapped in her direction. "Did *you* ever have a miscarriage?"

That was the problem with perceptive teenage daughters. Now they were both looking at her, and she didn't want to lie. "I did," she said. "It was heartbreaking."

"When?" Sophia asked. "Was it when you got so sick, right when you bought the hotel?"

Ria bit her lip, then slowly nodded.

"Does Dad know?" Sophia clapped her hand over her mouth. "Wait—it was Dad's, wasn't it?"

"Of course it was Dad's! And, no, he doesn't know. And I'd like to keep it that way for now."

The sound of the school bus rumbled by. "Come on," Kaitlyn said to Sophia. "We have to get going or we'll be late."

"Just leave the dishes. I'll get them." She put a hand on Sophia's shoulder. "Chin up, honey. Your family stands behind you. You're going to do fine."

"Come on," Kaitlyn said as she went into the front room. Then: "Navy! Hi, girl! Oh, hey, Dad. We're late to school. See you after."

"I'm going, too—don't worry," Sophia said, and they both rushed out the door.

Ria dried her hands on the dish towel and walked into the front room, where Drew was still standing in the entry-way. "Well, it wasn't seamless, but I got them both out the door and to school. Sorry you made a trip over here when you weren't needed."

He didn't answer. When she looked at him, she saw that there were white patches on his cheekbones, a sure sign he was clenching his teeth. "What's wrong?"

He lifted his chin, and when the words came out, they were cold as ice. "You had a miscarriage."

Ria's stomach seized up as she stared at him. She'd needed to tell him the truth, not to have him find it out himself. Not like this.

But, ready or not, it was showtime.

CHAPTER NINETEEN

A VOLCANO OF fury rumbled inside Drew. He followed Ria into her kitchen, Navy at his side. "You had a miscarriage? And you just now told the girls not to tell me?"

And what really burned was that they'd agreed without question, as if he were a child who had to be protected from the truth. How did Ria portray him to the girls when he wasn't around?

"Drew. I never meant for you to overhear—"

The volcano inside him exploded. "What else haven't you told me?" He shouted the words, louder than he'd ever yelled at Ria. "You've taught them disrespect. For their father. Not to mention your disrespect for your husband!"

The yelling felt good, familiar. This was how his dad had kept them all in line. This was the sound of a family.

No, it's the sound of someone who doesn't know how to be in a family, someone who isn't classy enough for the likes of Ria.

The nagging voice inside made him even angrier. He didn't want to think about his inadequacies. "You've *never* respected me. Never thought I was good enough. But this, this lying…getting our girls in on the lies… You're worse than I thought."

Ria didn't answer. She was banging pans. An aroma of coffee and toast and melted butter pervaded the room.

He walked closer, maddened by the scent of her, furious

that she seemed to be doing dishes, ignoring him. "You lost our baby and you didn't tell me?"

The banging pans went silent.

"Why not? You didn't get rid—"

"No. Of course not." But there was something in her voice. "Sit down, Drew. I'm not going to talk about it while you're looming over me like that."

No class. Bad at relationships.

He might lack class, but he knew better than to physically threaten a woman. Stomach churning, neck hot, he made his way to a chair and sat down.

"Coffee?"

"No," he snapped, even though he wanted some. Beside him, Navy flopped down to the floor and let out a sigh. "Tell me. The whole story."

He heard her pouring coffee, opening the refrigerator, adding cream. A chair scraped across from him, and then she nudged his hand and he felt a warm cup. She'd gotten him coffee even though he'd said no.

She cleared her throat. "I didn't want the baby."

Her words crushed him, stifled whatever he'd opened his mouth to say. Even with Sophia, when she'd been surprised by an unplanned pregnancy, she'd wanted the child right away. How could she have changed so much?

How could she not want his child? It was the ultimate rejection.

Grief struck him then, a knife in his gut. They could have had another child. It would be, what, two by now? He pictured Sophia at that age, Kaitlyn. Toddling, learning to walk, starting to run and say no. Starting to become the people they were now. His throat went tight.

"I feel awful about it now, but put yourself in my shoes.

We'd just split up. I had to support the girls, raise them mostly alone. I couldn't add—"

He heard accusation in her voice, more reinforcement for what was wrong with him. "Raising them alone was your choice. I offered joint custody. You chose to move here instead."

"Right, because you worked all the time, and odd hours. You couldn't have had the girls at your place half the week, like you suggested, unless you wanted them to be alone for long stretches of time. Teenagers need more supervision than little kids, in a way, not less. And there wasn't money to support two full residences, anyway."

Blood pounded in his head. "Like you've done such a fantastic job of supervision. One suicidal and one pregnant."

He heard her suck in a breath. Navy whined and walked over to her side of the table, tags jingling.

The silence went on, and as his pounding pulse slowed, he reviewed what he'd said. Blaming her for the girls' problems had been a low blow. He raised a hand. "I take equal blame, if not more. I disappeared on them."

She was still silent.

"But why didn't you tell me about the baby? Don't you think I deserved to know? I was the father!" Again, grief pushed at him. He'd always wanted another child.

"Yes, of course. I should have told you. But…" She trailed off.

"But what?"

Outside the house, traffic was starting to pick up, people headed for work, parents driving their younger kids to school. A cold breeze hit him, and he realized that he, or the girls, must have left the door open.

"Two things," she said finally. "One, I didn't tell you because I felt awful about it. Terrible, terrible guilt. I'd been working night and day on the motel, getting it ready to re-open. Physical work. Not moving things—I knew better than that—but scrubbing floors and walls, cleaning carpets, carrying out trash. Morning to night. And plus, I kept thinking about how I couldn't manage a baby, not right then." She paused. "I think that's why God took him away from me," she said finally, her voice choked.

Drew's breath caught. "It was a boy?"

"Yeah. They do a test on the…" He heard her swallow. "On the remains, to see if there was a genetic reason for the miscarriage."

"Was there?"

"No. Nothing they could determine."

Drew sat trying to process it all.

Ria had gotten pregnant with a baby boy. It must have been the last time they'd made love, which he remembered as clearly as if it had happened yesterday. It was an unplanned, unprotected encounter, now that he thought about it, while he'd been packing his things to leave. Passionate, intense, for both of them. He'd thought maybe they'd patch things up.

But the next morning, they'd immediately started fighting again and he'd carried his boxes out to his car and left.

She must have found out that she was pregnant within the next couple of months. "I still don't get why you didn't tell me," he said, pushing from his mind the thought of her, pregnant and alone, working day and night to start a new business, because she needed money to support their children.

"I didn't tell you because you'd have blown up, just like you did today!" She sounded exasperated. "All the macho crap. Yelling and criticizing and blaming. I couldn't deal with it."

His blood rose in him again. "That macho crap is what a man is."

"No, Drew," she said, "that's what you and your father *think* a man is, but it's not true. Macho men are fragile. You have to keep the truth from them, because they can't handle it."

"I'm nothing like my father!"

There was a tap on the back door, and Navy let out one sharp bark. "Ria?" came a male voice. "Did you know your door's standing open?"

Ted Taylor. For all the world as if he came here all the time. Did he? Did she spend time with him after the girls had left for school?

Iron bands tightened around his gut.

Ria's chair scraped and he heard her walk across the room. "Hey, Ted," she said, her voice easy, "it's not a good time."

"Can we meet later?" he heard Ted ask.

"Sure," she said, sounding distracted. "I'll give you a call."

Wasn't that nice and friendly? It sounded like they got together all the time. Drew stood, his chair banging back behind him, as she closed the door behind Ted and walked back into the room. "I thought there was a chance we could get back together," he said, "but now I see there isn't."

"Drew—"

He waved a hand. "All this secrecy. Telling the girls to keep secrets from their father."

"That was wrong," she said quickly. "Both things. I should have told you."

Now she said it—now that he'd already found out.

Now that she didn't need him, because she had another boyfriend.

He'd gotten optimistic, thought he'd changed enough that they could fit together. But even if he *had* changed, she'd never see him that way. Whatever she said, whatever nice words she whispered to him, she still didn't think him good enough for her. Her actions plainly showed that.

His hope of a reconciliation—his *foolish* hope—faded away, replaced by a churning mix of disappointment and jealousy and rage.

"You're not who I thought you were," he said. "Even after we split, I respected you. But now I see you're nothing but a devious, disrespectful, cheating—"

"Cheating?" she broke in. "Drew, I'd never—"

"Was that baby even mine?" he interrupted, rewarded by her audible, choked gasp. His arrow had hit the mark.

"I'll be here for the girls," he said, putting ice into his voice, "but I want nothing to do with you. You hear that? Nothing."

As KAITLYN AND Sophia reached the school grounds, Sophia slowed down. "There he is," she said in a low voice.

Kaitlyn glanced up at the small crowd of students hanging out in front of the school. It was cold, but still, most of them would rather stay outside than begin the cooped-up school day early.

Tyler and his two sidekicks, squirrelly little Kyle and take-off-your-sweater Chris, stood at the top of the steps beside the main entrance like a king and his courtiers, surveying the scene.

Kaitlyn looked at her always-confident sister. Now her shoulders were slumped, and she had swollen eyes and no makeup. No armor. It was completely obvious that something was wrong.

Stupid Tyler Pollackson had done this to her.

And Sophia had let him, for Kaitlyn's sake.

Kaitlyn's jaw clenched and her hands wanted to form

themselves into fists. "Just don't look at him," she said to Sophia.

Sophia nodded and clutched her arm. "Walk in with me."

Even though Kaitlyn would've normally veered off toward the school's other entrance, she stuck with her sister. It was getting close to first period, and now there was a steady flow of students into the building.

Tyler, Chris and Kyle hadn't moved. As Sophia and Kaitlyn got close, the three boys immediately started nudging one another.

"Keep walking," Kaitlyn murmured to her sister. "We're almost past them."

At the last minute, Sophia slowed down. She looked up at Tyler, her face hurt and vulnerable, though she pressed her lips together, obviously trying to hide her feelings.

Kaitlyn winced as the significance of Sophia's expression came clear to her. Sophia had slept with that jerk. She was pretty sure that Sophia had been a virgin before. Tyler was her first, and that had to mean something to Sophia.

Obviously not to Tyler, though. Kaitlyn shot him the glare that Sophia owed him.

Tyler gave her a quick, reflexive sneer. Then he reached out a hand toward Sophia, a grin on his face.

"Leave her alone!" Kaitlyn stepped past her sister, positioning herself between Sophia and Tyler. "Come on. Let's just get inside," she said to Sophia.

But Tyler put out a meaty arm now, blocking them. The students behind them veered past into the building without even a complaint about the slowdown in traffic.

That was because you didn't complain to or about Tyler Pollackson, not if you wanted to survive the day with your face, pride or reputation intact.

No boy should have that much power. Especially no

boy as mean and egotistical as Tyler. Her own lip curled into a sneer.

He studied her and frowned, and she could tell he was thinking—not something he was especially known for. But after a minute, realization crossed his face.

Kaitlyn guessed what it was about, immediately.

He knows I know.

Was that good or bad for Sophia? She took a chance on it being good and lifted her chin. "That's right. I know what you did, and if you don't leave her alone, I'll tell my dad."

He raised an eyebrow and tilted his head. "Your *blind* dad?"

"Burn," Kyle said, then glanced at Tyler and Chris as if to make sure he hadn't stepped on their toes.

Chris laughed.

Kaitlyn's pulse rate skyrocketed and her muscles quivered.

Now the rest of the students had gotten inside the school, except for a few smokers and vapers grabbing a last dose of nicotine.

Kaitlyn sucked in a deep breath. She'd find a way to get back at them, for disrespecting their father in addition to everything else. "He may be blind, but he's smart. So is my mom."

"You better not tell them anything," he warned. "I know just how to get you in trouble, too." He gave her a meaningful grin, reached out and plucked at her sweater.

Kaitlyn's bravado leaked out of her and her stomach cramped. The video. She'd almost forgotten about it. She grabbed Sophia's arm and marched inside on weak, quavering legs.

After she dropped Sophia off, she met Venus and Sunny at their usual spot, a bench near the school library. She filled them in on what Tyler had said and how obnoxious all the boys had acted.

"Can you tell your parents?" Sunny asked. "If you just tell them about the video, it'll be over with, or at least out in the open, and they can help you."

"No. No, I don't think so. Dad's better than he was, but I still think this will make him crazy."

"He'll get over it," Venus said. "Until you come clean, Tyler, or whoever has that video, has power over you. And you don't want a guy like that having power."

The bell signaled that it was time to start class, so they all headed toward their lockers.

A text pinged into her phone. She looked at it.

You have until 12:30 to decide. Love, TomDickandHarry.

But who *was* he? Was he Tyler?

Or, as Sophia had thought, a combination—probably Tyler, Chris and Kyle?

Decide what? she typed.

Whether you take your sister's place.

Kaitlyn sucked in a breath. TomDickandHarry had to be Tyler. And he wanted her to do the same thing Sophia had done.

"What's wrong?" Venus grabbed her phone and studied it.

"Give that back!"

But Venus held the phone away from her. "Girl, you need help. Me and Sunny here are going to help you." She studied the text again. Then she spoke to Sunny. "This dude TomDickandHarry wants her to do what her sister did." She scrunched her face. "What did your sister do? Is it what I'm thinking?"

Kaitlyn blew out a breath and spread her hands. "It's not mine to say."

"It's what you're thinking, then," Sunny said in a matter-of-fact tone.

"You've got to say no." Venus put a hand on her shoulder. "You get that, right? You've got to say no."

"Well, but…" Kaitlyn thought of what the guys had on her. What dirt he might have on Sophia. Oh, man, she hadn't even thought of that. If the boys had videoed Kaitlyn taking off her shirt, what had they videoed of her sister?

"Give it to me," she said, holding out her hand for the phone. "I have to stall him."

"Stalling will never work with a jerk like that," Sunny said. "You have to be forceful. That's what I learned from my mom." She grabbed the phone from Venus and typed in a message, and then, to Kaitlyn's horror, she hit Send.

"No! What did you say?"

Sunny handed her the phone. NO WAY was the message she'd sent.

Venus looked over Kaitlyn's shoulder and then high-fived Sunny.

"Don't worry. We'll stand by you," Sunny said.

"That's right. We got your back," Venus added. And then Sunny split off to go to her regular class while Venus and Kaitlyn went into their classroom.

Kaitlyn sneaked glances at her phone all morning, but there was no more activity. So maybe Sunny had been right. Being firm had been the answer. Still, she had a sick feeling in her gut, a feeling that kept her mind from focusing on her studies. Erica scolded her twice for daydreaming.

If only this were just a daydream, not a nightmare. Twelve thirty couldn't come and go fast enough.

Her throat was so dry, her stomach churning so hard, that she couldn't eat anything. After lunch, they headed into their activity period. That was good, because Kaitlyn didn't feel like she could focus on science or math. Maybe it would be something interesting, something to distract her from her fears.

The activity period took place in the gym, with various groups clustered around, most kids sitting on the floor, a few of the athletes shooting hoops. Kaitlyn sat down with the film club Sunny and Venus had talked her into joining and relished the solid feeling of her friends beside her. It felt good to be flanked by Sunny on one side and Venus on the other.

She craned her neck, trying to see Sophia, but she was nowhere in sight.

"...start with some previews," Sissy, the girl in charge of the movie club, said.

The bell rang. Kait glanced reflexively at the clock. Twelve thirty.

TomDickandHarry had said she had until twelve thirty.

And her group, of at least thirty students, was going to watch previews. Cold prickles rose on the back of her neck, and she jumped to her feet. "I need to talk to Sissy," she said, trying to squeeze out past Venus.

"Girl, what's wrong?" Venus grabbed her hand and looked up into her face.

"I gotta check on what Sissy's showing," Kaitlyn said and twisted away.

But it was too late. The video started. As if in slow motion, Kaitlyn looked at the TV screen to see a familiar green sweater. Hers. Then the camera flashed up to her smile, shy and idiotic, now displayed before the whole film club. She watched it like you'd watch a train wreck, saw her hands reach to the bottom of her sweater and start to pull it off.

"Wait a minute," Sissy said. "This isn't the video I meant to show."

"Leave it on," said a couple of the boys, nudging each other. The group's laughter and hooting drew the attention of kids from nearby groups.

The video went on, because Sissy was having trouble locating the phone she was casting from.

Of course she was. Because someone tech savvy—Kyle?—had switched up the signals.

Kaitlyn should have looked for an off button, should have tried to find where the screen was plugged in, but her arms felt made of rubber. There was nothing she could do about it. Her worst nightmare was playing out, right here, right now.

Kaitlyn sank down onto the floor at the edge of the group and let her face fall into her hands while the sound of laughter and catcalls washed over her like sickening waves.

Beneath it, she heard the voices of a couple of supervising teachers, the click of heels walking toward them. Kaitlyn looked up just as the video disappeared.

As the teachers reached them, an innocuous movie preview started to play on the screen.

The boys were too slick to get caught. She buried her face in her hands again.

Around her, everyone continued talking and laughing, paying no attention to the screen now.

"Kaitlyn. Are you all right?" Erica knelt beside her and put a gentle hand on her arm. "What's wrong?"

She looked up to see Sunny and Venus approaching, looking concerned, and suddenly she was terrified that they'd tell Erica what was going on. That would only make things worse.

"I'm fine," she said, forcing a smile. Then she looked at Sunny and Venus and gave a minuscule shake of her head.

"If you're sure," Erica said doubtfully. She went over to a group of giggling kids, knelt down and started talking to them.

"Girl, you should tell her," Venus said. "Mrs. Harrison's cool. She'd figure out what to do."

"No way." Kaitlyn shook her head. "I'm not getting any adults involved. They'd just make everything worse."

"Okay, then," Sunny said. "We've got to find out who's doing this ourselves. And then…" She looked from Kaitlyn to Venus and back again.

"And then what?" Venus asked.

Kaitlyn's upset and rage morphed into determination. "And then we stop them."

"I'm with you," Sunny said, "but how?"

"I don't know yet," Kaitlyn admitted. "But between the three of us, we'll figure it out. They'll be sorry they ever messed with me and Sophia."

"And with *us*." Sunny put out a hand to pull Kaitlyn up from the floor. "Come on, girlfriend. We've got work to do."

The sick feeling in Kaitlyn's stomach intensified. They had to do something. Because if they didn't, Mom and Dad would find out, and her fate in her family as well as at school would be sealed.

CHAPTER TWENTY

AT DINNER THAT NIGHT, Ria realized that something new was going on with the girls.

Ria had cried a lot today herself, in between filling in for a cleaning person who'd called off and checking in guests and working on financial spreadsheets, trying to figure out how to keep the motel going another few months.

She was glad she'd been able to stay busy, lest she descend deep into the darkness that loomed just under the surface. Drew's finding out about the miscarriage had been bad enough, but he'd as much as accused her of cheating on him.

Talking with him about the miscarriage had brought up all the grief she'd felt about the loss of a baby.

One daughter was pregnant and the other had attempted suicide and was, according to her teacher, still having some problems with boys in the school. The sense of failure on every front threatened to overwhelm her.

Now, as she served the girls take-out Chinese that none of them really wanted, she studied their swollen eyes and knew their days had been awful, too.

Gentle inquiries had yielded nothing. She'd have to approach the issue, or one of them, head-on. "What's this about a video?" she asked them.

Kait flinched, and the two of them glanced at each other.

"What are you talking about, Mom?" Sophia asked in a too-innocent voice.

"Erica told me there are some rumors going around involving a video, or a couple of them."

They glanced at each other again. "It's nothing," Kaitlyn said. "Probably just someone being mean, like usual."

"Why do I get the feeling you're brushing me off?" She pointed at Kait with her empty fork.

"Because you always think we're brushing you off." Sophia took more rice and stirred it in with her kung pao chicken, making a mess Ria knew she wouldn't eat.

"How am I supposed to help you if you won't tell me what's going on?"

"This isn't about you, Mom, so leave it!" Kaitlyn stood. "I'm not that hungry. I'm gonna go upstairs."

"I'll go up, too," Sophia said, shoving away her plate. "I need to do some homework before we go to Dad's."

Ria pressed her lips together to keep from yelling at them, calling them back, forcing them to talk to her. They were too old for that. It didn't work.

Fighting down a sense of failure, she sent Drew a detailed text explaining what Erica had said about the rumors and asking that he try to talk to the girls.

No more hiding, no more keeping secrets. If he could deal with it, great; if not, he'd have to cope with the same feeling of failure she had.

Mechanically, she got up from the table, dumped the food into plastic containers and put it away. She straightened and cleaned up the kitchen, then walked through the downstairs, picking up clutter the girls had left lying around. Found a headband Sophia had been looking for last week. She carried their things upstairs and put them in stacks outside each girl's door. Stood with her hand poised to knock at Kait's and then changed her mind and walked back downstairs.

She found a text from Drew, just as cool and professional as hers had been: Thanks. Will talk to them at 7 when they arrive.

She looked at her watch—6:50. And sure enough, Kaitlyn came down the stairs with an overnight bag. "Soph! Hurry up!" she yelled upstairs.

"Coming, coming." Sophia came partway down the stairs, turned back for the schoolbook she'd forgotten and then trotted down.

"Bye, Mom," Kait said, and Sophia echoed, "Bye, Mom." They looked a little perkier than they had at dinner. The prospect of going to Drew's must have cheered them up.

Getting away from her must have cheered them up, she thought glumly. "Love you," she said, hoping for hugs but settling for pats on the back as they went out the door. "Text when you get there."

She stood watching them walk down the road, under the streetlights. By the time they were out of sight of home, they were more than halfway to Drew's place, and he would be waiting for them.

She swallowed hard and turned back toward the house, but stopped when a car turned into her driveway, its horn honking.

She watched it come to a halt. Three doors opened, and Erica, Bisky and Amber got out.

Ria stared. "Um, hi, guys."

"Get in the car," Erica said. "We saw your girls on the way, so we know you're home alone tonight. We're doing a girls' night out."

"I don't think—"

"Your mom and Mary are meeting us there."

"But…why?" Ria looked down at her faded jeans and plain sweater. "I'm not dressed to go out."

"You're dressed fine for the Gusty Gull," Amber said. "People practically wear their bathrobes there in the off-season."

"Plenty of folks go there in fishing clothes," Bisky contributed. "Come on, girl. Live a little."

"I don't..." She sighed. What did it matter? And it was nice of them to come and get her like this.

Ten minutes later they'd joined Mom and Mary at one of Pleasant Shores' few waterfront bars that remained open year-round. A three-woman band played in the corner, peppy dance tunes but not too loud. The mixed-age crowd was mostly eating dinner, although a couple of twenty-something women danced with eighty-year-old Henry Higbottom on the edge of the dance floor.

Ria felt a little better already, just getting out and being among her friends. "So, whose idea was this?" she asked the others.

"Mine," Erica said promptly. "I could tell when we talked earlier that you were worried about the girls. I didn't want you to be alone."

Amber elbowed her sister. "But it was *my* idea to come here, where there's music and men," she said. "Old lady here would have had us staying home for salad and light beer." She looked around the crowd speculatively. "It's not easy to get a date in Pleasant Shores, but we're for sure not getting one if we huddle up in somebody's living room."

"I don't want a date," Ria said automatically, then frowned. If things were over with Drew, truly over, was she going to have to get back out on the dating scene?

Perish the thought.

"Did the girls shed any light on those rumors?" Erica asked.

Ria shook her head. "I wonder if it's the same boys who were bothering Kait before."

Bisky frowned. "I thought Pleasant Shores Academy was supposed to be so great. Turns out there's as much bullying there as anywhere else."

"Did Sunny say anything?" Ria asked.

"Are you kidding? Do you think my kid would talk to me about something important in her life?"

It was a relief to Ria to know she wasn't the only one who had problems communicating with her girls.

Amber seemed to tune back in to the conversation. "Boys bullying girls. Gee, that's a surprise."

"I was hoping it'd get better as time went on," Mom said, "but apparently not."

"Toxic masculinity. It's an ongoing issue." Mary held up her hand to get a waitress's attention. "White wine for me, Connie."

"What the heck is toxic masculinity?" Bisky asked.

Mary gave her a wry look. "Pretty sure you see it every day down at the docks," she said.

"Men show off to impress other men in all different places and lines of work," Amber said. "Though it's sad if it's happening at the high school. Not surprising, but sad."

"Really sad when it affects your daughters," Ria said. "And it's worse now, because anything that happens gets spread on social media. Although I haven't seen anything on Kaitlyn's and Sophia's social media. I do monitor it."

Erica wrinkled her nose. "Unfortunately, I think most of the kids have fake accounts or other ways to get around what their parents are looking at."

"We all have to do everything we can to help our young women," Mary said. "It's not something any one family can conquer alone. Believe me, I know."

Ria glanced at Erica, who was studying Mary with interest. Talk about rumors. Everyone said Mary had a complicated past, that somehow she had ended up with a lot of money but no family at all. She herself never talked about any of it, but she occasionally dropped the tiniest clue.

There was a tap on Ria's shoulder, and when she turned, there was Ted Taylor. He was smiling, looking happy. "It's great to see you here. I didn't think you frequented places like this."

"When her friends drag her here she does," Amber said.

"Then she has good friends." Ted held out a hand to Ria. "Care to dance?"

"Oh, I couldn't…" She looked out at the dance floor and realized that while they had been talking, it had filled up.

"Go for it, girl," Amber said.

The rest of the women nodded, except for Mary, who just tilted her head and raised her eyebrows.

Ted was looking at her in an admiring way. It was obvious he really liked the way she looked. But he also seemed to respect her as a businessperson and to enjoy talking with her.

He was a nice man and would be thought of as a catch by many women. Tall, fit and wealthy, with good manners and a great car. Unfortunately, though, he wasn't Drew. And though she knew she would have to get over her ex, she couldn't rush it. Her heart was too raw, her feelings for Drew still too strong. She stood and beckoned Ted over to a quiet spot along the wall. She didn't want to reject him in front of a group of women; it had taken courage for him to approach her.

"I appreciate the offer," she said. "But I'm not ready to dance with you." She held his eyes steadily while she said it, so that he would realize she meant more than dance.

He met her gaze and then slowly nodded his head. "I get it," he said. "Thanks for being honest." His words were a little clipped; he wasn't happy.

Ria didn't feel especially happy doing it, either. But it was the right thing to do. Like it or not, her heart belonged to someone else.

"WHAT'S THIS ALL ABOUT, Mom?" Drew asked on Tuesday night as he walked through the door of his childhood home and into his mother's embrace. The old kitchen was steamy and fragrant with the smell of something baking. "Is that pecan pie?"

"Yes, your father's favorite," she said.

"Uh-oh." Mom always used food to butter Dad up. What was she angling for now, and why had she gotten Drew involved?

Drew had had to scramble to get a ride into Baltimore and would probably have to hit up his dad for a ride home, but Mom had made this dinner invitation sound important. As he inhaled the familiar scent of shredded beef stew, heard the radio playing oldies and felt his mother's arms around him, he knew he was home.

Maybe being home would help soothe the guilt and anger and worry that welled up in him every time he thought about Ria, Sophia and Kait.

He hugged Mom back, then let her go but kept one arm around her shoulders. "Are you okay? Is Dad?"

"I wanted to try getting everyone together before Thanksgiving, to get your father ready."

"Everyone?"

He felt her conspiratorial nod. "Your brothers are coming."

Drew's eyebrows shot up into his hairline. "Does Dad know? And ready for what?"

"For a big Thanksgiving dinner with all of us together. Mike, Stevie and his partner, Ria and your girls, and you."

"Ria won't be coming to any Thanksgiving dinner I'm at," he said flatly, taking a step away from her. "We're not getting back together."

"Why not?" she asked. "When we visited and I saw you together, even for just a few minutes, it seemed like you were…well, getting close."

"No." Though he'd thought so, too.

"But the girls said you're spending a lot of time together as a family."

Drew thought of the meals they'd shared, of giving out candy on Halloween, of Ria surprising them with braille Scrabble. "That's just for the sake of the girls," he said.

"Oh, but I was so hoping you would get back together. I really want another grandchild, and you and Ria…"

Her words stabbed into him, interrupting his fantasy. He'd wanted another child, too.

"She disrespected me," he said. "Leave it at that." No matter how he felt about Ria, he wasn't going to reveal what she had done.

"That doesn't sound like her." A sizzling noise from the stove. "Oh no, the rice!"

"Let me help you, Mom." He moved toward the stove, but she reached out a hand, holding him back.

"Just sit down, honey. Don't you worry about the food—that's my job. I just don't think Ria would ever disrespect you. She had all the respect in the world for you. I could see it in her eyes."

"Leave it alone." He sat down at the kitchen table where he'd had so many meals. This room had been the center of their home, the little house that Mom and Dad had bought when they first married. When Drew and his brothers were growing up, it had been bursting at the seams with one bathroom and just two bedrooms. Drew had helped Dad finish the basement one winter just so he could have a place to escape from his little brothers.

There was more sizzling from the stove, and the smell of ham, beans and rice mingled with the familiar fragrance of *ropa vieja*, the Puerto Rican shredded beef stew that she had learned to make for Dad.

Ria had learned to make it, too, just to please Drew. Back when she had wanted to please him.

"Are you sure you didn't just imagine she was dis-respecting—"

"She overworked herself until she lost our baby, and didn't even tell me!"

Mom made a faint little sound, and Drew was immediately sorry he had lost control and said such a thing, true though it was. He was even sorrier when he heard his father banging into the room. "What's this about losing a baby? Your wife lost a baby from working too hard?" He didn't wait for an answer. "I always knew it was wrong for her to work like she did. She wanted to wear the pants and this is what it got her."

"No, that's not it." He felt a major urge to defend Ria, even though the effort would be lost on his traditional father. Women worked all the time. And the reason she had to work so much was their divorce.

It was your fault you didn't take care of your family.

A burning smell caught his attention and interrupted Dad's tirade. Then the back door opened and Drew heard what he hadn't heard in almost two years: his youngest brother's voice. "Hey, everybody. Hey, Mom," he said, and Drew heard the sound of him kissing Mom.

"You better fix this meal. I don't eat burnt." Dad stomped out of the room. The basement door slammed, and Drew could hear Dad's footsteps pounding down.

"Oh no, just let me try to get this food under control," Mom said.

"Let me help," Stevie said.

"No, no. You men relax."

That was Mom. Drew turned toward his brother and lifted his head a little, trying to see him, catching a blurry outline. He held out a hand. "Stevie, it's been too long."

There was a pause. Then Stevie gripped his hand and shook vigorously. "Yeah, man, it has. I…I heard about your vision. I'm sorry."

"I'm dealing with it okay." And for the first time, Drew realized that was true. His vision loss seemed like more of a pain and less of a horrible fate, these days.

"I should have come to see you but… I didn't know how…how you'd take things. My 'lifestyle,'" he added, and Drew could practically hear the air quotes. "You're a lot like Dad."

"Not in every way." Drew lifted his chin. It was the second time lately that someone had assumed he was like his father. And while he loved his dad and had tried to emulate him in many ways, he was seeing more and more problems with Dad's worldview. "I'd like to meet your partner," he said to Stevie.

"You would?" Stevie sounded shocked. "If you mean it, that would be great."

"Looking forward to it," Drew said, and it wasn't a lie. He knew it might be uncomfortable for him, just because it was a big turnaround in how he viewed his brother.

But blood was blood, and Drew would accept Stevie for who he was.

And then the back door opened again, and there was Mike, clapping both Drew and Stevie on the back, hugging Mom, opening pot lids that shouldn't be opened and stirring sauces that shouldn't be stirred and generally blundering into the middle of everything like he always did.

That spurred Stevie to help, too, and Drew managed to set the table by feel and by remembering exactly where Mom kept things, which hadn't changed in twenty years. Then he sat down, making space for the others to get the meal on the table.

Mom yelled down the stairs, and Dad stomped up instantly, like he'd been waiting. "What's this?" he grumbled. "Everybody's doing women's work."

"Welcome to the twenty-first century," Mike said. "Good to see you, Dad."

Dad didn't answer, and he still hadn't greeted Stevie. Instead, he took his seat at the head of the table. "Ria always did the cooking for *you*," he said to Drew.

"Not really," Drew said. "We both cooked."

But Dad was on a roll. "In my day, men were men. Not like you thrcc."

There was a little silence in the room, and Drew wondered whether his brothers would get offended and leave.

But they didn't. They just kept passing dishes and serving themselves. Like always, Mom tried to smooth things over. "You're just hungry. Once you have some food, you'll all feel better."

The soothing tone reminded Drew of the way Ria had sounded when she'd told the girls not to tell Drew about her miscarriage. Mom was always trying to keep peace between her husband and sons, and for the first time, Drew realized that she might be the most mature and sensible of all of them.

"You know, Dad," Stevie said, his voice mild, "if it wasn't for Mom's pecan pie, I'd be out of here." Drew could just imagine what he was thinking, that it would be a huge disaster for him to bring his partner to a family event.

"There's pecan pie?" Dad asked, his tone brightening.

Mike snorted. And as they struggled through the rest of the dinner, buoyed only by Mom's fabulous cooking, Drew wondered: Just how much *was* he like Dad? And if he was, did it mean he'd alienate his daughters just as Dad had alienated his sons?

CHAPTER TWENTY-ONE

"It's the only way to catch him in the act, Sophia," Kaitlyn said late Tuesday evening as she tried to shake her sister's restraining hand off her forearm.

They were standing with Venus and Sunny in front of Chris's upscale waterfront home. Dark had fallen and a cold wind blew in off the bay.

"I don't like it," Sophia said, shivering. "You don't know what he's going to be like, in his own home. What if he's pushier than before?"

"I can handle it." Kaitlyn shrugged and twisted out of Sophia's grip. She *did* feel like she could handle it. She felt more angry than scared.

That second showing of the video had made her wild to solve the mystery: Who was behind it? If they were right that Chris was at the center—after all, he starred in the video, since he'd been the one persuading her to take off her shirt—then they would be able to convince him to delete it by threatening to report him to the cops. Chris had played into their hands by offering up a surprise invitation to Kaitlyn to come over to his place and hang out, an invitation Kaitlyn viewed with suspicion. But if they could get the evidence they wanted, it would be worth it.

She and Sophia had had to trick Mom and Dad to get out here in the evening. Mom thought they were staying at Dad's house again, and Dad thought they were at Mom's house, and since the two of them didn't seem to be speaking, Kaitlyn was crossing her fingers that it would all work.

Though their obvious animosity was a bit of a bummer. She'd thought for a little while that her parents would get back together.

"I've got Mom and Dad on speed dial," Sophia warned. "If you get in trouble, I'm calling them right away. And then we'll have to tell them everything."

Kaitlyn winced. No way did she want Mom and Dad learning about the video or, God forbid, seeing it. That was motivation enough to get in, get it done and get out.

She sucked in a deep breath, looked into Venus's and then Sunny's confident eyes for strength and walked up the sidewalk to the pillared front porch. She rang the bell, and it chimed through the house.

Maybe nobody would be home. Maybe Chris wouldn't be home and she wouldn't have to do this.

But, no, she wanted to do this.

The door opened into a dark entryway, and a tall man gestured her inside. "You must be here for Chris," he said. "I'm his dad. Let me take your coat, and I'll go get him."

The voice was familiar, and she shoved her hair out of her face and looked up at Chris's father. "Hey, you're Mr. Taylor," she said. "My mom is a friend of yours. Ria Martin."

"Then you must be, let's see—are you Kaitlyn?" he asked, and when she nodded, he gave her a half smile. "Pleased to meet you," he said, then turned and trotted up the stairs.

So that was a relief. If anything went wrong, her mom's friend would be here to help. She thought about texting that to Sophia and the girls, but now Chris was coming downstairs.

"Hey, you came," he said. He was smiling, but not in

a nasty way. He seemed genuinely pleased. "You want a soda? Something to eat?"

"No, thanks," she said. Hopefully, this wouldn't take long.

"Let's go downstairs." He opened a door, then called back into the front of the house, where his father had disappeared. "Dad, we'll be in the den," he said.

He led the way into the basement, and Kaitlyn's heart jumped. How could her friends check on her here? The plan was that she stay in an area they could watch—emphatically *not* upstairs—but they hadn't discussed the possibility of Chris having a basement, something you rarely saw in this area of the shore. There *were* windows down here, but they were high and small.

"Have a seat," Chris said, gesturing toward a big couch. He turned on the television, its screen practically as big as a movie theater's, and without asking her opinion, he clicked on some action-adventure thing.

Then he sat beside her on the couch, very close, and slid his arm around her shoulders. "I'm really glad you came over," he said in what he probably thought was a sexy voice.

"Yes, I wanted to talk to you," she said. "What did you know about that video?"

He pulled back a little, lifting both hands like stop signs. "That's nothing to do with me. I had no idea anyone was filming it."

"That's a little hard to believe," she said. She looked around. "How do I know you're not filming now?"

"I'm not. I wouldn't do that."

"Mind if I look around?" Kaitlyn was really winging this. She had wanted to get him to admit his guilt or to be able to discern it, but now that she was in the situation, she didn't feel as sure that it would work. He seemed like he might really not know where the video had come from. So she peeked behind furniture to make sure no one was hiding and watching. She even looked behind the giant-screen TV.

Was that a rustle outside the window? She went over and stood on her tiptoes, but she couldn't reach it.

It was a little creepy. But she reminded herself that it could be Sunny and Sophia and Venus, keeping an eye on her. And besides, Mr. Taylor would help if she got into any trouble.

"Come sit by me," Chris said. "I really, really like you, Kaitlyn. You're so pretty."

She studied him. How had she ever thought compliments like that were sincere? It sounded like such a line.

"I just want to be your boyfriend," he said. "You know, like, exclusive."

She tilted her head to one side, standing in front of him, arms crossed. "That's what you said before," she said. "But after I took my sweater off, you didn't want anything to do with me."

"Why would you say that?"

"Well, you ignored me in school, for starters," she said.

"I must not have seen you. I would never ignore you."

Did he think she was stupid? "I have a phone number. You could've texted me, or gotten in touch with me on social," she said. "Hey, what's your username on Frock?"

"I don't have one," he said, sounding sulky. "Look, are you going to be nice or not?"

"That depends. Are *you* going to be nice?" She squared her shoulders. This was kind of fun. "What does 'nice' mean, anyway? Doing exactly what you want, regardless of my feelings?"

He stood up and came over to her, and she thought he was going to apologize, but instead he put his hands on her shoulders and pulled her to him. He pressed his mouth to hers and his tongue went inside her mouth immediately. She shoved at him and turned her face away. No fair that her first French kiss was so disgusting. "Stop it!"

He grabbed her chin and forced her face back to his. He kissed her again while his other hand strayed toward her chest.

She shoved him harder than before. "Mr. Taylor! Hey, Mr. Taylor!"

Heavy footsteps upstairs made relief wash over her. When Chris grabbed for her again, she put up her forearm like a barrier. "Don't touch me. Your dad's coming down."

Chris cocked his head to one side, listening. "I don't think so," he said.

Kaitlyn listened, too. Mr. Taylor's footsteps were now headed upstairs, not down here. Had he not heard her?

"Mr. Taylor!" she yelled again, but the footsteps didn't slow down. An ugly possibility occurred to her: Did he maybe not *want* to hear her?

"My dad doesn't care," Chris said, confirming her fears.

Now Kaitlyn's heart was pounding, her throat dry. *I'm on my own.*

When he came at her again, she remembered the self-defense videos Mom had made her and Sophia watch, and she lifted her knee just at the right moment. He gave a yelp and bent double.

That was supposed to incapacitate a guy, but she hadn't kneed him hard enough, apparently. He straightened up, his face full of rage. Now he came at her not even trying to act amorous. He put a hand on her chest and shoved her backward and she landed on the couch.

He loomed over her. He was going to pin her. She yelled as loud as she could. "Sunny! Venus! Sophia! Help!" She gulped in a breath. "Mr. Taylor! Help me!"

Upstairs, the doorbell chimed.

It distracted Chris for a moment, and Kaitlyn rolled away and scrambled over the back of the couch, putting it between them. Then she turned and ran as fast as she could up the stairs and burst out of the basement just as Sophia came into the entryway.

"Leaving so soon?" Mr. Taylor looked at her, eyebrows raised.

"Your son just jumped me," she said. "Didn't you hear me yelling?"

"I saw it through the window," Sophia said. "He grabbed her and kissed her and pushed her down onto the couch."

Mr. Taylor looked uneasily at his son, who'd followed Kaitlyn upstairs. "You didn't do that, did you?"

Chris shook his head. "Nope. I mean, we made out, but…that's why she came over."

"That's a lie," Sophia said, lifting her chin. "And we saw you shoving her around. We were watching through the window."

"That's pretty weird," Chris said. "Who watches other kids making out?"

Mr. Taylor glanced toward the basement door and then back at them, his forehead wrinkling. "I think you girls had better leave. You're making ridiculous accusations that you can never prove."

"Leaving sounds like a great idea," Kaitlyn said to Sophia, and they turned and walked out the door.

On the ornate porch, Kaitlyn leaned against one of those ridiculous pillars. Her heart drummed, hard and rapid, and she couldn't catch her breath.

"Are you okay?" Sophia asked.

"I'm okay, except…" Kaitlyn sucked in air, her heart rate

calming, finally, a little bit. "Except I didn't get the answers I need. He was a jerk, but he didn't admit to anything."

Sophia bumped her shoulder into Kaitlyn's. "Not to worry," she said. "Sunny and Venus got the whole thing on video. Including some stuff that's going to surprise you."

"I DON'T WANT to take a walk," Sophia said Thursday morning when Ria walked into her bedroom. "I'm still sick."

"If you're well enough to watch movies on your computer, you're well enough to go for a walk." Ria looked around the clothes-strewn floor until she found a hoodie and a pair of athletic shoes. She handed them to Sophia. "It's a nice day, and we'll both feel better if we get outside. And that was our bargain."

"You said I could stay home if we *talked*," Sophia whined. "Not *walked*."

The truth was, Ria didn't much want to walk, either. She would have rather spent this Thursday morning hiding out in bed and binge-watching some mindless drama. Nothing that included a love story, because that would make her think of...

As soon as her mind turned to her ex-husband, she forced it away again. Reality TV, that was what she'd watch. A chef competition show or maybe *Hoarders*.

But she didn't have that choice, because she was a mom. Ten cantankerous minutes later, they were strolling along the rocky beach.

The breeze was stronger here, cool enough that Ria was glad she'd put on a thermal under her hoodie and insisted that Sophia do the same. The November sun was bright, but too weak to warm them much. A couple of fishing boats were visible up the peninsula.

She looked sideways at Sophia, who was trudging along,

head down, and love for her oldest daughter, now struggling with such adult issues, filled her heart so full that it actually ached. She put an arm around Sophia's shoulders. "We need to talk about the baby," she said. "Have you thought about what you want to do?"

Sophia glanced at her, then kicked a rock. "A little," she said cautiously.

"Good. Because you're thinking for two now. What's best for your baby, as well as what's best for you." She was watching Sophia's face, so she saw her mouth turn down. "Do you want to raise it yourself?"

Sophia nodded. "Of course I do!"

Ria rubbed Sophia's back a little as they walked. "Okay. So let's imagine there's a football game next year, your senior year. First one of the season, and you have a new baby. Can you go?"

"Sure! I'll take it with me. Or..." She frowned. "Do new babies cry a lot?"

"A lot of them do," Ria said. "And they sleep a lot, too. Being in a loud stadium might not be good."

Sophia looked over at her. "That's okay, because you and Dad will watch the baby. Right?"

Ria pursed her lips and shook her head. "I can't speak for your father, but, no, I wouldn't be willing to take care of your baby on the weekend so you can go have fun. Besides, you'd have just given birth. You'd be nursing, most likely."

Sophia's hand clapped to her mouth. "I'd be fat!"

Ria winced. *This is on you*, she told herself. *You did this.* "You do gain some weight with a baby, but being so young, you'll lose it fast."

"I'd get a babysitter," Sophia said.

"Okay, that makes sense. What's the cost of a sitter these days?"

Sophia's forehead wrinkled. "I've done it for ten dollars an hour."

Ria nodded. "So your night out will last, what, four hours? So that's forty dollars, plus whatever food you buy at the game, so about fifty. Where will you get the money?"

"From you and Dad?" Sophia asked hopefully.

Ria shook her head. "Remember how this year I paid for only half of your recreation and you earned the other half? And we talked about how you'd pay all of it senior year. That still holds."

"Mom!" Sophia kicked another stone, hard. "I could work at the motel," she said, her voice sulky.

"But who will take care of the baby while you work? And for that matter, while you go to school? You'd probably need to do cyberschool, which would be tough while you were taking care of a baby, but it could be done."

A muscle clenched in Sophia's cheek, and Ria's stomach twisted. She had no idea whether she was doing the right thing, having this talk with Sophia. She wished she could have discussed it with Drew. Missed his insight.

She looked upward, watched a gull soar overhead, letting out its mournful caw. "Look," she said, "I'm not saying you can't do it. And Dad and I would help, for sure, with the baby's expenses, like food and medical care and supplies. But there wouldn't be extra, financial- or time-wise, for us to also take care of the baby while you work or go out."

"So you're saying I couldn't do either one?" Sophia sounded indignant. "That I'm basically stuck at home?"

"Right." Ria hesitated. "I'd worry about you feeling isolated if you cyberschooled and couldn't go out with your friends. But I would support you if that's what you decided to do. And your friends wouldn't forget you. I'm sure they'd come see you and the baby."

Sophia let out a snort. "Yeah. Once."

"You could do library programs for young parents. They're free. You'd meet other mothers you could get together with. Make new friends."

"Not as young as me," Sophia said.

"Right, not too many."

Ria felt like she'd said enough, on that topic at least. She remembered all too well being in Sophia's shoes, and how overwhelmed she'd felt when her mother had confronted her with all the decisions she needed to make.

The difference, besides the fact that she'd been a few years older, was that she'd had Drew. Drew, who, the instant he'd learned she was pregnant, had taken it on as his responsibility. He'd insisted that he'd be involved no matter what and that he would pay his financial share. But what he'd wanted to do was to get married.

That option had been a balm of comfort to her as she'd struggled with all the uncertainties. And while marrying him had brought its own set of challenges—planning a hurry-up wedding, learning to be a wife, dealing with his family—he'd been at her side, so she hadn't faced them alone.

In the four days since she'd revealed her pregnancy to the family, Sophia had adamantly insisted that she didn't love the father of the baby and he didn't love her, that she didn't want him involved. Nonetheless, Ria felt she ought to bring it up one more time. "These decisions should be made with the father," she said.

"No way. Do you know anything about adoption, how it works?"

Relief surged over Ria, because that was the choice she hoped Sophia would make. "I know you can have a say in who the adoptive parents are, what they're like. And usually you can know how the baby's doing, even see the child sometimes as he, or she, grows up."

Sophia opened her mouth, then closed it. "I'll think about it."

"Good. I know you'll figure out the right thing to do. And Dad and I are both here to talk it all through." She put an arm around Sophia's shoulders and squeezed one more time. "Lunch at Goody's?"

"Yeah." Sophia was looking at the ground. "Hey, Mom, if I tell you something, can you keep it to yourself? I mean, total cone of silence?"

Sophia's serious tone prickled Ria's nerve endings. "Unless someone's at risk," she said.

"No one's at risk. I promised I wouldn't tell, but I have to tell someone," Sophia said. "See, there's this video..."

CHAPTER TWENTY-TWO

DREW WAS BREATHING HARD, his feet slapping the boardwalk, sweat dripping down his chest and back.

"Bike coming," Stevie said, and Drew felt the slight swerve in direction through the tether they'd rigged up out of an old towel.

"All clear." And Stevie moved back to the middle of the boardwalk, with Drew following suit.

"Let's pick it up," Drew said as he accelerated, and he felt Stevie rise to it, speeding up so that he could be slightly in front of Drew. The physical exertions felt great. And, yeah, Drew felt a little idiotic being leashed to his brother like a dog, but, hey, if it allowed him to run again, he'd take it.

"There's…a bench…up here." Stevie slowed down, breathing hard. "Let's rest."

Truthfully, Drew didn't mind. He hadn't run outside since losing his vision, and the treadmill just didn't have the same exertion quality. He flopped down beside his brother. "Thanks, man. Glad you came down." He lifted his face to feel the cool breeze off the bay, and a little warm sunshine, too. He could smell something fishy, and grease from a food truck, and his brother's sweat.

Stevie's phone call had surprised him, but it had made him happy. He still felt bad that they'd fallen out of touch. When Stevie had said there was something they needed to discuss, Drew had gladly invited him to drive over on his next day off, and now here they were.

Stevie went over to the food truck and got them both bottles of water. When he came back, he handed one to Drew and opened his own, and they both took long swigs.

"Wanted to talk to you about something," Stevie said. "Something you said the other night at Mom and Dad's."

"Yeah? What's that?"

"Mom told me Ria had had a miscarriage and that it was Ria's fault. You sure about that?"

Drew almost spit out his water. "She told you that?"

"You know Mom," Stevie said.

"I do. So, yeah, Ria said it was her fault. She was doing hard physical labor, trying to open the motel she's running, and it was too much for her."

"Look," Stevie said, "I did an OB-GYN residency." He said it not like some expert but like a humble younger brother.

This was what Stevie had wanted to discuss? Drew had figured there was some problem he needed help with, probably something to do with Dad. Instead, Stevie was focusing on Drew's life, his issues.

"I saw a lot of miscarriages," he said now. "Women tend to blame themselves. Those units have social workers or counselors come in all the time, partly for that reason. It's hard on women, and sad."

Stevie's words sent a prickle of guilt up Drew's spine. He hadn't really thought about how difficult it must have been for Ria, having a miscarriage and having to deal with that alone. He'd gotten defensive and angry the moment he'd learned about it. With good reason, but still.

"It probably wasn't her fault," Stevie said.

Now his brother's knowing tone was getting annoying.

His *little* brother's. "She was doing heavy cleaning, carrying bags of trash, working long hours," Drew said.

"Women all over the world work hard and have babies," Stevie said. "Think of farmers in the rice paddies, or people that work in factories where they don't have any insurance. They work right up till the day they give birth with no problem."

"Yeah, but… Ria isn't exactly a peasant woman."

"Did you know that about one in four pregnancies ends in miscarriage?"

"Really?" Drew shook his head. "No, I didn't know that. But the thing that really makes me mad is that she didn't tell me. Didn't think I could handle it, didn't trust me. I deserve to know."

"*Can* you handle it, though? Did you handle it well when you found out?"

Drew was getting really irritated with Stevie's comments. "I got angry," he said. "But that was about the deception. Not the miscarriage itself."

Stevie was quiet, and Drew wished he could see the expression on his brother's face. A couple of women walked by, talking rapidly in Spanish. It sounded like they were pushing a baby carriage. Behind them on Beach Street, cars moved, just a few of them, slowly.

"Did you know Mom had a couple of miscarriages?" Stevie asked.

"No." That surprised him. She'd never mentioned it. "When?"

"One before you, and one after me," Stevie said. "I just found out last night, when Mom and I were talking about Ria." He paused. "But she kept it from Dad, so don't tell him."

"What?" Drew felt his jaw drop open. Since when did

something like that happen to a wife and the husband not know about it?

And how weird was it that Stevie's words to him were almost the same as Ria's words to their daughters? *No, Dad doesn't know, so don't tell him.*

"Mom kept it from him," Stevie said, "because she didn't think he could handle it, thought he'd be angry and blame her."

Thought he'd be angry and blame her.

Didn't think he could handle it.

Drew gripped the edge of the wooden bench, hard. A rough spot dug into his finger.

Didn't think he could handle it. "I'm just like him, aren't I?"

Stevie blew out a loud breath. "No, not in most ways. Like, you're not calling me names because I'm gay. But you did screw up in a Dad kind of way, with Ria."

In other words, he'd made accusations and gotten angry before he'd heard the whole story. "I guess I did."

"And Ria's great, man. You were great together. That's why I came down here, to tell you... Fix it up, man. For your kids, and also for you and Ria."

Drew felt like his world was spinning. Things he thought he'd known to be true weren't true. Things had happened that he had no clue about.

"Dad always wanted us to be so macho," Drew said slowly. "But if macho means people have to protect you from things, protect you from the truth..."

"Then it's not so big and manly after all." Stevie patted his shoulder, so lightly that Drew wasn't even sure he had felt it.

"You haven't seen the girls for a couple of years." Drew felt his throat constrict a little. He hadn't made much of an effort with Stevie, but Stevie had taken it upon himself to come and set him straight, not because of self-interest but so Drew could have a better life.

"I'd like to see them," Stevie said. He hesitated. "Jerome would like to meet them, as well."

"Jerome, huh?" Again, Drew wished he could see his brother's face. "You're serious with him?"

"Been together two years," Stevie said. "We're happy."

"Good," Drew said. "I'm glad." It was true. He wanted Stevie to be happy and have a good life, including someone to share it with.

He wanted that for himself, too, but he'd screwed it up. "We'll get together. The girls would love to see you. And I'd like to meet Jerome, too."

They picked up a couple of hot dogs from the food truck and went back to Drew's place, ate them and drank a beer each, watched a little football. All the while, Drew was thinking, figuring things out.

He had said awful things to Ria out of anger, anger that she had kept the truth from him. But his mother had kept the exact same kind of truth from his father. Sometimes women thought they knew what men needed better than men did themselves.

Maybe they did.

On the other hand, he didn't want to have to be treated with kid gloves. Didn't want to be that fragile.

He saw Stevie off with a thank-you and plans to get together again soon, but he was distracted. He couldn't stop thinking about what a jerk he'd been.

He and Ria might have had a chance. Mom had seen it and wanted it. Stevie had seen it.

More important, Drew had wanted it, and he'd thought she did, too.

Drew *still* wanted it. He wanted to reconcile with Ria, live the rest of his life with her, in the worst way.

He loved her.

He had to do something to fix his mistakes, but he couldn't make up for what he'd done with a simple little apology.

He had some planning to do.

"SHH, THEY'RE COMING!" Kaitlyn crouched just inside the tumbledown crab shanty and peered out into the darkness.

"Stations, everyone," Venus said in a fake British voice and giggled, and there was shuffling on the boat behind her.

"You're so weird," Sunny said.

"Shh!" Sophia hissed.

A couple of people walked by the docks. A man and a woman, talking. Not the boys. "False alarm," Kaitlyn called over her shoulder.

"I can't believe they agreed to give us money to take the video down," Venus was saying inside the crab boat's cockpit.

Kaitlyn duckwalked to the doorway so she could talk to the others. "Remember, that's not the main point of tonight. We want to, one, educate them, and two, get footage of them that we can hold over their heads."

"All of them," Sophia said. "Because we got Chris on the basement video, and a little bit of Kyle, but not much to scare Tyler." She put a hand to her stomach in a seemingly unconscious gesture of protection. Sophia had admitted she'd told Mom about the sweater video, which had made Kaitlyn mad. But apparently Mom hadn't freaked out. And Kaitlyn couldn't stay mad at Sophia when she was trying to deal with being pregnant by a real jerk of a guy.

"How much money did they offer?" Sunny asked. Although she was letting them use her family's boat, and fishing shack, for tonight's escapade, she'd been the last to arrive and hadn't heard all the details.

"A cool thousand," Venus said.

"What? Let's take it, split it!"

Sophia waved a flat hand back and forth. "No. It's more important to teach them a lesson. We want to make sure they never do this again."

"You don't know what it's like to be poor. What my family could do with a thousand dollars…" She looked at each of them in turn. "Never mind. I can see I'm outnumbered."

"And it wouldn't be a thousand dollars if we split it four ways," Sophia reminded her.

"None of us have much money," Venus said, "but money isn't everything."

"Hey, you there?" The deep voice made Kaitlyn jump.

"They're here," Venus whispered unnecessarily, and she and Sunny dived to their hiding places.

Kaitlyn was sweating and forgot her lines. But Sophia put a hand on her shoulder, and when she spoke, her voice was calm. "It's about time. Do you have the money?"

"We've got it," Chris said.

Just hearing his voice made Kaitlyn cringe. He'd really scared her for a minute there, down in his basement, and she'd been trying not to think about it. His arrogant tone brought it all back.

"Bring it here." Sophia sounded cool and collected. "We have booze."

"Yeah?" There was some murmuring between Chris, Tyler and Kyle.

Kaitlyn pulled herself together. "We want to party, no hard feelings," Kaitlyn said, "as long as you give us the money first."

"See, they're hot for us," Tyler said, and one of the others laughed.

Kaitlyn bit her lip to keep from screaming out: "In your *dreams*, you jerk!" But she kept control. They had a job to do.

She glanced over at her sister. Sophia's eyes narrowed and her fists clenched, and Kaitlyn felt a brief, gleeful moment of sympathy for Tyler. He'd picked the wrong girl to love and leave.

The boys climbed aboard and Sophia pulled out the beers she'd stolen from Dad's fridge. They were both hoping he wouldn't be able to see that his stash was diminished, but it would be typical of a former cop to keep a count and notice the shortage.

They'd worry about it later. It wasn't like they were actually going to drink it, especially Sophia, who was being super careful of everything health-wise since her visit to the ob-gyn.

"Boats creep me out," Chris muttered as they came aboard.

"Yeah, because you never learned to swim, ya idiot," said squirrelly little Kyle.

"Money, please." Kaitlyn held out a hand.

"Delete the video first," Tyler said.

"Both at the same time," Venus suggested as she emerged from the shadows. "Why don't you show them the video while I count the money?"

Strangely enough, Venus's presence and practical tone seemed to reassure the boys. They climbed the rest of the way on board and into the covered cockpit and handed an envelope to Venus.

There was a rumbling, and then the motor sprang to life.

"Hey!" Chris said. "Who's starting up the boat?"

"Oh, Sunny is here, too."

"You wouldn't know me," Sunny contributed from the cabin where she'd gone to steer the boat. "I'm just a dock kid."

Kaitlyn glanced at Sophia and noticed that her cheeks flushed. It hadn't been long ago that she'd held the same view of dock kids. Now that she was getting to know Sunny, though, that had to be changing.

"Here, have a beer," Sophia said, tossing one to each boy as the boat swung out into the bay. "And let's roll the video."

It was the scene with Kaitlyn and Chris in the basement, a little dark since it was obviously shot from the window well. Kaitlyn felt like squirming when she saw herself, especially when Chris tried to kiss her.

"Right there," Venus said, pausing the video. Then she scrolled backward, played the last bit again and paused it. "Right there. That was your first mistake."

"Yeah, you should have just ripped off her shirt," Kyle said and laughed a nasty laugh.

Sophia, crossing the cabin to get a soda, banged her hip into his arm just as he was lifting the can to his mouth, and beer gushed out onto his shirt and jeans. "Oops," she said.

"Hey! Now I'm gonna smell like booze and my mom is gonna know."

The girls ignored him, and Venus played the video forward again. Within thirty seconds, she stopped it. "You can't hear it, but it's easy to read Kaitlyn's lips," she said. "She said, 'Stop it.'"

"And when a girl says *stop it*, she means it." Never had Sophia's patronizing big-sister tone been such music to Kaitlyn's ears.

Chris looked embarrassed, and then he lifted a hand as if a new idea had come to him. "It's like I told my dad," he said. "Why'd you come over if you didn't want to, you know, get some?"

Kaitlyn put her hand to her chin and looked upward as if she was seriously considering his question. "Let's see, could a girl visit a boy for some *other* reason than that she wants to make out with him?" Then she glared at Chris. "I wanted to get you to admit to being in on the sweater video and agree to delete it everywhere," she said, "not because I have any interest in you as a boyfriend or a date."

"That's not right!" Chris said. "You tricked me."

"Tit for tat," Sunny said from the back of the boat.

"Yeah." Venus grabbed Kyle by the scruff of the shirt and yanked him into a standing position. "We found this little creep in the window well filming everything. He said you put him up to it. Just like you got him to video Kait the first time."

"So who's tricking whom?" Sunny asked.

"The difference is," Sophia said, "we were better at it than you were. That's all."

"Let's go on with the show, ladies, shall we?" Venus asked. "These boys have so very much to learn, and time is short."

"I don't want to watch the video. I want you to delete it," Kyle whined. "I've got beer all over me and I don't wanna ride in a boat. It makes me nauseous. I *told* them we shouldn't come."

"I don't think we'll be able to delete the video," Venus said with mock regret. "I noticed that the cash you gave us was twenty dollars short. We'll be maintaining access to it."

Tyler laughed meanly. "We'll be ready to roll with Kait's video, too, then."

"I don't think so," Sophia said. "I've got two of your three phones right here."

"What?" Chris and Tyler fumbled for their pockets.

"Hey, she does have it—give it back," Chris said.

"She's a good pickpocket," Kaitlyn said, grinning.

Sophia held the phones over the water. "If you don't delete the videos of Kait now, and from everywhere," she said, "the bay will delete them."

"They don't have my phone," Kyle said, holding it up.

Sunny had slipped up behind him. "Now we do," she said as she grabbed it out of his hand. "And let's be clear. We know you can find the video again and download it. But if you do…" She made a grand gesture toward Venus.

"If you do, I'm going to use my video skills to enhance the video we have of you guys," she said. She pointed at Kyle. "And I got photos of you in the window well, so you're included, too."

Kaitlyn restrained a smile. The thing the boys didn't know was that this whole exchange was being recorded. More evidence was building up, even as the boys tried to argue with them. Finally, they'd have something on Tyler as well as the other two jerks.

"You boys might need time to think about all of this," Sunny said. "That's why I'm towing our rowboat. It's real comfortable. Why don't y'all spend the night out here on the bay in that, and you can let us know your decision in the morning?"

"But they won't have their phones," Sophia said, pretending concern.

"They're really loud, though," Kaitlyn said. "You might even call them loudmouths. I bet if they yelled for help for a long time, someone would hear them. Once they get towed back to land—oh, you didn't think we'd give you oars, did you?—they can let us know what they think."

Tyler's face had been getting redder and redder. Now

he stood and dived—not at Kaitlyn, but at Sophia, knocking her over.

She clutched her belly as she fell down.

Chris gave her a little kick.

Fury and fear rose and overflowed like lava inside Kaitlyn. She rushed Chris, wrapped her arms around him from behind and started hauling him back toward the rowboat. Sunny saw what she was going for, grabbed his feet, and together they dumped him there, then shoved the rowboat far enough away from the crab boat that he couldn't climb back on.

"We gotta get Tyler next," Kaitlyn panted. "He could hurt Sophia."

They rushed back to the others and found Sophia sitting up. "Are you okay?" Kaitlyn asked, kneeling beside her.

"Yeah, but I don't think he is." She pointed at Tyler, who was writhing on the floor, clutching at his crotch. As they watched, he retched and actually vomited a little.

Venus shrugged. "I wanted to see if he actually had gonads," she said. "Surprisingly, he does."

"I can't swim," Chris moaned from the boat behind them.

Sunny shone a flashlight back at him. "I think he might have wet himself," she told Kaitlyn quietly.

"Wow." He'd gotten seriously scared. Good. A taste of his own medicine.

Venus put a boot on Tyler's back. "Now, we can leave you boys out here or we can have your promise that you won't do anything like that again."

"Our money," Kyle whined. "I got that out of my bank account, and my mom will kill me if she finds out."

"So…" Venus said. "You were somehow planning to get that back off us, after you got us to delete the video?"

Kyle nodded. "He said it'd be a piece of cake." He pointed at Tyler.

"Well, it won't," Sophia said sharply. "Personally, I think you should make a donation to a domestic abuse fund."

"And another to the watermen's relief fund," Sunny added. "I know you want to help all the dock kids and their families."

"Five hundred each?" Venus suggested.

"Yes, yes, we'll do it. Just don't leave us here," Chris begged.

Tyler still hadn't said a word. He was just moaning and squirming, very quietly, on the floor of the cockpit, clutching at the front of his pants.

"Oh, and all of this is on video," Sunny said, "so if you ever get a hankering to do something to any woman, involving video or not…it goes live."

Watching Tyler moan and Kyle cry and Chris beg to be taken to shore, Kaitlyn didn't feel guilty at all. She high-fived her sister and the other two girls and, as Sunny turned the boat back toward the docks, felt a great satisfaction in her soul.

CHAPTER TWENTY-THREE

"So, APPARENTLY, the girls have a plan to take care of these boys who've been bullying them," Ria told Mary and Julie at the bookstore late Thursday evening. The shop had closed hours ago, but Mom and Mary had been working on preparations for the Christmas shopping season, and Ria had brought a couple of bottles of wine to celebrate their hard work. And, admittedly, to get access to their sympathetic listening ears.

"Did you find out what happened?" Mom asked.

"I'm sworn to secrecy. But suffice it to say...a lot of it's related to body image and sexuality, and it's my fault."

Julie and Mary looked at each other. "Any time a woman says it's all her fault," Mary said, "I'm a little doubtful, because our society has designed things to make us feel guilty."

Ria forced a smile but didn't answer. She didn't want to disrespect Mary by saying that society didn't design anything.

"I can tell you're skeptical," Mary said. "I can recommend a couple of books to read that will go into detail."

"She can *always* recommend books," Mom interjected.

"But think about it," Mary went on. "Advertising that makes us feel like our housekeeping and our skin and our parenting are inadequate, and that we should purchase some product to fix that. TV advertisers are incredibly talented at making their messages compelling."

"Well, sure, that's true," Ria admitted.

"And then the unrealistic images we see in the media. Looks, for one thing. It's all airbrushed. Believe me, I know."

Something about the way she said it made Ria study her with curiosity. Mary was slender, with long white hair and incredible bone structure. "Are the rumors that you were a model true?" she asked her.

The older woman opened her mouth, then shut it again. Looked from Ria to Julie and then back again. "Just between us?" she asked.

They both nodded.

"I was," she admitted. "Not the most famous, but I did runway modeling and had a couple of magazine covers before..." She broke off.

They waited.

"It's all in the past," she said, brushing her hands together in a washing motion. Clearly, the mystery of Mary was going to remain a mystery. "For now," Mary went on, "we're focused on you, Ria, and your tendency to blame yourself for things that aren't your fault."

"But one of my daughters was tricked into a...a compromising video," she said, "and you both know she tried to take her own life."

Mom's eyes widened. "A compromising video? That doesn't sound like Kaitlyn."

Ria waved a hand back and forth. "Forget you heard that, because I promised Sophia I wouldn't tell. She insists they're handling it themselves. The point is, her worries about her body made her vulnerable to a couple of bullies—and, no, I don't know who they were. Meanwhile, Sophia is pregnant."

Mom had already been told, but Mary put a hand to her mouth. "Oh, dear," she said.

Ria nodded. "Don't you see that it's all about body image, about being a woman, about sexuality? If I didn't struggle with all of those things so much—"

"Honey," Mom said, "we *all* struggle with those things."

Mary nodded vigorously. "Most women do. You'd think fashion models would be exempt, since they're considered so beautiful, but they're all obsessed with weight and worried about aging and uncomfortable getting naked around a man for fear they won't live up to their cover shoots, which, of course, they won't."

"Interesting," Ria said. Could it be that she wasn't unusual in her discomfort with her body? Was she maybe not as special and unique as she thought?

The idea of other women sharing her problems made her feel less alone and less ridiculous.

"And if some of it *is* your fault, passing those worries from mother to daughter… Well…blame it on me," Mom said. "I dieted all through your childhood and caved in to your father's opinions about what women should look like, and I'm sure it's had its impact on you."

"Dad's views sure did," Ria said. Then she thought of something. "Do you know, the last time he saw Kaitlyn, he told her she ought to hit the gym."

"I've *told* him he shouldn't comment on the girls' looks," Mom said.

"Me, too. And I dragged him aside and called him on the gym comment, and he said it had nothing to do with weight—he was just making conversation."

Mom rolled her eyes.

"Even if that were true, which I'm sure it's not," Mary

said, "a young girl—any woman, really—is going to interpret that remark as a cut."

"Exactly. Kaitlyn did." Ria shrugged. "Nothing we can do about Dad, or about the media, right at this moment. But I've been thinking they need to ramp up their antibullying awareness campaign over at the school."

"You're right," Mom said, "and the kids also should be reminded about the consequences of sharing videos of underage girls. It's a criminal act."

"Even if the perpetrators are underage?" Mary asked.

"Yep. I'm almost sure. Earl would know."

"Maybe," Mary said, winking at Ria, "you and Earl should put some kind of program together for the kids."

Mom's face colored just a little. "I suppose we could."

"And I could do a book display here in the store," Mary said. "Just raising awareness in the town generally. Even if the boys involved never crack a book, some of the adults in their lives surely do."

"That would be wonderful," Ria said. Impulsively, she stood and hugged first Mom, then Mary. "Thank you so much for taking this on like it's your own project. It means the world to me."

What would she do without Mom, and without women friends like Mary? When she was with them, she felt so much stronger, more capable, more empowered.

So much more like a good person, rather than a screwed-up misfit.

If only she could carry that feeling into her work and her love life.

"I'm curious about one thing." Mom put a hand on Ria's arm. "What's going on between you and Drew? It's not my business, but I was getting the feeling you and he were…" She looked at Ria's face and trailed off. "Not so?"

Ria shook her head rapidly. "There was a thought of that but…it's over." She got up and started cleaning up their wineglasses to avoid questions about it.

She was processing tonight's discussion, though, regarding her own situation just as much as the girls'.

What if she could live her life without feeling guilty or inadequate?

What if she wasn't too fat, just like a model wasn't too fat? What if she just had a curvy body?

Even worse, she'd been blaming herself for a whole lot more things than her daughters' inherited bad feelings about their bodies. But what if she was wrong to blame herself?

Mary had said that women always tended to take on too much responsibility.

An image of herself in the hospital after her miscarriage came into her mind, and for once she didn't let herself push it immediately away.

Instead, she let a little compassion creep in for the woman huddled in the ER with silent tears dripping down her face, making calls on her cell phone for other parents and Mom to take care of the girls while she went through "a minor medical issue."

Even when she'd felt so weak and terrible about herself, she'd actually been kind of strong. There was even a chance that the miscarriage *hadn't* been her fault, or not entirely. Her doctor had said as much at the time, but she'd ignored him, too distressed to take it in.

Drew had always said he liked her body, and when she thought about it logically, she had no reason to disbelieve him.

But he'd been quick to blame her for the miscarriage, and he'd hurt her by suggesting the baby hadn't been his. That, she didn't deserve. She regretted keeping the miscarriage a secret from him, but given his reaction, she was almost glad she had. At the time, she couldn't have handled his disapproval.

Now she was stronger, and she could, although it made her sad.

There was a pounding at the door, and Mary stood and lifted a hand to both Julie and Ria. "Let me get my gun," she said, "and then I'll see who it is."

Ria raised her eyebrows at Mom, who half grinned and shook her head, looking fondly at the older woman who was now fumbling behind the cash register.

"Mom! Grandma! Let us in!"

"Never mind," Ria called to Mary. "It's the girls."

Julie hurried to the door to let them in. Not just Sophia and Kaitlyn, but also Venus and Sunny burst into the bookstore, half dancing with delight. "We did it!" and "Wait till you hear, Mom!"

They proceeded to tell a wild tale of trickery, guile, a boat trip and getting even. They interrupted one another and laughed and sometimes shouted. "We have it all on video, too," Kaitlyn said. "Stuff they won't want anyone to see. Chris Taylor wet himself!"

"And Kyle Sprang, the little genius, cried."

"Wait a minute," Ria said, a prickling sensation going up her spine. "Chris Taylor? Ted Taylor's son?"

"Yeah, but don't expect Mr. Taylor to do anything," Kaitlyn said. "He was there last night when Chris was trying to push me around, and he didn't lift a finger to help me, even though I *know* he heard me yelling."

"She was loud," Sunny said. "We heard her, and we were outside."

"And *he* was just sitting in the living room," Sophia

said. "When Kaitlyn told him what happened, he acted like she was lying."

"What?" Ria stared, opened her mouth to speak, then closed it again. She thought back over what she'd known of Ted, years ago and again in the past month. Was he really that kind of a man?

She'd always thought Ted was *nice*, a good guy. But if he'd let his son come close to assaulting an innocent girl, had ignored her cries for help... She clenched her fists. "Ooh, I could strangle him. I'd like to put him behind bars, but...he'd just deny it, wouldn't he?"

"You leave Ted Taylor to us," Mom said, looking at Mary.

"That's right," Mary said. "If these girls can execute such a wonderful comeuppance for the boys—and make no mistake, Ria, they learned that strength and problem solving from you—I'm sure we can think of something suitable for Ted."

As she looked at their conspiratorial grins, Ria's clenched fists relaxed. She knew they'd get him but good.

She took the girls home then—Sunny to her house, Kaitlyn, Sophia and Venus to her own, since Venus didn't live close and needed to sleep over so she could make it to school more easily the next day.

She was proud of them. They'd handled the problem themselves in a way no adult would have thought of, but more effectively than if she or Drew or, for that matter, the police had taken over. The boys had been scared into never doing such a thing again by the threat of the ultimate adolescent punishment: humiliation in front of peers, on social media.

The punishment fit the crime exactly. And meanwhile, looking at Kaitlyn laughing with Venus and Sophia, Ria realized that the process of figuring out and executing the punishment had helped Kaitlyn to heal and regain her confidence.

She'd never seen her girls get along as well as they were right now. And Kaitlyn had developed a couple of wonderful friendships in the process. Both Sunny and Venus were girls with intelligence and heart, and they'd influence Kaitlyn in a good way just as she would them.

Ria was filled with gratitude as she said good-night to them and went upstairs. Her girls would be all right. And that was the main thing, the most important thing.

She was also incredibly grateful for her mom and Mary, their wisdom and love. Tonight, they'd helped her take a few more steps past some of her worst hang-ups.

She undressed and, as she reached for her nightgown, caught a glimpse of herself in the full-length mirror. Turning away was practically a reflex, but she caught herself. Slowly, she turned back.

The body she saw wasn't anything like you'd see in a fashion magazine. But, according to Mary, even models' real bodies weren't like that. Ria had always known intellectually that models' figures were unusual and unattainable by most women, but she hadn't known it in her heart.

She looked at her breasts, her stomach, her thighs. No one would call her slender, but she could see that, in another era with different values, her body would have been considered pretty.

Which meant that there was no real, objective truth about who was beautiful and who wasn't. Again, that was something she'd known, but not *known*.

She had so much to think about. Hearing the girls laughing and playing music downstairs, she acknowledged, again, how much she had to be grateful for.

She pulled on her nightgown and got in bed, and there, she admitted to herself that there was only one thing missing.

Even when she and Drew had been at their most contentious, they'd always hugged and kissed good-night. It had always felt good to have him warm in the bed. She'd loved to look at his face, relaxed in sleep, and had considered herself the luckiest woman in the world to be married to such a handsome man who, beneath everything else, was a good, loving, protective person.

His issues, which he'd shown in their fight over the miscarriage, had proved too great for them to be together, and now, alone, she could admit how much that hurt.

She guessed she could be grateful that Drew, or her spontaneous relationship with him, had saved her from Ted Taylor, whose actions toward her daughters had shown a flaw at the core of him. And she would always be thankful that Drew had given her her daughters, her lovely, smart, growing-up daughters.

It was just that she was lonely. Lonely for Drew. She hugged a pillow to her chest, buried her face in it and let herself cry.

DREW'S HANDS WERE so sweaty that he nearly dropped his water glass. A family Sunday lunch at DiGiorno's might have been a big mistake.

Ria had gone along with the girls' insistence that they go there, but she'd clearly been uncomfortable, and with their history there, no wonder. She hadn't eaten much and the conversation had been stilted, despite the girls' good moods and best efforts.

Around them, tables full of people talked and laughed,

and everyone seemed to be having a better time than the Martin family.

Now Kaitlyn's phone chirped, and she gave a little squeak of surprise that sounded completely fake to him. He felt Sophia kick her under the table and realized that Sophia agreed with him.

The person they had to fool was Ria.

"Mom," Kaitlyn said, "Venus and Sunny are at Goody's and they asked if me and Sophia could come—can we?"

"When we're finished here," Ria said.

"But they want us to come now. Ple-e-e-ease? I'm done eating." Silverware clinked and dishes scraped across the table.

"Me, too," Sophia said and pushed her dishes away, as well.

No answer from Ria. "I think it would be okay," Drew said. He didn't want to overrule Ria and put her in a bad mood, but he really wanted to make this happen the way he'd planned.

"Fine," she said in a tight voice.

"Thanks, Mom!" The two of them left, Kaitlyn squeezing his shoulder in a vote of encouragement.

Ria cleared her throat. "Are you about ready? I think I've eaten my fill, too."

"I'd like to order dessert," he said.

She sighed loud enough for him to hear.

Might have been a mistake. But he'd wanted this restaurant, where she'd first told him she was pregnant. And he'd wanted to come in the daytime because the huge windows facing the bay let in enough light that he could see a little, better than he could anywhere else.

Sweat collected on the back of his neck. Where was the waiter who was supposed to implement the next step?

And then he smelled it: roses.

The slight clink on the table indicated the placement of one vase, then another. Simultaneously, their lunch dishes were cleared away. If Drew's orders had been followed, there should be four dozen roses, all the colors of the rainbow. He narrowed his eyes, and he could just see the bouquets' blurry shapes. He reached out to touch a delicate flower.

"What's this all about, Drew?" Ria's voice sounded a little higher pitched than usual.

He listened to ensure that the waiters were gone, then reached across the table and found her hand. "I'm sorry for what I said before. About the baby possibly being someone else's. I was an idiot, and that was wrong."

"It's fine. You didn't have to do all this. Although," she said, and he felt her shift and lean forward, "the roses are gorgeous and they smell wonderful."

She was softening a little, but there was more to say. Much more. "Listen, I was wrong about everything. I talked to Stevie and learned a lot about miscarriages. He said they're incredibly common and most women blame themselves, but that really often, they can't be prevented. And that doing physical work couldn't have caused it."

"Thanks," she said, her voice quiet. "My doctor at the time said something like that, but I didn't believe him."

"I hope you do now. It wasn't your fault, and I was wrong to say it was, or even agree with you that it was."

"Okay, but... Drew, did you...? Why'd you pick out this place to apologize?"

He shot up a quick prayer. This was it. "I've been doing a lot of thinking about the first time we were here."

"Yeah?"

He kept ahold of her hand. "I'll never forget when you said you were going to have a baby."

"It was definitely intense," she said dryly.

"Do you remember what I said?"

"Drew—"

"I said *we're* having a baby. And after I asked if you were okay, I said, 'There's no one I'd rather make a baby with.'"

"Drew," she said, tugging her hand away. "Stop. This is painful."

Gloom threatened to overcome him, like the cloud that had just covered over the sun. He felt like giving up. But he'd promised himself he'd go through with it, because he would never know unless he asked. He'd prayed about it in church today, asked for strength and courage, and now he called on it. It was a different kind of strength and courage than his father respected, but it was probably more important.

He leaned forward as the sun came out again, and he could see her, a blurry outline. "It's still true," he said. "There's no one I'd rather parent with."

"Drew."

"But back then," he struggled on, "I had no idea. I didn't feel worthy of you. I knew you were forced into it, and I took advantage of that because it was the only way I could marry you."

"I thought *you* were forced into it."

"Do you remember what else I said? 'It would be a dream come true if you'd marry me.' And it was. For all the problems, it was."

Ever since he'd lost his vision, he'd struggled with his self-worth. He defined himself differently now, because he had to—he couldn't chase down criminals and shoot a big gun. The redefinition was good, but one thing had stayed steady: he wanted to be the man of the family, to keep it together. He had to make that effort, even though Ria was still silent, and he was pretty sure that wasn't a good sign.

"I was wrong to yell at you and accuse you, and I'm sorry." At least he'd get that much out, make it clear to her. "I can't promise I'll never lose my temper again, but I'll work on it. I'll try never to take it out on you like that."

She cleared her throat. "I was wrong to keep the miscarriage a secret," she said, almost in a whisper. "I'm sorry, too. Sorrier than you'll ever know."

He reached across the table and found her hand again. Squeezed it. "I love you, Ree," he said. "Now more than ever. We've both learned so much, grown so much. We understand that life is full of problems and challenges, and that people are full of flaws. Knowing that...we could have a richer, better marriage than ever before. And we have this history together...two beautiful girls..." His voice choked a little.

He covered it by getting down on one knee and pulling the box out of his pocket. The room had fallen silent, and he hoped that was because most folks had left, not because they were watching.

He opened the box and held it out to her. He heard her sharp intake of breath. He'd had to jump through a lot of hoops to get this done, but he'd taken her old diamond ring—thrown at him in a fit of anger—and had it reset in a rose-gold frame with two rubies, one on each side. Rubies for each of their girls, who had assured him it was beautiful.

"So, um...will you marry me?" he asked, then rushed on so she wouldn't say no right away. "I promise I've grown and I'll keep growing. If you say yes, I'll work to make our marriage stronger all the time, stronger than ever." He looked up, intently, and at this angle, with the bright sun, he could see her face better than he had since he'd lost his vision. It was blurry, but he could see enough to reach up and touch her cheek.

Her face was wet.

"Oh, Drew…" she breathed out, and then her voice seemed to give out.

"If you don't want to," he said, "if I'm not enough, I won't bother you or bring it up again. Being married to a man with my disability would be a challenge. I'm working on some job opportunities, but nothing is sure yet."

She reached down, and he felt her soft hands, one on either side of his face. "I want it more than anything," she whispered, then kissed him.

Joy exploded inside him like fireworks.

There was applause all around them, but it faded into the background as he stood and pulled her to her feet and kissed her thoroughly, kissed her tears away, and tried to breathe through the swelling happiness in his heart.

"Did she say yes, Dad?" Kaitlyn called from across the room.

"Are you marrying him?" Sophia chimed in.

And then their daughters crashed into them, laughing and crying, and he reached out and pulled them into their embrace, pulled his family together. Gratitude filled his heart. "She said yes," he said. "Thank God, she said yes."

EPILOGUE

Ria had never had such a thankful Thanksgiving in her life.

First and most of all, because her girls were doing so well. She'd had incredible talks with both of them. Kait seemed so much stronger than even a month ago, and Sophia was wrapping her mind around the idea that she was pregnant, starting to plan.

They'd discussed the bullying and the boys endlessly, as a family. She and Kaitlyn and Sophia had wanted to puzzle out what motivated them to target Kaitlyn and then Sophia as they had.

Drew had helped them to understand the way boys tended to try to establish a hierarchy among themselves, often through sports, but sometimes through teasing and insulting others. Boys who didn't feel good about themselves could be the worst of all, hiding their vulnerabilities under a tough exterior and gaining a certain type of popularity from being jerks.

That could be the case with Tyler, for sure. And Kyle had gained prestige from having a popular boy like Tyler as a friend.

Chris's was a different story, in some ways sadder, because it was so common. His dad wasn't an awful man; he just held some unfortunate views that Chris had embodied, trying to get his father's attention and approval.

It made Ria want to smack herself for going to dinner with Ted and letting him close enough to think of as a friend. But she was realizing that it was just a mistake, and that she'd probably make more mistakes, and that was okay.

Obviously, she wasn't going to consider Ted's offer to invest in the motel, which was presumably off the table now, anyway. But that was okay. She'd decided to accept the motel as it was—old-fashioned and retro—and make the most of it, rather than trying to change it into something different. That seemed to be a theme with her these days. She was accepting herself for who she was, too, imperfections and all.

She put a huge bowl of mashed potatoes on the table in front of Drew, who was already seated at the head. She squeezed his shoulder, and he reached up for her hand and kissed it.

They couldn't display tons of affection, of course; they had guests. Besides the girls, Mom was here, and she'd invited the police chief, Earl Greene; the two of them were carving the turkey. Erica and Trey were here, with Sophia sitting between them.

Erica's sister, Amber, sat across from them, her daughter, Hannah, beside her, watching Erica and Trey with a little smile on her face. Amber looked good, healthy, and there was word she was working on a new writing project that consumed her. All the same, there was a little of the lost waif about her still, and that tugged at Ria's heart.

She wanted everyone to be happy the way she was happy.

The front door opened again, letting in frosty air, and there was Stevie, Drew's brother, and another short-haired, bespectacled man.

"Your brother and Jerome are here," she said to Drew, and he stood immediately and went toward the door. Ria watched while he greeted both of them, then hugged Stevie and made small talk with Stevie's partner.

It was completely normal, not a big deal. But for Drew, coming from the background he'd come from...well, it made Ria proud. She walked over to welcome both new arrivals and admire the pies Jerome had brought. She was just closing the door when there was a shout. Bisky and Sunny, along with Bisky's older sons, jumped out of Bisky's pickup and hurried to the door, Bisky carrying an incredibly fragrant tureen. "Oyster stew?" Ria asked with delight.

"My specialty. Taught Sunny to make it, this time."

Kaitlyn and Sophia helped put away everyone's coats, and the newcomers joined everyone else at the table. They stood and held hands to pray, each person offering thanks for something good in their life.

She, Drew and Kaitlyn all named their restored family. It wasn't technically restored yet—she and Drew planned a Christmas wedding—but for all intents and purposes, they were together. Drew was spending almost every minute here, and even Navy seemed to feel this house was her new home.

They sat down and passed food, and talk was general while they enjoyed it and ate their fill.

"I have something to announce," Drew said as Ria served dessert. "As of next week, I'm to be a curator at the new watermen's museum."

"That's great!" and "Terrific news" rang out around the table, along with some scattered applause.

"I have something to announce, too," Sophia blurted out and then clapped a hand over her mouth. She looked at Ria, then at Trey and Erica. "Can I tell everyone what we've been talking about?"

"It's your call, honey," Erica said.

"Okay. Erica and Trey might…well, I think almost for sure…they're going to adopt my baby."

"Oh, how perfect!" Mary clapped her hands.

"We'd still get to see him," Kaitlyn said. "Or her."

"I think it's a girl," Sophia said.

"Either way, we'll love the baby so, so much," Erica said. "I can't tell you how happy and grateful we'll be if this all works out. We never thought we'd get to raise a child."

There was champagne then, to go with their pic and cobbler, and lots of general talk. Sunny and Kaitlyn had taken Navy to her first agility class, and they made everyone watch while she wove between chairs and jumped over a low coffee table, then sat up on her hind legs for a treat.

But after the meal was over, in the kitchen, Mary pulled Ria aside. "I just wanted you to know that Ted Taylor is making a nice donation to the Gender Violence Awareness Fund," she said. "And your mom made an informal arrangement with Earl for Ted and his son to go through a training course. Sexual Harassment and Gender Violence. If they complete it to Earl's satisfaction, it'll end there, but if not, Kaitlyn might need to produce evidence of what Chris did."

"That's perfect," she said. "And you're perfect. Thank you for everything you've taught me throughout this whole ordeal. You're amazing."

"Just putting my vast life experiences to good use," Mary said, her eyes growing distant for a moment. Then she shook her head a little, smiled and put both hands on Ria's shoulders. "You're feeling good about Drew, then? And about Sophia and the baby?"

"Yes. Wonderful about Kaitlyn, as well. Wonderful about everything."

"You're raising two terrific girls," Mary said warmly.

As the older woman turned away to talk to someone else,

Ria felt a prickle of awareness and knew that Drew had come into the room. Sure enough, he touched her sleeve, then slid his arm around her shoulders. "Mary's right," he said. "You're raising two terrific girls."

"*We're* raising them," Ria corrected. "You're a good man, Drew Martin."

"I'm a lucky man," he said, tugging Ria closer to his side. And as they walked through the house, talking to their friends, they stayed like that, side by side.

It was how they'd go through life together. They'd lost it for a while, but they'd found it again.

Ria could think of no better reason to give thanks.

* * * * *

ACKNOWLEDGMENTS

I HAVE MANY people to thank for their help with this book. First, my agent, Karen Solem, who looked over my initial ideas and suggested that Drew should come to the Healing Heroes cottage due to an injury resulting in vision loss. The idea caught hold of my imagination, but I gained the courage to go forward with it only when my friend and fellow writer Sally Alexander, who lost her vision in her twenties, similar to the way my character did, offered to hold my hand every step of the way. I owe a big debt of thanks to Sally for her ongoing assistance, and to my former student, writer Jessica Minneci, who read the full manuscript and offered a completely different perspective on blindness and how to best depict it. The book is much improved by their suggestions; all remaining flaws are my own.

My portrayal of teenagers owes much to my work with them at Seton Hill University, but the greatest thanks are due to my daughter, Grace. Not only has she been expressive and outspoken through all the ups and downs of adolescence, but she continues to fill my home with lively, laughing teenagers. She is the best daughter anyone could ask for, the light of my life. Sadly, not all teens are as resilient and upbeat as Grace is fortunate enough to be. Teen suicide is a complex problem that manifests in various ways, and it has touched my family's life most painfully. Kaitlyn's suicide attempt is a call for help that's quickly answered, and my prayer is that more and more young people are able to reach out in a less drastic way to get the support they need.

Bill, you made my research trips to Maryland's Eastern Shore delightfully fun. Jonathan, Jackie, Karen, Colleen, Kathy and, of course, Sally, your gentle but pointed critiques improved every chapter you read.

I am grateful to the team at Harlequin for the opportunity to write these books, especially my editor Shana Asaro, editorial director Susan Swinwood, the art department, and the sales and marketing crews. Most of all, I am thankful to my readers; your enthusiasm and encouragement motivate me to push past the challenges and make my writing the best it can be. Thank you for spending some of your precious leisure time with me in Pleasant Shores.

*Read on for a sneak peek at the next book in
The Off Season series,* Christmas on the Coast, *from
Lee Tobin McClain!*

CHAPTER ONE

AMBER ROWE WOKE up to the sound of a child crying and pushed herself to a seated position on the couch. Was it her daughter, Hannah?

Heart pounding, she looked around the living room of her little beach cottage and then checked her phone—11:15 p.m.

Outside, a dog barked, a tomcat yowled and the November wind rattled. Amber shoved her fingers through her hair, reflexively pressed at the scars on her abdomen and sucked in a deep breath, let it out. She'd been sleeping so heavily, dreaming.

It hadn't been her daughter crying. Hannah wasn't a small child anymore, but a thriving college freshman two states away.

She heard the dog bark again, closer, and the same howling cat. Or… She cocked her head, listening.

Was that a cat or a child?

Shoving her blanket and travel books aside, she crossed the living room, flipped on the porch light, and then opened the door and peered out. "Hello?"

Silence for a moment, and then one deep, baying bark, shockingly close, made her jump. She peered into the darkness just beyond the porch light's circle and saw a big, dark dog.

Then the wail of a child pierced her heart, and she rushed

out onto the porch. She made out a small form hugging the dog's neck.

"Hey, buddy, what's wrong?" She kept her voice warm and soft, knelt to make herself smaller and less frightening. "Do you want to come in?" She held out a hand, too concerned about the child to be afraid of the large dog.

The child—a little boy in superhero pajamas—buried his face in the dog's neck and continued sobbing, flinching as a gust of cold wind ruffled his hair.

This wouldn't do. "I have hot chocolate," she said, leaning forward enough to touch the child's arm.

The dog growled.

She pulled her hand back. "Don't worry. I have a biscuit for you, too." She kept a canister of them for Ziggy, her sister's goofy goldendoodle, and King, her brother-in-law's German shepherd.

"His name's Biscuit," the boy mumbled, turning his head sideways on the dog's neck to look at her.

That rang a bell, but she couldn't stop to think about why. "Come inside and we'll find your parents." She held the door open and gestured, and the boy came in slowly, the dog beside him. Both of them had muddy feet. The boy, who looked to be four or five, politely wiped his shoes on the mat before following her across the room.

They reached the kitchen and she was glad to note that his sobs were slowing down. "You have a seat and I'll start some hot chocolate. And we'll get Biscuit a biscuit." She filled a cup with water and stuck it in the microwave, then shook her tin of dog treats.

Biscuit—a ridiculous name for what appeared to be a bloodhound—lifted his head and sniffed the air, but didn't leave the boy's side.

She extracted a large dog biscuit and held it out to the

dog, and he took it delicately despite the strings of drool hanging from his droopy jowls. He flopped down on the floor and started to crunch. Apparently, he'd decided she wasn't a danger to his charge.

"I'm Miss Amber," she said, smiling at the child. "What's your name?"

"Davey," he said, studying her with big teary eyes. "Cold."

"Of course you are." She stepped into the living room, grabbed an afghan off the couch and wrapped it around his shoulders. Then she fumbled in the cupboard and found instant hot chocolate and some stale marshmallows, pulled almond milk from the fridge. The microwave dinged and she fixed a steaming, chocolaty mug for the boy, cooling it with the milk.

She sat down kitty-corner from him, the dog between them, and slid the mug close. She'd made it too full—it had been a while since she'd had a little one—but he knew to lean forward and slurp rather than picking the mug up. He'd stopped crying, though his face was still wet with tears.

"Where are Mom and Dad?" she asked.

He pointed to the sky.

Oh no. "In heaven?"

"Mommy is," he said and slurped again.

"Where's Daddy?"

His lower lip trembled. "Daddy was scary."

Her heart gave a big thud and her hands tightened into fists. "Did Daddy hurt you?"

He shook his head vigorously.

Amber blew out a breath and tried to think. Even if the child's father hadn't hurt him, a father being scary was cause for concern. And the boy was obviously lost. Calling 911 made the most sense, except that a police car with sirens would wake the neighborhood and probably scare the child all over again. She pulled her phone from her back pocket, scrolled and tapped her brother-in-law's name.

He answered immediately, his voice hoarse with sleep. "Amber? You okay?"

"I'm fine, but I have a…situation." She explained what had happened, keeping her voice calm and quiet, aware that the little boy was listening.

"I'll be over," he said and clicked off the call.

Suddenly, footsteps pounded up her front steps. "Davey! Davey, are you in there?" came a man's frantic yell.

"Daddy!" Davey ran to the door and Amber hastened after him. Scary Daddy wasn't coming in here without an explanation.

Davey tried to open the door, but she put a hand on his shoulder. "Step over there a minute," she ordered firmly and opened the door a crack.

There was a wiry man, barefoot, flannel shirt open over a thermal, dark hair disheveled.

He cleared his throat. "I'm trying to find my son." He looked past her, scanning the room.

"What makes you think he's here?" She tried to keep her voice steady.

"Yours is the only light on in the neighborhood. If he went outside, he'd go toward somewhere that was lit up."

The bloodhound brushed against her leg on his way to the door, tail wagging.

"Daddy!" Davey pushed past her, too, and reached for the storm door handle.

She stilled his hand. "Davey said you were being scary."

The man let out a big breath, his tense face and shoulders relaxing, and she realized she knew him. She tilted her head to one side. "Are you…?" She frowned, trying to remember his name.

"Paul Thompson. You interviewed my wife a while back."

"That's it." And the husband she remembered had seemed like a nice guy. And she remembered… Yeah. She knew way too much about his personal life, but now, that wasn't relevant. "Come on in." She held open the door.

He walked in and swept his son up into his arms. "Davey, Davey, Davey. You know you're not allowed to go outside after dark." He tightened his grip on the boy and rested his cheek on the top of the boy's head. "You scared your old dad."

"Sorry, Daddy." The boy looked totally relaxed in Paul's arms.

"Come on into the kitchen," she said, leading the way. Somehow, she didn't want little Davey to go off into the darkness with the man who'd been scary, even if Paul seemed like a perfectly nice guy. She gestured them both to the table. "Davey was having some hot chocolate. Want some?"

"Uh, sure." His eyes skimmed over her and then he quickly looked away, leaning down to scratch the bloodhound behind his big, droopy ears.

At that point, Amber realized she was wearing a skimpy crop top and workout tights. Nothing to hide her bony, boyish form. She started another cup of hot chocolate and then ran out to the coat closet to grab a hoodie and pull it on. As she walked back into the kitchen, she heard father and son murmuring together.

"You were yelling loud," Davey said. "You said, 'Get down, get down, get help!'"

"I *did*?" Paul pressed his lips together.

"I'm sorry I watched a shooting show. But you were 'sleep in your chair and it came on and I…I just wanted to see the soldiers." Davey started to cry again.

"Hey, hey, it's okay," Paul said, grabbing a napkin and using it to wipe Davey's tears, cuddling him close. "I wasn't mad. I was having a bad dream."

"Some dream," Amber commented as she pulled boiling water out of the microwave and stirred hot chocolate mix into it. No marshmallows for Dad; she'd put them all into Davey's cup.

She was pretty sure Paul was telling the truth. There was no guile in his rugged face, and his body language was open. He was obviously able to be affectionate with his son, who seemed to adore him. There was no way to fake that.

Davey picked up his half-empty mug and guzzled hot chocolate.

Amber met Paul's eyes over the boy's head.

"Thank you for taking him in," he said. "I panicked when I woke up and he wasn't there."

"He had a good escape buddy in Biscuit," she said lightly, smiling down at the dog who'd flopped onto his side. It looked like he'd decided the humans could take over for now.

A car pulled into the driveway beside the house, spewing gravel, and then she heard heavy footsteps, this time coming up the back steps.

Paul leaped to his feet and pushed Davey behind him. In his hand was a gun she hadn't known he was carrying, and her heart gave a great thump.

"Put the gun down," she forced out through a dry throat.

Davey knelt on the floor behind Paul, wrapping his arms around his knees. "Scared," he fretted, rocking back and forth.

Biscuit stood, the hair on his back bristling up as he watched the door.

"Police. Open up." Trey's voice outside the door was authoritative, loud.

Heart pounding, Amber gulped, then stepped in front of the door. She was facing Paul and directly in his line of fire, but she was praying he wouldn't shoot a woman. "Everything's fine," she said to the rigid man whose eyes were glued on the door behind her. "It's my brother-in-law. I called him when Davey came over. He's a cop," she clarified when Paul showed no sign of relaxing his fighting stance.

Davey was sobbing quietly.

"Everything's fine," she repeated.

"Amber! Open up!" Trey pounded on the door again.

"Just a minute," she called over her shoulder, and then she frowned at Paul. "I'd appreciate it if you'd put your gun away."

His eyes narrowed. He slid his weapon into a holster inside his jacket but kept his hand on it.

"Why don't you just sit down," she said quietly. "You're scaring your son." For whatever reason, she didn't want Trey to come in and find this man an utter basket case, someone who should have his kid taken away from him.

Paul's head drooped for a minute and pain crossed his face. "Sorry," he said. He looked back at Davey and it was as if a switch flipped; he knelt and picked the boy up and held him close. "It's okay, buddy. Everything's okay."

Curiosity licked at her. She waited until he'd pulled Davey back onto his lap and rubbed a hand over his head, soothing him, before opening the door to her very tense, angry brother-in-law.

The feel of his son in his lap—safe, warm, *alive*—helped Paul get his heartbeat back to something resembling normal.

He tried to make his face look normal, too, to stop sweating, but the big guy at the door was a cop and clearly on high alert. He'd almost certainly seen Paul's weapon, because he was watching Paul with narrowed eyes. So was Amber.

Of course they're watching you. You acted like a madman.

Just as he'd done on the job, leading him to be here in a little shore town in a program designed to help him heal.

At least Davey was calming down. Paul focused on his son, used a napkin to wipe his tears and held it to his nose. "Blow. Real hard. There you go." He wiped Davey's nose. "You're fine. We're all fine. Okay?"

Davey looked up at him, and Paul's heart seemed to warm and grow. He didn't deserve the trust in his son's eyes, but he'd try to live up to it. He stroked Davey's hair.

"Everything okay here?" the guy asked Amber.

"Yeah. I think so." She backed away from the door and beckoned the guy to come farther in. Her hand was shaking. "Sorry to call you out so late, but Davey, here, came to visit me, and then his dad showed up a few minutes later."

"Hey, buddy." The cop walked slowly in their direction, smiling at Davey. He stopped a good eight feet away and knelt down, hand subtly near his waist where, almost certainly, a weapon was concealed. "My name's Trey. I'm a police officer, just making sure everything's okay."

Davey nodded and looked up at Paul, his face solemn. "It's okay. My daddy's a cop, too."

Paul blew out a breath and tried to smile at the officer. He shifted slowly, held out a hand. "Paul Thompson. Staying in the cottage next door, and Davey took a notion to come outside while I was dozing on the couch."

"Trey Harrison." The officer reached out and shook his hand, looking directly into Paul's eyes. Then he refocused his attention on Davey. "It's late to be outside by yourself. You're, what, five?"

"Four." Davey held up four fingers. "I have a birthday coming. Then I'll be five." He held up five fingers now, to illustrate.

"Wow," Amber said, moving over to the counter and leaning against it. "Five is big."

"Sure is," the cop, Trey, agreed.

Davey nodded, his face solemn. "Daddy said I can have a party."

Now that the immediate danger was past, shame licked at Paul's insides. He was a poor excuse for a father, scaring his son like that, but he was all Davey had. And Davey couldn't take another loss, not after losing his mother two years ago.

Paul's whole life centered, now, around protecting his son.

"Daddy, you're squeezing me," Davey said.

Paul loosened his grip. "Sorry, kiddo. You had me scared." He let Davey slide to the ground and watched him as he cuddled against Biscuit. Thank heavens for his loyal former K-9 dog. How terrifying might Davey's late-night excursion have been without the big bloodhound for company?

"Sit down, Trey. Want some coffee?" Without waiting for an answer, Amber turned and reached high for a cup, her hoodie rising to reveal a thin slice of skin above those skimpy leggings. Women shouldn't wear them, Wendy had always said; she'd thought them too tight and revealing. Paul had agreed, just to keep the peace. He hadn't been the best husband in the universe, but he'd known enough not to defend other women's revealing clothing choices to his wife.

He looked away and realized that Trey had seen him

checking Amber out. He hadn't been; he'd just noticed what any guy would notice, probably including her brother-in-law. Still, his face heated. He didn't need to add "creepy old guy" to the list Trey was no doubt making in his head.

Not that he was that much older than Amber. Ten years, maybe?

But ten years could be a lifetime.

Amber put coffee in front of Trey and then looked at Paul. "Want a refill of hot chocolate? Or some coffee?" She glanced down at Davey. "I'm thinking he won't need a refill."

Indeed, Davey was resting his head on Biscuit now, his eyelids fluttering like he could barely keep them open.

"Thanks. I'll drink what you made before." He wrapped a hand around the still-warm mug.

Trey pulled out his phone and started texting. Apparently, he'd decided Paul wasn't an immediate threat. "Letting Erica know everything's settled down," he said to Amber. "She's worried."

"Take a pic so she knows I'm okay," Amber said and struck a pose, her own coffee cup lifted in a toast as she pasted on a big smile. "And then I'll fix you some eggs. It's the least I can do, calling you out in the middle of the night."

That last was directed at Trey, and again, Paul felt shame. "Sorry to get you up, man," he said.

Trey shrugged. "Goes with the territory." He snapped a photo of Amber and went back to his phone, and Paul once again had to tear his eyes away from Amber. She was a character, all right: hair frizzing out wildly behind a colorful headband, tattoos up one arm, and those bright flowered tights that fit her so well.

It wasn't just her clothes or hair, though. He remembered thinking her a little eccentric, in a good way, when she'd come to interview Wendy. Then, she'd worn a dress and some kind of jacket and boots, all professional.

But she'd gotten Wendy laughing more than he'd heard her laugh in months, and when he'd looked in on them, he'd seen that Amber had pulled off her wig of long hair and was showing it to Wendy. Her head had been completely bald, just as Wendy's was.

Amber had beckoned him in and shown them both pictures of her variously styled wigs in all different colors, suggesting which would best suit Wendy.

Now Amber's hair was chin length, and he had to assume that it was natural, since she was wearing it home alone in the middle of the night.

She pulled eggs and a loaf of bread out of the refrigerator, set butter melting in a pan and turned as if to ask them something. Then her eyes fell on Davey, now asleep. "Want me to put him to bed on the couch for a little bit?"

Paul didn't want his son out of his sight. "He's just as comfortable sleeping on Biscuit. Do you have a blanket, though?"

She nodded and reached around him for an afghan lying across a kitchen chair. Before Paul could take it from her, she'd knelt and tucked it around Davey, as tenderly as any mother would.

Paul swallowed. Davey needed a mom. Maybe after Paul pulled himself together—if he ever *did* pull himself together—he'd try to meet someone. Another Wendy, sweet and steady and pure. Only without cancer.

Amber rose gracefully to her feet and kind of danced over to the counter, set a frying pan heating with a chunk of butter in it and then broke eggs into a bowl with one hand.

"So, you two know each other?" Trey's voice was friendly,

but Paul could hear the wariness underneath. Trey was still evaluating whether Paul was a risk to his son.

And the man was well within his rights. It was Paul who'd done something wrong. "Not well," he said. "Amber interviewed my wife for her book."

Amber beat the eggs to a froth with a big silver utensil, poured them into the pan and pulled a small bundle of something green out of the fridge. She snipped pieces into the eggs, then turned to face them. "Davey said she's in heaven," she said quietly. "I'm sorry for your loss."

"Thanks." He flashed back on Wendy, fixing eggs for breakfast. Not like these eggs—just plain ones—but it had been sweet to have someone cooking for him.

"Sorry, man," Trey said. "How's Davey handling it?"

"He's resilient, like all kids." Paul looked down at his son. "But it's taken its toll."

"On both of you, I imagine." Amber turned back to the counter and sliced thick pieces of brown bread.

What could he say to that? "How'd the book do?" he asked Amber. "What with all that's been going on, I haven't had time to look for it."

"It did great," Trey chimed in, sounding proud. "In fact, she has an offer to do another one. You going to go for it?"

Amber stirred the eggs, turned off the burner and spun around to face them. "Pretty sure I am."

"This next book project seems kind of risky to me," Trey said. He reached across the table and started reading the spines of a stack of books. "Nepal, Tibet, the Himalayas…"

"Well, mostly Delhi and Calcutta," Amber said, smiling. "But I do hope to squeeze in some side trips. They want me to do another book on cancer patients in South Asia," she clarified to Paul. "How they do with non-Western medicine."

"Wow. So you're going to, what, live there?" Paul couldn't fathom it. He'd wanted to travel, a lifetime ago.

"More like a couple of long trips," she said. "I'm excited."

"Cool." Amber was way far from his comfort zone and his type. The odd little flutter of attraction he'd felt was just one of those opposites-attract things.

Amber scooped eggs onto two plates, added slices of bread to each and brought them over to the table.

"You're not eating?" Paul asked.

"She never eats." Trey took a big bite. "Even though she's a great cook."

"I do so eat," she said in a play-whining tone that told Paul she and Trey were close. "Just not in the middle of the night."

Paul dug into the eggs, flecked with spices and rich with cheese, and realized he hadn't had dinner. Had he fixed something for Davey? Jeez, what kind of...? Yes. He'd cut up a hot dog, stirred it into some mac and cheese. Not exactly healthy, but at least he wasn't starving his kid.

Amber sat down at the table with them and pulled out a big map. "See, I want to start in Delhi. That's where my publishers have some contacts. But I'd like to get out into the countryside, too, see how people manage disease when they don't have access to modern medical centers." She was running a red-painted fingernail over the map as she talked. "And then I'll be so close to Nepal, I have to make a side trip there." Her eyes sparkled.

"I don't like the idea of you traveling alone," Trey said. "Neither does Erica."

"I'll start out alone," Amber said, "but I doubt I'll be alone for long. There's a big expat community in most of these places, so it's easy to find friends to travel with."

Trey shook his head.

Paul kind of admired that loose attitude toward planning a trip, especially to the other side of the world. "I don't think I could do that," he admitted.

"Well, you couldn't. You have responsibilities here." She nodded down at Davey. "But my nest is empty, and except for helping out with the Cottage, I'm free to pick up and go anytime." Something flashed across her face and then was gone.

Maybe some of her enthusiasm could be bravado. Maybe she was traveling alone because she didn't have anyone to go with.

For just a minute, that wide world of adventure beckoned. He'd never even left the country.

But no. His job was to be safe and keep his son safe, not go globe-trotting.

"So you're staying in the Healing Heroes Cottage?" Trey asked, and Paul realized the man was still observing him in the guise of making conversation. Probably deciding whether to call child protective services.

Paul couldn't blame him. What had happened tonight hadn't just scared Amber; it had scared Paul as well, badly. It made him wonder whether he was, in fact, fit to parent a child.

Paul couldn't let something like that happen again. And he also couldn't jump up and pull his weapon every time someone knocked on the door.

He looked directly at Trey. "I had a nightmare, and that's what scared Davey. I'm getting counseling for PTSD and I'm to do volunteer work here in town. That's the deal with the Cottage. My old boss set me up for it." He hated revealing even that much, but his symptoms were too obvious to ignore. He couldn't act like he didn't know he had a problem. He cleared his throat. "I'm thinking maybe I should give up my weapon for now." He pulled it out, slowly, and laid it on the table.

Trey had tensed, but as soon as Paul's hands were away from the gun, he nodded and scraped the last of the eggs off his plate. "I can hold on to it, if you'd like."

He didn't like it, not one bit. But he couldn't risk carrying when he was so obviously out of control. "Thanks."

"Think you're okay to take care of him now?" Trey asked.

Paul rubbed a hand over his face. "I have to be. I'm all he's got." His own words made him straighten his spine. He had to buck up, because he could lose everything. Worse, Davey could.

He needed help, and he had to get it here, or else.

Don't miss Christmas on the Coast
by Lee Tobin McClain!

IF YOU ENJOYED THIS BOOK
WE THINK YOU WILL ALSO LOVE

LOVE INSPIRED
INSPIRATIONAL ROMANCE

Uplifting stories of faith, forgiveness and hope.

Fall in love with stories where faith helps
guide you through life's challenges, and discover
the promise of a new beginning.

6 NEW BOOKS AVAILABLE EVERY MONTH!

"I'm sorry I was distant before. That was just me being foolish."

Samantha didn't ask what he was talking about; she obviously knew. "What was going on?"

Corbin debated finding some intellectual way to say it, but he wasn't thinking straight enough. "I got turned upside down by that kiss."

"Yeah. Me, too." She glanced at him and then turned to put a stack of plates away.

"It was intense."

"Uh-huh."

Now that he had brought up the topic, he wasn't sure where he wanted to go with it. For him to go into the fact that he couldn't get involved with her because she was an alcoholic... Suddenly, that felt judgmental and mean and not how he wanted to talk to her.

Maybe it wasn't how he wanted to be with her, either, but he wasn't ready to make that alteration to his long-held set of values about who he could get involved with. And until he did, he obviously needed to keep a lid on his feelings.

So he talked about something they would probably agree on. "I was never so scared in my life as when Mikey was lost."

"Me, either. It was awful."

He paused, then admitted, "I just don't know if I'm cut out for taking care of a kid."

Her head jerked around to face him. "You're not thinking of sending him back to your mom, are you?"

Was he? He shook his head slowly, letting out a sigh. "No. I feel like I screwed up badly, but I still think he's safer with me than with her."

She let the water out of the sink, not looking at him now. "I think you're doing a great job," she said. "It was just as much my fault as yours. Parenting is a challenge and you can't help but screw up sometimes."

"I guess." He wasn't used to doing things poorly or in a half-baked way. He was used to working at a task until he could become an expert. But it seemed that nobody was an expert when it came to raising kids, not really.

"Mikey can be a handful, just like any other little child," she said.

"He is, but I sure love him," Corbin said. It was the first time he had articulated that, and he realized it was completely true. He loved his little brother as if the boy were his own son.

"I love him, too," she said, almost offhandedly.

She just continued wiping down the counters, not acting like she had said anything momentous, but her words blew Corbin away. She had an amazing ability to love. Mikey wasn't her child, nor her blood, but she felt for him as if he were.

If he loved his little brother despite the boy's issues and whining and toddler misbehavior, could it be that he could love another adult who had issues, too? He was definitely starting to care a lot for Samantha. Was he growing, becoming more flexible and forgiving?

He didn't know if he could change that much. He'd been holding himself— and others—to a strict high standard for a long time. It was how he'd gotten as far as he had after his rough beginning.

Corbin wanted to continue caring for his brother, especially given the alternative, but the fact that Mikey had gotten lost had shaken him. He didn't know if he was good enough to do the job.

Samantha's expression of support soothed his insecurities. He wanted love and acceptance, just like anyone else. And there was a tiny spark inside him that was starting to burn, a spark that wondered if he could maybe be loved and fall in love, even with a certain nanny.

Don't miss
Child on His Doorstep
*by Lee Tobin McClain, available August 2020 wherever
Love Inspired books and ebooks are sold.*

LoveInspired.com

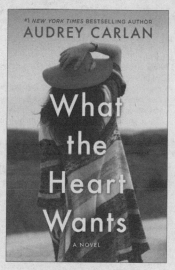